MW00882978

By: Rebecca Gober & Courtney Nuckels

Clean Teen Publishing

PROJECT ELE

Cover Design by: Marya Heiman

Typography by: Courtney Nuckels

For more information about our content disclosure, please utilize the QR code above with your smart phone or visit us at

www.cleanteenpublishing.com.

ONE

Waiting in line totally bites!

What's worse than waiting in line? Waiting in line, outside in the stifling heat with escalating temperatures. The only relief being a hand held battery operated fan and a portable misting machine that ran through our daily ration of water in less than two hours.

Beads of sweat drip down my face, causing my eyes to sting. My dad faces his fan so it hits the back of my neck. He always looks composed and collected, but even he isn't immune to this sweltering weather. His salt and pepper hair is plastered to his head with sweat and his usually vibrant green eyes show telltale signs of heat exhaustion.

"They could have at least left the patches up until we had a chance to apply for entry. Maybe then the heat wouldn't be this stifling." Our neighbor in line, Mr. Leroy mumbles. The patches that cover the holes in the ozone layer is all everyone talks about lately. They are the only thing that keeps us all from burning to a crisp. Mr. Leroy is an elderly man with leathery skin, shiny grey hair and beady brown eyes. He walks around all day in only a pair of plaid boxers and a 'wife beater' undershirt. Some of the older women scoff at his choice of attire. It doesn't faze him though; he says that dying of heat stroke while waiting in line to see if you pass inspection would defeat the purpose entirely. While I may agree with Mr. Leroy on that part, I have to say that honestly, he gives me the heebie-jeebies. He wears a nasty frown twenty-four seven and always reeks of stinky old man sweat. My mom assures us that he's just a cranky old geezer with a thousand conspiracy theories and that he has nothing better to do other than share them with us.

"You know Lee, they are doing the best they can. The virus is spreading at rapid speeds and they have no choice but to begin the heating process to stop it." My dad says this, not bothering to remove the annoyance from his voice.

"Is that why they let all of the rich ones in first?" Mr. Leroy asks with a cynical expression. "They've been in there for two weeks already and the rest of us 'lower class' just now got invited to the party."

I catch my dad rolling his eyes behind Mr. Leroy's back. It makes me grin, especially since he always gets onto me when I do it. My parents are none to happy to have Mr. Leroy behind us in line. Up until Mr. Leroy opened his mouth, my parents had done their best to shelter us from the impending doom that we were all facing. Mr. Leroy on the other hand, couldn't care less that we are 'merely' children as my mom would put it. He voices his distaste for this whole situation, which he deems completely the government's fault, whenever he so feels like it. With him running his mouth non-stop, my parents had no choice but to tell me most everything. My four year old little brother, Sebastian, is too young to understand. At fifteen, I truly feel I can handle the truth. Well, at least I think I can. To be totally upfront, I'm scared to death, but I'm dealing with it the only way I know how: Pretend, I could care less. It's a hard facade to pull off though.

We've had a rather closed off life for the past few years, as have many children. With the fear of the virus looming over everyone's heads our parents had kept us inside our home for the most part. We had stopped going to a formal school by the time I was ten. Now we are home schooled online. Of course I never truly understood why we were forced to stay inside our small home all of the time.

Millions have already died, with thousands more dying daily. The government was forced to implement Project ELE. Don't ask me who ELE is because I have no idea. I asked my dad once who she was, his expression went dark as he replied, "All you need to know is that you don't want to meet her." I didn't ask him again after that. After all, if ELE scares my dad, I'm sure she would terrify me.

With Project ELE in place we only have another seventy-two hours before the temperatures are predicted to increase above one hundred and seventy degrees, which will most likely kill the remaining survivors outside of the F.E.M.A. shelter. Our bodies are not meant to withstand that kind of heat, neither is the virus. Currently the temperature is at one hundred degrees and some of the people in line have already faded away because of it. Fading away from heat stroke seems like a more pleasant way to die than to experience the excruciating death caused by the virus. It's an eerie feeling watching people that have died being whisked away on a stretcher with a white sheet draped over their bodies.

This shelter is our only hope to survive this thing. All remaining power that wasn't diverted for Project ELE has been re-routed or conserved to run the few F.E.M.A. shelters across the country. The line to our shelter is running at a snail's pace. There are so many tests stations to go through before people are permitted to enter the shelter where we will supposedly spend the next three years or until they can get the patches back up, whichever comes first.

Before you can enter the shelter they have to verify that you are not infected and that you are fit to survive. Mr. Leroy says repeatedly that this is not the place to bring the weak or weary and it's especially not the place to bring the sick.

This whole business started with the sick. A virus brought forth from a cure. They thought it would work, that it could heal everything. Cancer, diabetes, depression, the flu, even the common cold could be healed by 'The C.U.R.E.' or Counteractive Universal Recovery Elixir. It did work for several years, until a super virus came along that not even our precious 'C.U.R.E.' could fix. My mom says that we weren't meant to live forever. Not that we could live forever even with the 'C.U.R.E..' Meaning that we couldn't cheat death by curing everything the world suffered from.

The super virus killed off more than half of the world's population. No country was safe from this air born virus; it only takes a measly few days to die once infected. In an attempt to kill off the super virus, the United Nations agreed to pull down the patches that they spent over a hundred years perfecting. Obviously I wasn't around when the patches first went up to cover the giant gaping holes in the ozone layer but I heard that it took a tremendous amount of energy and power to put them up in the first place. It is said that the entire world worked together back then and went for a full month without electricity of any sort in order to put the patches in place. This is another reason why they are diverting all of the energy now and not allowing us to stay in our homes. They need that power to put the patches back up after the warming does its job. On a side note, the project for creating those patches a hundred years ago was also called Project ELE. It's kind of creepy if you ask me.

Scientists anticipate that with the patches gone it will cause a long-term heating of the earth's surface that will hopefully kill off the virus. They aren't sure if the plan will work, but obviously with the temperatures rising daily, it seems to be. They don't know what the long-term effects will be on the planet after they cause this heating, but the United Nations deemed the possible reward was worth the risk.

Mr. Leroy said that the earth will never be virus free and that this whole scheme will most likely end in the destruction of all life on earth, as we know it. My dad says that Mr. Leroy, or Lee as he calls him, exaggerates.

"Willow, it's time for bed." My mom says. I look to my dad hoping he can make the call to allow me to stay up a little longer but he just shrugs. I roll my eyes, like a normal teenager would, and head over to our tent. I carefully unzip the tent door and cool air piles out. "Hurry, don't let out all of the cold air," my mom calls. I hurry inside and zip the door up again.

F.E.M.A. passed out portable cooling units to the families with small children yesterday as temperatures exceeded the hundred-degree mark. Mr. Leroy said that they only want the younger ones. He doesn't even know why he's wasting his time in this line when they are just going to stamp a big old DECLINE across his passport card. He says it's all about the survival of the fittest. The young ones who can one day re-populate the planet. I asked my mom what Mr. Leroy meant about re-populating the planet. She wouldn't answer me so I asked Mr. Leroy when she wasn't looking. Unfortunately, he answered me without hesitation. Gross! I could have gone the rest of my life without having that talk with Mr. Grumps-a-lot! I wish I could scrub my memory out with soap and hot water. Scratch that, soap and cold water, ice-cold water. Yes, that would be nice.

"Wello," Sebastian calls out.

"It's Willow!" I say a little too harshly. His big blue eyes tear up and his face crumples into a sad puppy dog look. It breaks my heart. My little brother is the chink in my 'all-attitude-twenty-four-hours-a-day-teen-armor.' "I'm sorry Sabby, I'm just a little grumpy tonight." I apologize. I lay down next to him on the small air mattress that we share. My parents sleep on the hard ground, but all of the children get air mattresses, which gave Mr. Leroy one more reason to complain about the 'travesties of his existence,' as he calls it.

"It's okay Wello. Mommy says we need to sleep when we're grumpy." He pats me softly on the shoulder as if he's the grown up reassuring me. My little brother is a little too cute for his own good sometimes. He's going to be a heart breaker one day; at least that's what all of the old ladies say. Sebastian has huge cherub cheeks, big bright doe like blue eyes and soft brown curls that are long enough to fall in front of his eyes. We look so different. I'm wiry and thin with hallow cheeks, brown eyes and caramel colored hair that has a mind of its own. I sometimes find myself envious of Sebastian's perfect ringlets. My hair seems to twist and bend every which way leaving me no choice but to throw it under a cap or into a ponytail.

"I'm not grumpy cause I'm tired, I'm grumpy because I'm too old to be going to bed at eight o'clock." I throw my arms across my chest in a physical gesture to prove my frustration.

Sebastian turns over and cuddles next to me. "I not tired eter." He says with a yawn.

"Love you Sabby." I say as I watch his little eyelids droop heavily.

"Wuv you too Wello." He says before he drifts off

to dreamland. Right now he looks like the poster child for innocence. I wonder if I will ever feel that innocent again. Sometimes I wish I could go back to the days when my only worry was what dress to put on my Barbie or whether my mom would let me have that extra cookie after dinner. This is the land of no return though; a land where the weak-minded aren't welcome.

I stare at Sebastian for a while then turn my sights on the shadows that dance across the white tent walls. I try not to think about the future, the insecure feeling I get when I hear people talking about the upcoming tests, but they weigh heavily on my heart. My father used to tell me when I was younger that I should tell myself a story when I felt scared. I know I'm getting older, but I justify the fact that it's okay to tell a story to the sleeping toddler next to me, just in case he's feeling as scared as I am. I reach over and sweep the tiny ringlets from his face with my fingers. With a voice just above a whisper I begin, "Once upon a time..."

TWO

"Numbers one hundred thirty nine thousand through one hundred forty five thousand please pack your belongings and proceed towards the entry gate."

A voice booms from a loud speaker.

"Willow, Sebastian, its time to get up." My mom calls cheerfully out to us.

I bolt up out of bed with excitement and immediately start packing my stuff. After waiting for so many days doing nothing, we are finally going to get to go inside! There are only so many games to play with a deck of cards. I pull my passport out of my bag to make sure it's still safe and examine the number that is stamped in red ink. I am number one hundred forty-four thousand and one. The number unsettles me; I don't like odd numbers.

"Sebastian, it's time to get up," I shake him slightly. He whimpers a little and sits up groggily.

"I still sleepy." He says rubbing his eyes.

"I know buddy, but today is the day we get to go inside." My father says to him. "Aren't you excited Sabby?" He ruffles my brothers little curls with his hand. Sebastian gives him a big sleepy smile.

"I bet you are excited Willow," My dad says to me.

"Yeah, well, it's okay I guess." I say trying to act like I could care less when inside I am jumping for joy.

"Yeah, uh huh." My dad jokes around and playfully tries to ruffle my hair; except his hand ends up catching a tangle in my wild mane. He begins pulling at my hair trying to untangle his fingers. "Sorry love." He says with a half-smile while I wince at the sensation.

"No biggie." I reply a little self-consciously.

As a family we all work speedily to pack our belongings. I help get Sebastian ready. In fifteen minutes we are all dressed, have our single bag packed and are out the door of the tent headed towards the food line. The morning air already brings a heavy heat and with the clear skies it looks like the rest of the day will be unrelenting. I decide that I'm not going to allow my heavily perspiring skin to bother me. Nope, today is going to be a good day. Since our number was called, we are granted an express pass to the front of the line to get our breakfast, consisting of some type of cold cream of wheat concoction and a bottle of water. I scarf down the cold cereal as if I haven't eaten for days. My mom gives me a sideways look and shakes her head. Instead of calling me out for my bad table manners she just jokes, "I guess someone is about to have a growth spurt."

"Yeah, I guess so." I smile back, a real smile this time. I can't help it; I'm too ecstatic that we will be out of this smothering heat soon. Plus, my mom seems to be in a much better mood than she has been for days. I can see the worry lines easing from her forehead now that our numbers have been called.

Once we finish our meals we head to the entry gate and get into yet another line. Fans run along the path of the line circulating the already hot air around us. You would think something like this would provide some sort of relief, but with as hot as it is out here, nothing can take our minds off the scorching temperatures. A few mister stations are set up a long the way for the children. Children can't handle the heat as well as adults can. Even though the heat is intense, this set up in line is much better than the one back at camp, because thankfully, this line leads inside.

"I love you all." My dad says while pulling us all into a big bear hug. Normally I would be grossed out at even the idea of enveloping sweaty bodies, but it feels good to have that physical affirmation that we all love each other.

"Wuv you too!" Sebastian calls out.

"I love you all so much," my mom says.

Everyone looks at me expectantly, "You guys know that I love you." I say trying to be nonchalant but meaning every ounce of it. I wouldn't trade my family for the world.

"This is it, we are going to make it." My mom says with relief pouring from her voice.

"Yeah, speak for yourself. Do you see how many people they are turning away? Ageist bastards; almost all of the ones leaving are over fifty." Mr. Leroy spits out venomously.

I turn back startled. I hadn't realized that he was standing behind us. My dad tries to diffuse the situation by saying, "Please watch your language around my children Lee. This is stressful for everyone but I'm sure the F.E.M.A. has their reasons for turning those people away."

"Yeah, their reason is that they don't give a crap about us. We are nothing but a number to them, a statistic." Mr. Leroy huffs.

"I'm sure they will let you in Mr. Leroy." I don't know why I speak up to comfort him, but I do. I can tell that under that grumpy old man exterior he really is just as scared as the rest of us. Perhaps he's a little lonely too. He mentioned that he lost his wife to the virus last year. I give him an awkward pat on his back. I know I'm giving up my tough girl, annoyed attitude but I don't want anything to ruin today. Today is about hope. We are all going to be just fine. His eyes lighten up just a bit and his posture relaxes at my touch.

"Willow's right, we all are going to get to go inside. Just you wait and see." My mom chimes in. I can tell that her face shows a little bit of anxiety but she's doing her best to remain calm for us.

"I don feel so good." Sebastian tugs on my mom's shirt.

My mom's hand immediately goes up to his forehead checking his temperature. Her face shows a look of displeasure. "Willow, I think Sebastian is overheating. Do you mind taking him to one of the mister stations?"

I nod my head and grab Sebastian's little hand, "Let's go Sabby."

He walks beside me lethargically toward the nearest

mister station; I end up carrying him most of the way. When we get there, I sit him down in the middle of the tent under the cool mist. “Raise your arms Sabby.” He complies and I pull his tank top up over his head. His little skin looks red and overheated. He’s had to spend almost every hour since we’ve been here inside our tent with the cooling unit on. My dad says that little kids can overheat much faster than adults. Plus, they don’t always know how to communicate when they are showing signs of heat exhaustion. Waiting in this line for the past hour has probably been the longest time he has spent outside in the elements. To help cool him down quicker I take his little yellow tank top and hold it up close to one of the sprinkler heads. Once it’s nice and wet I put it back on him.

“Tank you Wello.” He says sweetly. His hair has accumulated enough moisture that his ringlets fall down in long waves over his forehead. Little beads of mist form on his eyelashes. I can tell by his eyes that he is still not feeling well, so I have him lie down and rest his head in my lap. I brush his hair like my mother does for us when we’re feeling under the weather. Sebastian gives a slight smile and closes his eyes to my petting.

“Would you like some water for the boy?” I look up from where I’m sitting to see a tall sturdy boy who looks to be about my age, holding out a cold bottle of water. His hair is shaved so close to his head that I can’t tell what color it is. Tiny droplets of water cover his hair making his head look shiny. His skin shows a sun-kissed tan that tells me his parents didn’t lather him in the same sunscreen I had to endure. I look down at my white legs and grimace before looking back up at him. He has unusually dark eyes that appear to be black and long thick lashes. I didn't know people could have black eyes, but I guess this boy does. His bushy eyebrows rise in question and I realize that I'm staring. I blush at my apparent lack of social skills.

"Oh, sorry. Yes, thank you." I reach up to grab the bottle. "Hey Sabby," I cringe a bit realizing that my baby name for my little brother probably sounds childish. The boy standing in front of me didn't seem to notice so I continue. "Why don't you drink some water Sebastian?"

I put the bottle to his lips and Sebastian opens his eyes only long enough to take a few small sips then he closes them again.

"Is he okay?" The boy asks me.

I look from Sebastian to the boy. "Yeah, he's just over heated. He should be fine. He's not used to this heat, but we should be allowed to go inside soon."

"Yeah, my little sister Lillie has a hard time with this heat too." He gestures with his head over to a small girl sitting in the corner of the misting area. Her long orangey-red hair is pulled back in a ponytail. She's working on her dolls hair, trying to put it into a similar style. She appears to be around seven or eight years old.

"My name's Connor." He looks at me expectantly.

I just stare at him again. I don't know where my tongue went but I haven't really had a conversation with anyone my age in a long while. I'm a little out of practice. When I finally catch my tongue I say awkwardly, "Oh, sorry, I'm Willow and this is my brother Sebastian."

He stands there above me for a few seconds in silence. I guess he might be out of practice too when it comes to holding a conversation. That or we are both just as lethargic from the heat as our siblings are.

I clear my throat, "So, um, what number are you?"

"One hundred forty-three thousand and sixteen." He says.

"Oh, you are before us then." I reply noting the even number he lucked out with. He nods his head. Still not feeling much in the way of conversation I say, "Thanks for the water."

"Sure, no problem." He smiles a big goofy smile.

"Connor! Lillie!" A robust woman with curly red hair calls from outside the misting area. "It's time to go."

"Okay mom." Connor calls back to her. He turns back to look down at me. "Nice to meet you Willow. Good luck with the tests." I smile and wave goodbye to him as he turns on his heel to gather up Lillie. They both run out of the mister station to catch up to their mother hand in hand.

I look down at Sebastian who is sleeping noiselessly in my lap. Good luck with the tests. I hadn't even thought much about the tests that would be coming up soon. Nor have I thought about the fact that we could be turned away. I guess I just assumed everyone would be granted entrance, but even Mr. Leroy was saying that he's seen people declined. A sick feeling tumbles through my stomach. I take a few sips of water to help squelch the nausea.

"Hey honey, how's he doing?" My mom asks from

outside the station. She walks inside and bends down to feel Sebastian's head and seems satisfied with his temperature.

I answer anyhow. "He's good, he crashed out almost immediately. Someone gave me some water so I made him drink it before he went to sleep."

"You are the best big sister ever." She smiles at me. "Hey, have I told you today that you are my favorite daughter?" She leans in to give me a motherly hug.

"Yeah mom; I'm your only daughter." She says the same thing to me nearly every day and I reply in the same way too. I smile up at her and return her hug. "You are my favorite mom." I mean it too.

"Thanks honey." My mom pushes my wet hair back from my forehead. To pass the time, she pulls my tangled hair out of its ponytail and goes to work combing through it nimbly with her fingers. My eyes nearly roll back in my head at the wonderful feeling of her playing with my hair. It's such a comforting gesture that all of my earlier worries about the tests momentarily slip from my mind. We spend the next hour talking and joking around while my mom works all of the knots out of my tangled mess. She fixes my hair up into a beautifully braided bun. The time sped by so fast that when my dad comes to tell us that our numbers have been called we are pleasantly surprised.

"Time to get up Sabby." I gently shake my little brother, who hasn't budged, from my lap. He stirs slowly. My dad comes over and picks him up giving him a zerbert kiss on his cheek. Sebastian squeals with laughter.

My mom helps me stand up because my legs have

fallen asleep from sitting in the same position so long. I stomp around trying to get the blood flowing. Once all of us are standing my dad calls out, "Ready family?"

We all say, "yes," simultaneously and head back out into the heat, hand in hand. We walk towards the giant entry gates as a family in silence. The butterflies inside my stomach dance around in summersaults from anxiety and with every step we take I think, 'This is it.' I have no idea what our new home for the next three years will look like. I don't know what life will be like inside the shelter, but I do know it will be vastly different than my old life. The closer we get to the testing stations the more of the old me I leave behind.

The fortified steel gates surround us as we near the entry point. An enormous mountain sits before us. There is a straight line of tents that form a tunnel to the entry point leading us deep into the mountain.

"Identification please," asks a faceless official in a white biohazard suit with a F.E.M.A. nametag.

I fumble around my shorts pocket looking for my identification. Thankfully my dad pulls out my passport along with my little brothers and his. He hands them to the official who inspects it carefully. The suction of air that spits from his biohazard suit puts me on edge.

"Mosby family, report to testing station one." He points a stiff finger in the general direction of the first station. I follow behind my family feeling increasingly nervous with all of the white hazard suited officials walking about. I huddle closer to my dad.

Station one is marked with a giant red label that states, 'first testing station,' in bold block letters. Its entryway is covered with a large white curtain blocking the inside of the tent station from our view.

"Passports," An overweight official who is guarding the entrance requests. We comply by quickly handing him our passports. "The boy first," the man says blandly after skimming over our identification.

Another F.E.M.A. official, a woman whose name badge identifies her as a nurse, comes out to collect Sebastian. The nurse isn't flaunting the biohazard suit thankfully, which makes her look less intimidating. She does have her entire body protected by long sleeve scrubs, rubber gloves and a disposable surgeons mask over her mouth and nose though.

"No momma!" Sebastian clings to my mother's leg.

"Can I not go with my son? He's only four." My mom asks the nurse.

"No, I'm sorry but each person must go through the tests alone." Her answer sounds so genuine that I believe she may actually feel sorry that she's separating our family.

I lean down and whisper in my brother's ear. "Hey Sabby, if you can be a big boy and go with this nice nurse, I'm sure you will get a lollipop or a sticker after you are done." I don't know if it's true or not, but I figure if they don't offer him a treat I will find a way to make it up to him later.

He looks up at me with wide hopeful eyes and releases his grip on my mother's leg. "Okay Wello."

"I love you Sebastian. We'll see you in a few minutes." My mom bends down and gives him a big hug. My father and I each take turns giving him reassuring hugs. Then he puts his hand out for the nurse to lead him into the testing station. He looks back and says to us, "I see you in bit."

I try to convey a reassuring smile. My nerves are running haywire and the anxiety I've been feeling increases ten-fold while I watch my little brother disappear through the curtain.

The nurse comes back a few minutes later and asks for me. I give my mom and dad a hug, say: "I love you," and follow the nurse inside.

The light inside the testing tent is so artificially bright that I have to keep my head down in response. It takes a few seconds for my eyes to adjust to the brightness but when I do look up, I realize I haven't missed much. The nurse is leading me down a stark corridor made up of white curtains. We walk halfway down the isle before the nurse stops suddenly and jerks back one of the curtains. Inside the room is a simple exam table and a tray with a few creepy items on it. The nurse hands me a flimsy white hospital gown and tells me to change into it. I expect her to leave the room but instead she merely turns around to give me some semblance of privacy.

"What are all the needles for?" I ask while changing out of my clothes. The sight of all of the needles, some holding several different colored fluids, makes me queasy. I count twelve needles in all. Ten of them are standing up perfectly straight in a container with the needlepoint sticking up. Two of them are lying side by side next to the container. Those can't all be for me, right?

"We have to take blood samples as well as give you an immunization before you may enter the facility. Please make sure you remove all your undergarments as well." She adds kindly. Unlike the other officials, the nurse doesn't seem annoyed with my question.

"Um, okay. Uh, do I have to get all of those shots?" I ask feeling rather dreadful at the thought of getting injected with these foreign substances.

She laughs. "We only give you one depending on your blood test results." Then she adds, "Everyone who wishes to enter must be immunized. We will be in close quarters inside the facility and we need to make sure everyone is healthy." She answers.

Phew! I finish changing in silence and then clear my throat to announce that she may turn around. My legs are feeling so shaky that I decide to take a seat on the exam table.

The nurse takes out a plastic bag from underneath the table and puts my clothes, my shoes and even my underwear inside it. "Could I please have your hairband too?" She asks.

I pull the hairband out causing my bun to fall and some of the braid to come undone. "Will I get my stuff back?"

She looks at me apologetically, "Not if you are granted entrance to the facility. You will be provided new clothes inside." She closes the bag with a twist tie and sets it on the floor near the curtain.

My breath hitches at her mention of if I'm granted entrance. My heart starts pounding at an unsteady rhythm and my head feels all light and dizzy.

"Hey, it's going to be okay. Here put your head between your legs. You're panicking." She says calmly while guiding my head down.

My heart feels like it's going so haywire that it may just beat right out of my chest. Maybe I have the virus, I don't know, but right now I feel like I'm dying.

"Deep breaths honey. Here breathe in, breathe out, breathe in, breathe out." She strokes my hair in an oddly maternal gesture.

My heart becomes increasingly steady and I feel my body starting to relax again. "What was that? Am I sick?" I sit up with frightened eyes.

"No honey, you only had a panic attack. You'll be just fine. What is your name?" She asks.

"Willow." My voice seems a little unsteady still so I reiterate, "Willow Mosby."

"Nice to meet you Willow. My name is Nurse Laurie. You need to try not to panic like that again okay?" She says looking at me with concerned eyes.

I nod my head in compliance.

"You will be just fine. Don't worry and if you start feeling a panic attack coming on again, just take deep breaths and focus on calming your body." She pats my leg and then says, "They should be in soon. The testing only takes a few minutes."

"Thank you." I say to her. She smiles and exits the room.

I lie down on the exam table and stare at the ceiling, while taking deep cleansing breaths. I do my best not to look at the needles and strange contraptions on the table next to me. It's so hard to stay calm when I feel like my very world is catapulting out of control. This tent, the needles, the F.E.M.A. facility, the end of the world, it all scares me to death. Last week I was doing homeschool lessons with my mom and this week I'm facing the end of my life, as I know it. "Once upon a time, there was a girl..." I try to tell myself a story to make me feel less afraid but I'm interrupted when three F.E.M.A. officials enter my room. All of them are wearing identifications on their biohazard suits that mark them as doctors. Two of the doctors are male and one is female.

"Willow Mosby?" The woman asks.

I sit up and nod my head.

"We are going to run some tests, is that okay." She asks.

No! No, it's not okay! "Yes." I barely choke out.

They go about taking my vitals. The male doctor, the chubby one, sticks me with a needle none too gently and takes four vials of my lifeblood from me. I wince as he moves the needle around in my vein trying to get the blood to flow faster.

The other male doctor sticks some circular patches just above my heart and on each side of my forehead. A handheld machine relays whatever data he was searching for. They move so quickly that, just as the nurse declared, they were finished within ten minutes. All three of the doctors leave the room without saying anything.

That was so freaky! I look to the exam table and realize they took the container of immunizations with them. Only the two needles that were lying on the table remain. I wonder what that means. What if I was declined? What other reason would they have to not give me a shot? My heart starts accelerating again and my breath quickens. I throw my head between my legs like Nurse Laurie taught me. Taking long deep breaths I succeed in warding off another panic attack.

As if sensing that she was needed, Nurse Laurie opens the curtain and comes to my side. She places my passport just beneath my eyes to where I can read the bright red stamp that states ACCEPTED in bold print.

I look up at her with grateful eyes.

"See, I told you it would be okay," she smiles.

I nod my head, too relieved to speak.

"Okay, so I have to give you an immunization. Once I give you this you will be promptly taken to the facility. I have to read you a disclaimer first though, alright?" She looks at me waiting for my answer.

"Okay." I say a little unsure.

"You will receive one immunization that has not been thoroughly tested by the FDA. By accepting the immunization, you are hereby-releasing F.E.M.A. and or the FDA from any and all liability if this immunization results in adverse side effects or death. Willow Mosby, would you like to accept this immunization by your own free will?" Nurse Laurie asks.

I stare at her rather incredulously. I know that I wanted to be a big girl, being a teen and all, but should I really be left with this decision on my own? "Um, I need to speak to my dad." I say hesitantly.

"Your father has already signed the approval for you to have the immunization. However, we are giving every person over the age of fourteen the opportunity to decline if they so wish." She looks at me sympathetically.

I look at the needles holding the bright foreign liquid and then back up at Nurse Laurie. Clearing my throat, I say at barely above a whisper, "Yes, I accept."

She nods, and lifts up a needle with a dark green fluid that I hadn't realized she was carrying. She gently inserts it into my arm. While the mossy serum is pushed into my blood stream I take a closer look at the vial and notice that it's labeled PROJECT ELE, I shiver when she pulls the needle out.

"Do I have to have those two?" I ask pointing to the remaining ones that were not a part of the set of ten.

She looks at them like they are lethal and replies, "No, those are given as a parting gift to someone who is declined."

"A gift?" I ask skeptically.

"Willow, I don't want to scare you." She answers carefully.

"I was just...curious." I ask hoping that she will shed some light on such a strange 'gift.'

"The yellow one here is supposed to help sustain a life for three years. It doesn't protect against the heat but it could possibly allow someone a fighting chance if they found a way to keep their bodies cool and if they found an untainted food-water source. It's completely untested and it is doubtful that it will work, but we felt compelled to do something. Most countries aren't even providing such an immunization, but we fought for it. The thought of turning away so many is unbearable without the slightest sliver of hope." Nurse Laurie looks at me with sad eyes. I can tell that those eyes have seen a few too many people declined.

"What about the red one?" I ask.

She stares at me in silence for a few moments, deciding whether she wants to share the answer to that question with me. As if realizing that she's already past the point of no return, she answers: "The red one brings death. A swift and painless death."

My eyes bug out of my head, her answer startling me, catching me completely off guard. Why would anyone take the red shot?

"Look Willow, there is only a limited amount of room inside of the shelter and we can't afford to fill those spaces with someone who doesn't have the odds in their favor for survival. Many of the people who are being turned away have some strand, maybe even a latent strand of the virus. Usually those infected go to a hospital where they are pumped with morphine and other pain relieving drugs to help their exit from this life to be as painless as possible.

Dying of the virus is excruciating." Her eyes glaze a bit as if remembering something from her past. She shakes it off and continues. "This shot would bring a quick and painless death to the person if they so wish to take it." She studies me waiting to see if I am going to break down any second.

My eyes tear up but I remain stoically straight. How am I supposed to process that kind of information? Either way I decide that I will be strong. I have to be strong. Plus, I'm going inside. I've been accepted.

She gives me a sad yet proud smile and says, "You are a brave one Willow. I think you will make it through this just fine."

A guttural scream breaks out from somewhere down the hall startling both Nurse Laurie and myself.

"No!" The person cries. Not just any person, my mom! I jump off the exam table and run out of the room before Nurse Laurie can restrain me.

"Mom!" I yell. I can hear her cries coming from a few rooms down. I open curtains trying to find her and succeed in startling patient after patient until I find her. My mom is hunched over Sebastian holding him in a death grip. She's crying so hard that her back is shaking up and down. Tears spring to my eyes as the panic and fear runs cold through my blood.

"Mom, Sabby!" I run and cling to them. "What's wrong?" I look down at my little brother expecting him to be hurt or worse, dead. He's breathing just fine and looking at me with scared, tear filled eyes. He doesn't understand what's going on, how can he?

My mom doesn't answer me so I look around trying to find out what's wrong. My mom's passport is lying open on the ground. I breathe a huge sigh of relief when I see the ACCEPTED stamp that's splayed across it.

"No, no, no." My mom keeps repeating through her tears while stroking Sebastian's curls.

My dad throws open the curtain and runs in the room. "Alice, what's wrong, what happened?" His voice cracks ever so slightly. I can see that his eyes mimic the same fear mine do. My dad rushes to her side and falls to his knees.

"No, no, no." My mom continually whimpers rocking Sebastian back and forth.

My dad shakes her lightly to get her to answer. "Alice, please tell me what's wrong."

Her arms are holding Sebastian so tight refusing to let him go. I follow my dad's gaze down to my mom's hand. She's clutching something and as if answering my dad's question she lets the object fall to the bed behind Sebastian.

We both look down simultaneously to find Sebastian's cute four-year-old face staring back at us from his passport. Across the bottom of the picture there is a big, ugly, red stamp that states: DECLINED.

"No!" I yell, breaking down in sobs. I clutch Sebastian's back and throw my arms around my mom too.

"This can't be right!" My dad's voice cracks. He looks behind us to a doctor who is shaking his head.

"I'm sorry sir. Your son has been infected." His eyes look sorry, yet his expression remains controlled in a way that only someone who has had to declare families grim fates can do.

"No, he is coming with us!" My dad demands.

"I'm sorry sir, he cannot be permitted to enter the facility." The man replies. "I will give you a few minutes to say your goodbyes."

"Nobody is saying goodbye!" My dad grabs the front of the doctor's biohazard suit and pulls him so close to his face that you can see my dad's spit land on the clear face shield.

"Sir, remove your hands immediately." Another official standing in the entryway points a gun at my dad. My dad slowly holds his hands up and steps away from the doctor.

My eyes widen in pure shock.

"I'm sorry sir, but you need to say your goodbyes." The man who has a badge stating that he is security, states empathetically. He puts the gun away and escorts the doctor out of the room giving our family some privacy.

"They said they could give him a shot that would allow him to go peacefully, the bastards! They want to put my son to sleep like they would an animal!" My mom says pulling away from Sebastian only slightly. Her face is red and puffy and full of pain. Her eyes are filled with indignation.

"No, no, no." This time it's my dad's turn to be weak. His legs give out beneath him and he falls to the floor. He's crying so hard that his painful moans break my heart into tiny little pieces. My mom moves Sebastian into my arms and goes to kneel beside her husband.

I grasp onto Sebastian as if my life depends on it. He cries and holds me tightly. "Wello, Wello, I so scared Wello." He cries into my chest.

I brush his hair back from his forehead and kiss him on the cheek. "Look at me Sebastian." His giant blue eyes look into mine. I stifle the sob that threatens to unleash itself and say, "You are going to be okay Sabby. We will all be okay. Nobody is going to leave you alone. If you can't go inside, none of us are going inside." Tears of helplessness fall freely down my face.

"No, Willow. You are going inside." My mom looks up at me but keeps her arms around my dad.

"No way!" I yell. "There is no way! I will not leave him!" I yell it so loudly that Sebastian cowers and puts his little hands over his ears.

My dad sits up and wipes his eyes. He takes a few deep breaths, stands up and helps my mom up as well. "Willow, your mom is right."

"No dad!" I cry. "We are a family, remember?"

My dad's eyes are filled with sadness, pain and a hint of understanding. In that moment, I can tell he feels the same way I feel. I can see it there on his face. He comes over and puts his arms around the two of us. Placing gentle kisses on the top of Sebastian and my heads. He takes another deep breath and says, "Willow, you and your mother will go inside. Our family will carry on. I will stay with Sebastian."

"Absolutely not!" My mom declares. "I am staying

with Sebastian."

My dad turns to look at my mom. "Alice, I'll stay with our son. I can't just leave him. You go inside with Willow."

"No! I can't Henry. I can't!" She crumbles to the floor, the unrelenting sobs starting back up. My dad sits down next to her and pulls her into his arms. He strokes her hair and kisses her tenderly on her forehead, her cheek and her lips. My mom wipes her hands across her nose and says, "I can't do it Henry. I can't go inside and pretend that I didn't leave my baby out here." She sniffles and tears stain her cheeks.

"And I can?" My dad asks her incredulously.

My mom looks at him contemplatively and then answers. "No, I know it's just as hard for you as it would be for me. But, my other baby has a chance Henry. Things are only going to get harder and she needs her father. I know that I can't survive this, I couldn't. You are strong. You will survive. You will do it for me. You will do it for Sebastian. You will take care of our girl." My mom looks up at me with nothing but love and hope.

"No, mom, I need you too. I need all of you." I beg. "We will all stay. The nurse, she told me about the shots. That they could possibly help us if we don't make it inside."

My mom shakes her head and says compassionately. "It's possible Willow. Did she tell you that the other immunizations would negatively react with that shot and could cause death? You can't mix the two."

No, the nurse didn't tell me that! Granted, she

probably didn't think I needed that information since I was accepted, but still!

"I didn't take the immunizations Willow. So you are right, we do have a chance." My mom tries to muster up a smile. She looks to my dad whose eyes confirm that he did in fact take the immunizations.

"It's settled then. Sebastian and I will take the shot and we will do our best to survive this. You two will go inside and you will move on. If it is meant to be, we will find you." My mom kisses my dad passionately on the lips then stands up and pulls Sebastian and me into her arms.

"I can't go mom." I cry into her shoulder. My dad comes up behind me and joins in on the family hug. We cling to each other in a mess of limbs and tears.

"I love you so much." My mom cries.

"I love you," My dad whispers.

"Wuv you." Sebastian whimpers.

I take a deep breath and say a very shaky, "I love you."

This is it, the end of the world for me. I had known the second I entered this tent that my life would never be the same. I wish I had known that my heart would be ripped from my chest and trampled on. I wish I could cease to exist at this very moment, but I know I can't. I have to cling to the hope that my mom and my brother will make it. I have no choice but to keep moving on. I'm broken beyond repair but when the officials come to take my father and me into the facility I force my feet to move. I take one step and then another. My heart feels as if gravity is pulling it down so hard that eventually it may fall right out of my chest and becomc one with the earth. I look back down the long white hallway to see my mom and my little brother walking in the opposite direction. That's when I feel it fall, my heart, it's gone. My chest is only a hollow shell and it will never be filled again.

My dad puts his arm around my shoulders and together we walk through the heavily leaded doors into our new home.

THREE

The musty smell within the mountain shelter permeates my nose.

Small strands of single bulb lights line the main hallway illuminating the six-foot high tunnel. My dad keeps his head ducked down partially because of his height but my guess is that it's more due to his family having just been ripped apart.

There isn't much room to either side of us but we can still walk comfortably. I'm grateful in this moment that I'm not claustrophobic. We follow the string of bulbs slowly and cautiously taking turns, feeling the rock on either side of us. A damp artificially cool draft begins hitting our faces the further we get into the tunnel. A few feet later I begin hearing noises: people talking, water dripping, paper crumbling. Up ahead the lights get brighter and we are able to make out a few figures.

As we near closer to the figures their faces become more visible. Everyone looks rather emotionless and they are all dressed identically in pale green scrubs. While the scrubs look horrendous, it is a huge step up from those creepy biohazard suits. I guess since we have all passed the test, they no longer need to worry about contagions.

A plump woman with unusually frizzy brown hair greets us with an arm full of pamphlets. She is smiling broadly and has an uncalled for cheeriness to her demeanor. "Well, on behalf of F.E.M.A. we want to welcome you to your new home." She hands us each a pamphlet and continues, "Inside you will find instructions and information about life in the shelter. On page two there is a map. Please note which direction you are facing now: it's East. Room assignments are given on a first come first serve basis. May I please see your passports?"

My dad hands her our stamped passports.

"Okay, lets see here," she says while scanning the documents with her eyes. "Looks like you will be in the Blue wing; that's numbers 400 through 499." She continues by giving my dad directions to where the Blue wing is. "We ask that once you find your living quarters you write your name on the nameplate outside of the door and report to headquarters to log it into the system. Once you log in at headquarters you will be given your clothing allotment for your stay here. Any questions so far?"

My dad and I look at each other and shake our heads.

"Good," she continues. "Well, if you need anything, and I mean anything at all, just look for the hospitality officials dressed in green. Feel free to ask for me personally. My name is Mary and I'm always here to help." She gives us a huge smile as my dad and I struggle to return it.

It's strange how the world keeps going even when

your life is crumbling down around you. Mary's smile seems so out of place in my world. Doesn't she realize that we are still mourning what just happened moments before? Lord only knows how long it will take us to come to terms with everything, if we even can.

My dad puts his hand lightly on my back and ushers me away from Mary-smiles-a-lot. The tunnel we were in opens up into a large cavernous room. I look back at the tunnel exit and see two large steel enforced doors standing open. I wonder if they plan on locking us in here once the final entrants are accepted. The room looks to be the eating quarters due to the small salt and pepper shakers scattered about. My dad and I sit at one of the tables to examine the pamphlet. I quickly scan through mine but find the boring legalities of what is written far too complicated for me. I'll ask dad for the cliff notes version later. Instead I find the map and begin scanning all of the different amenities. I have a photographic memory, which allows me to memorize the layout quickly. It looks like they threw together a library, a cinema room, a cafeteria, a pool and a bowling alley. I find where they placed the rooms and it seems they are relatively scattered amongst the entire mountain. I scan down to find that there is an entire level, almost as big on the map as the level we are on and the level above us combined, that is under where we are sitting. The map points out locations like a garden, livestock, a chemistry laboratory, and nurse/doctor stations. The garden and livestock areas take up an entire floor. I guess that answers where our food will be coming from.

Below this section is another level that is marked: Storage.

"So dad, where do you think we should find a room?" I watch him scan his portion of the map.

"Well," he says pointing to the map. "The lady said we were in the Blue wing which is located here." He points to a spot on the map that is thankfully color coded. "I believe if we follow this hallway we should run right into it." He attempts to give me a small smile but it falls just as quickly as it started. We get up from the tables with maps in hand and head off to explore.

As we browse through the rooms in the Blue wing we find that they seem to be identical. There are two bunks, a dresser, a tiny couch, an end table and a small bathroom. There couldn't be more than three hundred square feet of space total.

We end up choosing a room near the elevators and my dad writes our names on the small board on the door.

"Can I have top bunk?" I ask my dad.

"Well, of course. I would rather have the bottom any day. These old legs aren't what they used to be."

"Then I guess I better take the bottom two dresser drawers since we don't want to risk those knees giving out when you bend to get your undies." I don't know where the joke comes from but it does lighten the air just a bit.

"Deal." My dad says.

I climb onto the bed and test the mattress. Not a Tempurpedic, but not bad either. I lay down staring at the ceiling. Oh how I wish I had some glow in the dark star stickers to affix to it like I used to have in my room. I close my eyes and pretend that I am lying in my bed back at home. If I try hard enough I can even hear my mom playing the piano softly in the study. The imaginary sound fades away and I open my eyes a few moments later to find the stark white ceiling staring back at me. I take a deep breath and my chest hurts. 'But this is my home now, remember?' I say to myself.

"Well," my dad begins rubbing his hands together. "My watch says it's fifteen till six and dinner is at seven, so we should head over to register our room and get our clothes before dinner."

I look down at my hideous hospital gown. Ever since leaving my mom and Sebastian back at the testing station, I've felt dazed, like this whole thing isn't reality. Everything feels so ethereal and perhaps at some moment I will just float up out of my body and realize that this has all been one horrific nightmare. My dad looks at me with concerned eyes and when I study how ridiculous he looks in his hospital gown, I understand that there is no way this could be a dream. No pinch will pull me out of this reality. "Yeah, well lets just hope that we don't have to wear puke green." I say to my dad. I see just the slightest twitch in his expression that on another day, with different circumstances would have turned into a smile.

He pulls out his gown and does a slightly lethargic curtsy then says, "After you my dear."

My dad is such an amazing father. I can see that whatever it might take from him, even if it's lying boldly to my face, he's going to be my rock in this situation. I can only imagine how crushed he is feeling right now. We take the elevator to the first floor. I grab my father's hand as we step out and walk down the long corridor towards the headquarters. He holds it so tight that I imagine nothing could separate us, ever. We are all we've got for now. If my dad is going to be a rock for me, then I sure as heck will be one for him.

The Headquarters looks oddly like a mall. Several different shops, or stations are set up in a square that raises two stories high. At least ten shops advertising different types of services are located on each level. From my viewpoint I can see an administrative office that takes up three shop spaces, a pharmacy, a counselor office, a physical therapist office, a small convenience store and three different clothing stores. What I can see from the storefront windows is that the clothing stores all carry scrubs like the pale green ones, but in several different sizes and colors. I don't spot a single pair of jeans in there.

I sigh and my dad squeezes my hand teasingly. We walk to the administrative offices and get in line behind the counter, which holds a large sign stating: Last Names M-O. In front of us in line there are three other families dressed in similar hospital gowns. I can't help but notice that the family directly in front of us seems happy and complete. And when I say complete, I mean there are four of them... in the same family. A small spark of jealousy mixed with a large spark of envy fills my heart. I watch as a small toddler hugs tightly to her mom's leg. A tear escapes my eye and my dad lets go of my hand for a second to wipe it away and then silently takes my hand and squeezes it even tighter than before. He feels it too.

The line passes quickly and when it's our turn a short red haired man waves us to the counter. "Last name?" he asks.

"Mosby," my dad answers then hands him both of our passports.

"Have you picked a room?"

"Yes, room 442." Says my dad. He knew my affinity to even numbers so he made sure to pick a room accordingly.

The man goes about typing at the speed of light onto his computer. A short minute passes then he says. "You will receive your schedules and work assignments tomorrow." He bends down and grabs something from beneath the counter. He pulls out two tablets and places them in front of us. "Please keep these tablets with you at all times. There is an orientation app on the front screen that will give you all of the information you need to know about your new life here." He presses the app on the screen of my tablet demonstrating how the touch screen works and then closes the app before the video loads. "If for any reason your tablet malfunctions, please bring it back here and we will get you a new one. Do you have any questions?"

Both my father and I shake our heads.

The man seems satisfied with our answer and hands the tablets to us. "You may now proceed to Clothing Room A to collect your new wardrobe."

"Thank you." My dad says and then together, with our tablets in hand, we head towards the row of clothing stores.

The temperature in the common area is a little too cold for my flimsy hospital gown so I am anxious to get something on with a little more sustenance. I will say one thing. I am thankful that they aren't the gowns with the opening in the back!

We come upon the nearest shop and enter in the front door, which has been propped up with a shoe for a doorstop. I immediately notice the lack in variation from one outfit to the next. It is as I feared. The only thing available is scrubs, they simply vary in color. A small beep sounds when we enter, triggering a chain reaction. Walking towards us, in the lead, is a tall, lanky, flamboyant man followed by two women succeeding closely on his heels.

He stops a few feet from us and begins to take us in. He looks us over like he would when making a selection for prime meat. He circles us muttering "mmmhmm," as he goes. He returns to his original position and snaps both his fingers twice. The women must understand what this means because the one on the left immediately hands him a tape measure while the one on the right wipes his brow. Oh brother, I think to myself. You've GOT to be kidding me.

"You," he points at me. "Come with me." Snapping his finger, he turns on his heel and walks off with a purpose. I sneak a glance in the direction of my father but he just shakes his head, mouth still propped open in a shocked expression. I turn my attention back to the disaster at hand and follow quickly behind the man that's about to disappear around a corner.

He stands me on a small stool and has me hold out my arms. The woman, whom I'm guessing is his assistant, comes in the room with a clipboard and pen. She nods her head and he begins taking measurements. He barks out the measurements as she writes them down. They go on like that for ten minutes or so. My arms are on fire by the time he tells me he's finished. I rub them trying to get the blood circulating again. The woman leaves the room for a moment and comes back with an armful of scrubs in her hands. She leaves them on a chair for me; then retreats.

"Which color you want?" She asks me. I'm taken aback by her accent, which is obviously foreign. Our borders have been closed for years, well, as long as I can remember at least. Since our government passed the 28th amendment all export and import shipping stopped as well as flights overseas. They felt foreigners held too much threat to our society after numerous illnesses wreaked havoc through our nation. Since then we've had a policy where no one goes in and no one goes out. It really sparks my curiosity knowing this woman could be from The Outside as we call it.

"Hmmm," I respond. "I think I'll take the periwinkle, the chartreuse and the indigo." Yes, there's a reason why I said that. I wanted to gauge if she was a recent immigrant or if she has been here a while. Chances are, if she's been here a while, she'd have to know at least one, maybe two of these colors.

She gives me a blank stare and then sets the clothes

in the chair. "You pick three and take to front." She turns on her heel and leaves the room.

Darn, thought I had her.

I change into the pink scrubs and when I throw my hospital gown into the metal disposal bin I hear a clinking sound. I nearly forgot! I hastily grab the gown and with a shaking hand I work on retrieving the item that I stowed away in its hem. I don't know how I worked it in there so well because it doesn't come out as easily as it went in. I work the fabric on the hem back and forth exposing it a little more each time.

A knock on the door startles me. The lady who gave me the scrubs comes in without waiting for me to answer. I have to shove the gown behind my back. "Ouch." I cry out as something pricks my hand.

"You okay?" She asks.

I nod quickly and with wide frightened eyes I say, "Can I help you?" My heart is accelerating and I feel nauseous.

"I was just checking on you since it was taking you a while to change." She studies me like I'm crazy.

"I'm fine, I need another minute." I say and tears start springing to my eyes as a dizzy sensation washes over me.

She hesitates and I can tell she is contemplating asking me more questions. Thankfully she doesn't. She just says, "Please try to hurry. There are more people waiting on the dressing rooms." Then she leaves shutting the door behind her.

"Crap, no, no, no!" I cry to myself as soon as she's gone. Tears are flowing out of my eyes as I pull my hands and the gown back in front of me. I look down at my left wrist and see the faintest sign of a puncture mark. "No." I whisper as my heart pounds like drums in my chest. I'm not ready to die! I pull the gown back up in front of me and work the item out of the hem quickly now. The needle had poked through and as I work it the rest of the way out I notice that most of the red serum is still inside it. Maybe none of it went into me. I tell myself trying to calm my thoughts down. I don't know why I took it from Sebastian's room but I did. I guess I did it because I didn't want him to have it. I recall the explanation from the nurse. It might seem selfish that I took it but I felt like I had to protect him. I know the nurse said how painful the virus could be but I can't imagine Sebastian's life being sucked out of him by a single shot.

I sit down and put my head between my knees while taking deep breaths. I tell myself over and over again that none of it was injected in me.

"Please hurry." The lady calls from outside the door.

"Just one more minute." I say out of breath as I sit back up. Standing I have to steady myself against the wall for a moment to allow the dizzy spell to settle. When the world stops swaying, I move into action. I take the needle to the metal disposal bin and empty the remaining serum into it. Red liquid stains the trashed hospital gowns in the bin making it look like they were used to clean up crime scene. Then I carefully wrap the empty needle up with my old gown and shove it down above the red stained ones.

I throw on my new pair of bright white tennis shoes and look at myself in the floor length mirror. My hair looks wild and crazy and my eyes are filled with worry. I keep telling myself that I will be fine. I grimace and then leave the dressing area.

I meet my dad at the counter and see him clutching his clothes for dear life. His face is crimson red, which just happens to match his new set of scrubs. He mutters something under his breath about being violated. A small smile forces its way onto my face.

"Tablets please," the man asks while ripping them from our hands. Why he even bothers to ask in the first place is beyond me. He plugs each tablet into a USB port that's connected to a laptop and begins punching away at something. Within a few minutes he disconnects them. "You will each get five pairs of scrubs per season, two sets of pajamas and five sets of undergarments. Obviously there are four seasons per year. We advise you to take care of your clothing; wash on a delicate cycle in cold water, dry on low. If for any reason you are unable to care for them properly and they are damaged, there are sewing kits available for purchase here and in the general store. But I advise you, they are very pricey. In addition to your regular clothing, you will receive one bathing suit per year and one pair of shoes per year. Additional footwear will be allotted for growing children if their sizes should change." He hands us back our tablets. We grab our new clothes and make our way back into the commons area.

My dad picks a table near the outside and we place our things in the empty chairs. My dad's eyes roam over to a line near the entrance of the meal serving area that currently looks to be closed. "Well, Willow, looks like we should probably get in line. They must be opening for dinner soon."

I give him a half smile and grab my tablet. I'm not sure if we'll need it, but if they said to bring it everywhere, then by golly, I'm going to bring it everywhere.

We wind up in line behind a lady who looks to be by herself. She picks at her nails and shifts her weight back and forth from the balls of her feet. She looks exceedingly nervous and her actions are causing my unease. Suddenly she turns and stares at me. I'm a bit too shocked to turn away.

"We should go. We really should go." She says in a hoarse whisper. My eyes widen a bit in surprise because in all actuality, there is nowhere to go. "Bad things are going to happen--really bad things. We should get out while we still can!" Her breathing becomes more labored as her eyes dart about looking for God only knows what.

I feel my dad's arm wrap around me and give me a slight squeeze. The woman turns back around and begins talking with intensity to a woman in front of her.

That was just bizarre, I think to myself. Her warning did conjure up the accident I just had with the needle. I breathe a sigh of relief knowing that most likely nothing entered my system. The nurse had said the serum would bring immediate death. I think I'm in the clear now that we've past the immediate time frame. I hope that no other 'bad things' will happen though.

A grinding sound has us all turning to stare at the closed, meal serving area. A large metal gate begins to wind itself up revealing a cafeteria like setup. There are serving people behind the counter in hairnets holding giant ladles. Trays are stacked to the right of them along with multi-portion style plates. The line begins to move as we all inch forward. I'm not too hungry myself, but I vow to at least attempt to eat what they serve.

Within a few minutes we finally make it to the front of the line. My dad and I each grab a tray and a plate and set them on the three metal bars. As we move down the line we are served a variety of different scoops of varying colors. I don't pay too much attention until we are at the end of the line. "Tablets," a woman says in a raspy voice. I hand her my tablet and she scans a barcode I hadn't noticed on the back. "Next." She hands me back my tablet and I struggle to carry it with one hand and my tray in the other. Surprisingly, I make it back to our table without breaking or dumping anything. My dad joins me a moment later.

We eat in silence--well, my dad eats and I move things around on my plate, hoping maybe he won't notice. The colorful mush looks worse than the food they served outside of the shelter. My stomach rolls with nausea and any thoughts of eating quickly fly out of the window.

To pass the time, I take out my tablet and find the calendar on the home-screen. I tap it once and scan down to our current time. It's only seven in the evening although it feels much later. The lack of sun in here makes it impossible to tell time without consulting a clock.

My dad finishes his meal, and then we both carry our trays to the dish wash station to place them in the bins. "Why don't we go back to the room?" My dad suggests. "Unless you want to check out the amenities?"

I look at his tired eyes and say, "Nah, we can check them out tomorrow." I feel relieved that the accident earlier today didn't have any effect on me and that there will be a tomorrow. All of the worrying made me exhausted though. It's taking everything I have not to just curl up in a ball and fade away. Sleep will do me good.

"NO!" I try to grab for my little brother's hand and it slips through my fingers. "Sabby!" I cry out to him as he starts sliding across the floor further and further away from me. Or is he being dragged?

"Wello!" He cries while reaching his little hands towards me, begging me to help him. His blue eyes are wild and filled with tears.

I try to stand up and run to him but a man in a biohazard suit is holding me down. I struggle with all my might to free myself but it's useless. My limbs feel weighed down and when I try to stand it feels like I'm fighting against gravity itself.

"Willow, it's okay." I turn to look at the man in the biohazard suit but he's gone, my dad is standing there reaching out to me. I try to reach out to him but the edges of my vision become blurred and I feel as though I'm on the verge of blacking out.

"Willow, wake up honey."

I hear my dad calling to me but I can't see him anymore, everything went black. An earthquake erupts and the world starts shaking. I'm too tired to open my eyes and take cover under my bed.

"Willow!" My dad calls again, his voice rises with concern.

I finally come to and pry my eyes open to find my dad shaking me. I look around dazed trying to decipher reality from dream.

"It's okay honey, it was just a dream." My dad says soothingly, pulling me into his arms. He's sitting on the edge of the top bunk with me. I take a few deep breaths and when the reminder of Sebastian being torn from my hands floods back into my brain, I break down. I sob into my dad's chest and cling to him as if he is my life force, the only thing keeping me attached to this world.

"Why dad?" I cry and bang my fist against his chest. "Why are we here?" I pull away from him and curl into a ball on my bed crying with all my might.

My dad doesn't answer me right away. He picks me up and cradles me in his arms like he used to do when I was a small child. I feel teardrops fall on my arms and when I look up at my dad I see that they are from him.

He wipes them away and looks at me with all of the love in the world. "Because we are meant to be here honey. That's why we are here."

"But we left them dad." I say barely above a whisper.

The guilt of the situation is weighing heavily on my shoulders.

I feel my dad's body shake ever so slightly and he does everything he can to not break down in this second. "I know." He whispers and looks away. He takes several deep, shaky breaths. "We will pray that they make it. That's all that we can do now is hope and hold onto faith."

"If they don't...make it?" I find myself choking on my last two words.

"If they don't then maybe they are being spared from a worse fate. We don't know why things happen in this life but everything is for a purpose. If they...don't make it." My dad chokes on his words too. "Then they will be in a much better place than here."

I stare into my dad's eyes. "Do you really believe that?" I ask.

He nods his head and says, "With all my heart."

With that I wipe away my tears and move back into a sitting position next to my dad on the bed. Hope, I repeat over and over again in my head.

"Willow, I am here for you. I will not leave you. I promise." My dad hugs me and I hug him back as hard as I can.

"I am here for you too dad."

"I know." He pats me on the back and then hops down off the top bunk.

"You need to try and get some sleep now. I love you."

"Love you too." I lie back down and fall into a dreamless sleep.

FOUR

I wake up to alarms going off in the hallway.

I open my eyes and see a sensor of some sort on the ceiling flashing a bright white light over and over again.

"We need to go Willow. Get up and change quickly please." My dad says calmly.

"All persons report to headquarters." A woman's voice calls out calmly.

I look up at the speaker system in the corner of our room. I look back at my dad confused. "What time is it dad?"

"It's around 5:00 am. It's okay Willow, you need to get dressed though. They said in the orientation video that we would have routine drills and assemblies. That's probably what this is."

I nod my head and quickly hop down from my bed. I grab an ugly pair of blue scrubs from my drawer and head into the bathroom to change. I cringe at the sight of my unruly curls and decide to throw them into a quick ponytail. Even when it's wrapped in a band, curls still manage to pop out on their own as if they can metaphorically do so.

A few minutes later we both leave our room, tablets

in hand and join the masses of people flooding in the same direction down the stairwells and into the hallways. I look around and everyone looks just as dazed and confused as I do. This must be the first drill or assembly they've done here. I hold onto my dad's hand as we are herded into the headquarters. We pass by the administration offices and clothing stores until we reach an area that I could of sworn used to be just a wall. Now it's completely open and beyond it is a gigantic assembly hall that has thousands of stadium style seats surrounding an elevated stage. It reminds me of a football stadium and it even comes equipped with a jumbo-tron above the stage so people can still see all the way up in the nosebleed seats. F.E.M.A security guards in blue uniforms direct us towards seats, which are at a first come first serve basis. We follow the crowd up several flights of stairs until my dad finds us two isle seats near the middle of the stadium.

It feels like hours pass before the entire stadium is fully seated. I fill the time messing with my tablet. I watch several short tour videos that familiarize us with the amenities and different aspects of shelter life. When the lights start to dim, I look up and find myself amazed by the shear magnitude of people that are being housed in this shelter. All of the screens of each person's tablets glow like large blue fireflies in this gigantic cavern. A hushed silence overcomes the crowd when the jumbo-tron flickers on and a man's face appears on the screen. Not just any man though, the President of the United States.

"My fellow Americans, by now you may know that

we are facing a global shift in our way of life. We must consider that we are a country who has sacrificed in the past, not only for our way of life but to help those around the world who in dire circumstances needed us by their side. Today I am asking you to find your greatest resolve and sacrifice once more for the greater good of all. As a country, as a planet we must do what is required of us to support the preservation of our species: the human race. Those of you currently isolated in shelters: know that you are not alone. In these uncertain times the greatest comfort we can have is hope, hope in the future we are all helping to save: generations, for our children and our children's children. Thank you for your dedication to our cause as a nation, a world and may God help us all."

The speech ends and the screen turns blue. We all patiently wait in silence. A few seconds pass and a new face appears on the screen. This one I don't recognize.

A middle-aged man wearing a white lab coat and sporting a greying goatee speaks up. "Good morning citizens of F.E.M.A. shelter three. My name is Dr. Jim Hastings. I am in charge of this facility and I'm on the board for Project ELE. By now you all should have received your tablets, rooms and clothing allotment. As we all get situated and schedules get made please remain patient, as wait times will be longer than usual. As you have probably noticed already, we are a city encased within a mountain. As with any city there are rules that govern and keep us safe. If you would all flip your tablet to the blinking icon on the bottom of your screen and follow along. We are going to be going over some different rules and expectations for the next hour or so. If you have any questions please type it in the space below and one of our government officials will respond as quickly as possible."

I watch as a blinking icon appears in the corner of my tablet. I press it and a slide show presentation appears with highlighted bullet points. I try and not nod off during the remainder of the session but figure my dad will fill me in on any necessary details when we're finished. Then, a topic appears on my screen titled, "Work Assignments." This sparks my attention.

"As with any city," Dr. Hastings drones on, "each of us needs to pitch in for the city to properly function. Upon entry we took your measurements and weight to be able to assign a proper job to each of you. Age and ability have also been taken into consideration." A new icon pops up onto my screen. "In a few moments a new icon will become available on each of your screens. These are your temporary job placements. I say temporary because some may need adjusting as time may dictate. In addition, your tablets will hold your daily schedule. Please make sure you are timely to all appointments. With that said, you are all dismissed."

In anxiousness, I press the small blinking icon and am taken to a new screen. In large block letters at the top it reads, RUNNER. Runner? I look over at my dad's screen and his says SANITATION DEPARTMENT. Ewwww, I think to myself.

My dad must agree because he groans. He looks over onto my screen. "Runner? They're making children work? What is a Runner anyway?" He looks up at me confused. I just shrug my shoulders.

"It's okay dad, I don't mind." I really don't. I've never worked before, this may be cool, especially if there's money involved.

"You should be in school." He starts ferociously typing into the question box on the tablet. He hits send and we both sit there waiting for a response. People slowly file by us to exit the auditorium, but we remain seated. There's really no use in joining the masses to wait in yet another line to exit the place.

An answer pops up on the screen. "You will find an app labeled EDUCATION on your tablet screen. This will go over our shelter educational programs. Do you require any additional service?"

My dad types in "no." He looks at his tablet and doesn't see an education app on it. We look at mine and find the app in the lower left hand corner. I press on the icon that looks like an apple. We watch the presentation on F.E.M.A. education opportunities. They call the program, "Learning For A Brighter Future." I'm not sure how bright it will be with only four hours of class per day. Only children under the age of fifteen are eligible for full day classes. At the end of the presentation an online application pulls up. It is there for me to apply for Select classes. This would grant me a full eight hours of classes in substitute of working.

I look to my dad hoping that he will allow me to just close the box. "No honey, you are applying." My dad says.

I let out an exaggerated breath. I don't mind working. Of course I've never had to work before so I don't know what to expect but I do know that I wouldn't mind not having to go to school for eight hours a day. It's not that I don't like school or anything, I just often find myself bored. With a photographic memory, I learn quickly and find the repetitive assignments and lectures annoying. Going to work would be a new adventure. Plus, it would keep me busy. If I'm busy then I won't have time to think of my mom or my brother. I push back the tears and begin filling in the applicable fields. After I press send we both stand up and head out of the auditorium.

The line to exit is much shorter now and we find ourselves in the hallway a few minutes later. Outside we locate several tables set up with cereal bars and cups of water. We each grab a cereal bar and a cup of water then head back in the direction of our room.

I nearly drop my cup when my tablet vibrates in my hand startling me. I look at it and see a schedule reminder flash across the screen. Report to room 231 for class. Great, another odd number. The time on my tablet says 9:00 am. I look over at my dad who is looking at his tablet as well.

He looks over at mine. "Okay honey, I guess this is where we part ways. Will you be okay finding your room without me?" We both learned during the orientation that we are only allowed three tardies per month. He shakes his head and says, "Never mind, I'm walking you there."

"No dad. I can find it, don't worry. See, this GPS map will lead me there no problem." I show him the flashing map on my screen. The green dot shows us where we are and the red dot shows the room that I'm supposed to report to. It's on a level above us. I don't really need the map since I've already memorized most of the layout, but it's nice to have.

"I don't like this at all. I shouldn't be leaving you alone. Are you going to be okay?" His eyebrows furrow in worry.

"I'll be fine dad. I've got this. I'm fifteen, nearly sixteen, remember? I can certainly find a room on my own." I smile even though I do feel the building anxiety at being separated from my dad so soon.

He looks at me and smiles. "Yeah, fifteen going on thirty! I have to remember how mature and smart you are honey. I know you can get there. Just stay safe. Find a friend in your class and try to stick together. I'd say don't talk to strangers but most everyone here is a stranger. So I'm going to say to go with your gut. You'll know who you can trust and who you can't. If you get any type of uncomfortable vibe from anyone just get as far away from them as you can. Okay?"

"Okay dad. I love you but we both have to go." I give him a hug and then we both take off in opposite directions. I look around and see other kids my age walking alone but the smaller ones are escorted by their guardians.

My stomach twists in knots as I walk along. I feel engulfed by the crowd and I have to work to control my breathing in order to avoid another panic attack. I take the stairs to my right and at the top I'm herded into a hallway filled with mostly children and teens. I look down at the timer on my tablet that says I have only a minute left to get to the room, so I pick up my pace. I reach room 231 with only seconds to spare and find that it looks like any typical school classroom except it's about three times as big. I slide into a seat in the back next to a girl with hair so blonde that it looks white. She looks really uncomfortable and avoids eye contact by pretending to be absorbed in whatever is playing on the screen of her tablet.

The bell rings and I gaze around the room to see that there are more than a hundred students. Even still, the desks are crammed so tightly together that we have very little personal space.

I set my tablet and my cup of water on the desk then open up my cereal bar. I stuff it down as quickly as possible not knowing the rules for eating in the classroom. I have to follow it up with water since the cereal bar was dry like cardboard. Yuck. On the flip side, at least my stomach won't be growling in the middle of class.

"Good morning class." A woman calls out from the front of the room. "My name is Ms. Thomas and I will be your teacher for the semester. We have only a short period of time together, so we will be working hard and fast during our allotted time. This class seems packed to the rim but many of you will be transferred out tomorrow when the Select class assignments are handed out."

A boy runs into the room out of breath, his back is facing us.

"Tablet please." Ms. Thomas holds her hand out

stiffly. He hands it to her. "Reason for tardy?"

"I'm sorry ma'am. I had to take my sister to class and it was on the other end of the hall." He says apologetically but his posture remains stiff and straight.

"Your guardian should take her next time." The teacher says sternly to him.

"Yes, ma'am. She only met her guardian yesterday. Our parents are not with us. I promised her that I would take her to her first class. I won't be late again." He answers.

Ms. Thomas's facial expression softens. She presses a few things on the screen then hands his tablet back to him. "I understand. Today's tardy will be excused. Please be timely going forward. You may take a seat now."

The boy turns around and starts heading towards the back of the room. I suddenly realize that it's Connor; the boy I met in the cooling tent outside. My heart hurts for his loss. Both of his parents are gone. I think about his little sister with the orangey red hair. That makes me think of Sebastian and I am barely able to contain the tears that threaten to flood my eyes. I can't imagine what Connor must be going through. He doesn't have his mom or dad anymore. And now he carries the responsibility of his little sister with him as well. The thought pains me.

Connor takes the desk next to mine. He seems surprised at first to see me, then his face softens and he gives me a half smile. I return it then we both turn to listen to Ms. Thomas's lecture.

The lecture drones on for an hour and a half. Most of the kids around me begin to get fidgety after thirty minutes or so. I watch as Connor draws furiously in a notebook completely ignoring Ms. Thomas. His legs shake violently up and down; you can tell he's trying to fight the urge to get out of his chair and run. I simply take my time observing others. The girl with the 'almost white hair' seems lost. Her hair covers her face and whatever it is she is doing with her tablet.

I pick up my tablet, which we are supposed to be taking notes on and turn it up so Ms. Thomas can't see. Let's see if this sucker has any games, I think to myself. But, alas, the screen is completely locked so I am forced to stare at the boring slide show flashing by at a snails pace. Note to self...bring an alternate activity next time.

"So as you can see class, some of these problems are national and some global. However they can all be tied together through arithmetic and simple science." My eyes fight to stay open while Ms. Thomas drones on. She is starting to sound like the teacher in those ancient Charlie Brown cartoons at this point.

Suddenly my tablet goes blank and so does everyone else's. "So for tomorrows class, you will meet here first thing and I will be sending you our syllabus."

A small bell rings in the classroom signaling our release. Everyone pops out of their seat and begins stretching their arms and legs. I look at a clock on the wall and note that it's lunchtime. Although I really don't need a clock to tell me this…my stomach is protesting already.

My tablet vibrates and a new schedule reminder pops up on the screen.

REPORT FOR WORK ASSIGNMENT:
HEADQUARTERS ADMIN OFFICE 213.

I groan inwardly, what's with all of the odd numbers? Also, where's lunch?

I remember my dad's advice about making a friend and sticking together. I catch Connor staring down at the map on his tablet. "So where are you headed?" I ask.

He looks up and his dark eyes lock onto me. I catch myself staring at them like I did the first time we met. I really haven't seen eyes that dark before. They're interesting and a little bit eerie.

"Um, I guess Headquarters." He looks back at his tablet to study the map. His finger taps the side of the tablet over again. Man, this guy's quite fidgety.

"Oh. I'm headed there too. I can show you where to go." I say.

He looks back at me and tries to offer up a smile but it falls short. "Thanks. I'm a bit directionally challenged."

"No problem, I am a human compass. Let's go." I say gesturing for him to follow me. Connor stops cold when we step out of class. He stares down the hall in the opposite direction and shuffles from foot to foot. He looks like he wants to bolt. It takes me a minute to realize what's going on and when I do, I place my hand supportively on his shoulder. "Hey, she's going to be okay Connor. Is that where Lillie's class is?" I nod my head in the direction of his stare.

He looks back at me surprised that I knew his sisters name. It takes a second for him to register that he introduced her to me once before. He clears his throat. "Yeah. I just...I don't know. I don't like leaving her there. She's scared." His eyebrows furrow together like he's contemplating what to do.

Aren't we all? I think to myself. "I'm sure she will be fine." I say trying to reassure him. "She's young and has probably made several friends already. You know how easy it is to make friends when you're little. She's safe in there." All kids deserve to feel safe. I push down the pain that strikes my chest at the thought of Sebastian out there somewhere.

Connor nods his head and then suddenly he notices my hand on his shoulder.

I feel the heat flood into my cheeks and I awkwardly remove my hand. "Well, we should get going." I start walking towards Headquarters. Without looking at my tablet he follows me as we twist and turn down some hallways, a flight of stairs and finally end up in the middle of Headquarters with a few minutes to spare. I look around at the sea of colors that surround me. People are bustling about, walking fast in their colorful scrubs to wherever their assignments are. I don't see any children like the first time we came here. I guess most of them are still in classes. We walk towards an escalator and get off on the second floor. I start heading toward my assignment then it hits me. "Oh, I should have asked. Which office do you have to report to?"

"Two-thirteen." He says looking at the address numbers on the outside of the administrative offices as we pass.

"That's where I'm going! Are you a runner too?"

"Yeah, I guess so." He looks around, once more seeming uncomfortable then walks ahead of me towards the office.

So much for small talk. I guess I can't really blame him. This whole place, this new life, it's overwhelming. I've not been separated from my parents in a long time and my guess is Connor hasn't either. Most children have been home schooled like myself and have rarely left the house. Our social lives consist of only what we've managed to maintain online through our computer. I think about how I put my hand on his shoulder and inwardly kick myself. That probably was really awkward for him. My parents were very hands on, total huggers who have no problem invading your personal space. With the virus spreading the way it did, physical contact is very few and far between, especially between strangers. I make a mental note to keep my hands to myself.

Connor pauses at the administrative office labeled: 213. He holds the door open for me and I pick up my pace as to not make him wait much longer.

"Thanks." I say with a half-smile. I look around at the room that isn't much bigger than the classroom we were just in. The walls are stark white and there are ten office desks that line the exterior walls. Adults sit behind the desks typing at the speed of light. They seem either oblivious to us or they just don't care. My guess is the former since looming stacks of files sit piled high on each desk. Several metal filing cabinets, a copier machine and a small break area make up the rest of the office.

Connor and I join the group of about fifteen others who are huddled in the middle of the office. They all surround a table with several sack lunches. We both grab one and start munching down on the peanut butter and jelly sandwiches and veggie sticks. I pull out a small juice box and down it really quick not noticing the particular flavor. This lunch set up reminds me of elementary school, except we are all standing and trying to devour our nourishment before our work assignments start. After I'm done I gaze around at the other people in the room. Nearly all of the people in the group appear to be around our age. I notice the girl from my class, the one with the pale blonde hair, standing apart from the crowd. She keeps her head down, looking at her tablet. Her nearly white hair once again covers her face. One of the teens in the group tells a joke and a lot of the others laugh loudly. Not feeling like much in the joking mood, I make my way over to the loner girl.

"Hey," I say. As if I yelled it out at the top of my lungs, she nearly jumps out of her socks. "Whoa, I didn't mean to startle you." I say looking at her surprised.

She looks at me with wide doe like eyes. Her eyes are an icy pale blue that makes her look all the more fragile. With her petite frame and porcelain skin color, she looks like a doll. Her mouth hangs open a bit awkwardly as if she doesn't know what to say.

"I'm Willow." I offer all the while forcing my hand to stay at my side. I had been taught to shake hands when

I introduced myself but I don't want to break this poor girl. She already seems shocked enough that I'm even talking to her.

I stand there with one of my eyebrows raised in question. She takes a second and then offers quietly, "Claire." She pushes her hair behind her ears.

"Nice to meet you Claire." I say carefully. "This is Connor." I point out Connor who offers a silent wave. She looks at him then quickly darts her eyes away. I barely catch the pink rise up in her cheeks before she lets her hair fall in her face once more.

I look over at Connor as if he could help but he just shrugs. This girl is probably the most skittish creature I've ever seen.

A man clears his throat and announces, "May I have your attention please." I look up to see a pudgy middle-aged man with balding black hair standing near the entrance of the office. His black scrubs make him look drab and his voice comes off as overly bored. "Thank you for coming. My name is Mr. Blake. I am the head of the administrative department. You have been selected as runners based on your age and estimated energy level. Runners are required to move at a fast pace throughout the entire shift, as you will be given multiple assignments to complete each day. Most assignments will be in the form of deliveries however you may be utilized in other forms of grunt work. This may include filing, cleaning, supply retrieval and so on. Basically, you will just do whatever you are assigned to do. Since this is a fast paced, on your feet type of job you will receive an extra allotment of shoes, which you can switch out as needed. Does anyone have any questions at this time?" The look on his face shows that he's not really interested in answering questions.

A tall lanky boy with red hair and a face peppered in freckles raises his hand.

"Yes." Mr. Blake drones.

"Um, sir, since this is my first job and all...um, does this mean we all get paid, like real money?" The boy asks. I perk up wondering the answer myself, not that I would even know where to spend the money in a place like this.

Mr. Blake looks at the boy as if he were a filthy, putrid smelling rag. "What? Are you saying that you don't want to serve your country, to pitch in for your community?" His voice starts to escalate. "Is it not good enough for you that you have been provided shelter, safety, food and clothes on your back?" He counts the blessings on his fingers as if he bestowed them upon us himself. "You could be on the outside! Do you really think that you deserve money for your services in here?" His harsh tone makes me jump.

The boy's shoulders slump and he looks like a scalded toddler. "No, sir. I'm sorry sir."

The boy cowers beneath his stare as Mr. Blake gives him the stink eye for a few more moments.

Mr. Blake asks again, "Any more questions?" He stares us all down one by one, sizing us up in the process. We all shake our heads profusely. "Good. Now, I do not have the time to sit here and hold each of your hands. I have already assigned Alec as a leader for this shift." A young man steps forward. I hadn't noticed him before. He's tall and muscular with caramel skin. His hair is the same color as Mr. Blake's, but that's where the resemblance stops. He has intense emerald green eyes that stand out in comparison to his dark features. He looks to be around seventeen years old.

Mr. Blake gestures to Alec and then continues. "You will each receive your assignments via your tablet at the start of your shift. Alec is here if you should have a question or if you require assistance at any time. You may see him shadow you on occasion. In order to run a smooth operation we require dedicated, hard workers. He is here to ensure that you are performing efficiently. Under performance can result in negative repercussions on your work history and could also result in other corrective measures being taken. Please remember that in three years, when we are released, most of you will be of age to work full time. Your performance inside this facility could dictate your job assignments out in the real world. In addition you will receive a small allowance for your services at the end of each week so I suggest you use it wisely." He glares at the boy who asked the original question. "With that said, I will leave Alec to finish with your orientation. If you need my assistance in the future you can find my contact information on your tablet. You should however, refer to Alec for your day to day operational questions." Without another word he turns and walks out of the office.

Alec stands there a bit uncomfortable at first. After a second a light bulb must have gone off in his head because he stands up straight and puts on his most adult-like tone to address us. "My name is Alec Blake and I will be leading your shift." Someone in the crowd groans. Instead of ignoring it, as I would have done, Alec cuts the person off at the pass. "Who has a problem?" The perpetrator is singled out when several people turn to look at the same lanky boy who had asked Mr. Blake about pay. This boy must have a death wish or something. "What's your name boy." It should sound funny having someone Alec's age call another kid boy, but it doesn't. He stares the boy down and rightfully displays his authority.

The boy shuffles from foot to foot and then answers, "Josh."

Alec stands up even taller than before and says, "Josh, I'm taking it that you have an issue with my obvious relation to the Head Administrator. I know what you are thinking, that I'm just in this position because of my father. You are probably also thinking that with your extensive experience and work history that you should be the one leading this team. Well then, since you are so ready to run things boy, why don't you finish leading this orientation?" He taps his foot and waits for Josh to step up.

Realizing that he wasn't asking a rhetorical question, Josh answers, "Um, I don't know how to."

"You don't know how to?" Alec raises his brows in question. "I thought that you knew everything? Way more than me at least." He points to his own chest jokingly.

Josh's eyes open wide and I nearly feel bad for him, but the boy's got to learn not to stick his foot in his mouth.

"No, sir. I'm sorry, sir." He stutters and his face reddens as he's put in his place for the second time in less than five minutes.

I find myself surprised to see Alec nod his head and move on. I kind of took him for the tough guy who will continue to drill the point home but he just earned a few respect points in my book for letting it go. "You may all address me as Alec. I figure that most of us are near to each other in age so there is no point in calling me Mr. Blake. With that said, I do still expect for each of you to respect my authority and to follow my directions. I have run small shifts before at my father's factory and you will find that while I may hold high expectations for each of my team members, I am also fair. Our motto as runners is 'Get it Done.' I expect for each of you to live up to our motto and to get the job done to the best of your abilities." For a young person, Alec does surprisingly well with public speaking. He makes eye contact with each of us as he's talking and remains in control. "If you will all look at your tablets at this time you will see that your assignments have been uploaded. Your assignments are pretty cut and dry so you should not need much direction to complete them. If you do need direction or if for some reason you are unable to complete your assignments in the allotted time, then you will need to contact me. You can page me by typing into the IM box at the bottom right hand side of your screen. This will activate your locator and I will come to assist you as quickly as possible. Your assignments will be linked to your GPS so you will receive directions on how to get to your destination. I hope that within a few weeks you will commit our shelter's map to your memory as this will help you complete your assignments much faster." Alec turns around and grabs something from a table behind him. He holds it up. "Each of you will receive one of these. This is a holder for your tablet which can be worn on your hip like this." He straps the black holder around his waste and then sets his tablet face out, into it. I try and stifle a laugh; it looks like a fanny-pack. "Since you will often be carrying items, this will allow you to have your hands free to complete your task. You will also receive a pair of earphones so you can get audio directions to your destinations. You will not have time, or free hands, to continually look down at your tablet map." Alec hands us each a holder and a set of white earphones. I don't know if I imagined it or not, but he gives me a short smile when he hands me mine. "Alright. Unless you have any questions, you may disperse and begin your assignments."

Nobody asks any questions. I strap the holder around my waste, taking notice of my awesome sense of style lately and then look at my tablet to find my first assignment.

There's a note on the top of the list to pick up supplies in Mr. Volmer's office to take to the library. I find a map posted on the wall showing office locations. I pin it to my memory where his office is along with the names correlating with the other offices in this space. Mr. Volmer is located at the far end of the Administration 'building.' I put the tablet in my 'fanny-pack' and kick it into high gear.

There's no telling how long this day will be or how many errands I'll be running.

After an exhausting amount of twists and turns I finally end up at the corner office. There's a nameplate on the door with Mr. Volmer's name on it and underneath it says, "Historian." Hmm, I think to myself. I wonder why this facility needs a historian. I knock softly on the door and wait 'till I hear a deep voice telling me to come in. I try and open the door but it stops after only a few feet. I attempt pulling back and opening it again only to be stopped short. "Umm, Mr. Volmer?" I ask.

"Yes, yes, come in," he says.

"Well, that's the problem sir. I can't seem to get the door open." It seems like Captain obvious came for a visit now. I hear some shuffling behind the door and what sounds to be crates of boxes being moved. The door opens a few inches more and a frazzled head sticks out. I'm assuming this is Mr. Volmer. He has white frizzy hair that sticks up in the places he isn't bald. He's sporting a serious case of male patterned baldness. His bottle cap glasses that cover most of his face magnify his eyes in a creepy mad professor sort of way.

"Yes, yes what can I do for you young lady," he asks while sizing me up.

"Uh, yeah, my name is Willow and it says here that you have something that needs to be delivered to the library?"

"Ah, yes! Hold on just a minute." He disappears behind the door and I hear more shuffling followed by sounds of several different book avalanches. Seconds later the door opens a little bit and I'm being given a large stack of books. "Here you go," he says as he nearly slams the door in my face.

"Um, thanks," I say to the door.

There are about ten books or so in the stack and they all have heavy brown leather covers. I shift their weight in my arms so they're more easily carried and set off through the labyrinth of offices.

It seems like forever since I've been to a real library. Obviously being holed up in the house for a few years made it hard for me to go to my favorite place. There's something about the smell of books that speaks to me. I still read a lot on my e-reader back at home but there's something about holding the paper in your hands. I take a second to enjoy the sight then I drop off the books to a librarian who barely glances up at me from her book to acknowledge the delivery. She signs off on my tablet and then sticks her nose back in her book. I can't say I blame her. I make a mental note to find my way back here when I have free time.

My next assignment blinks on the screen almost immediately after I step out of the library. Another delivery. Argh, my feet already hurt but I keep moving along. To be honest I haven't even thought much about my mom or my brother today. While I don't want to forget them, I'm still grateful to have the busy work. It takes the edge off.

Two and a half hours later, I've completed my tenth delivery. A message pops up on my tablet stating that my daily assignments are complete and that I may return to the Administrative Office. I walk in and find Alec sitting behind a desk, typing something into a computer.

He turns and looks at me with eyebrows raised. "Don't tell me, your tablet GPS malfunctioned. That's been happening all day. Give it here." He rubs his temple with his index finger and holds his other hand out for me to pass him my tablet. His face looks slightly annoyed at first but then his expression changes to wonderment when I hand him my tablet. "You're done?"

I look from side to side wondering if I did something wrong then say, "Um, yeah. I mean, yes sir." My dad always taught me to respect elders but it still seems odd calling a boy only a few years older than me at the most, sir.

"No, don't call me sir. You can call me by my first name."

"Oh, okay Alec." It's strange calling a supervisor by their first name, but I guess I'll have to get used to it. He gives me a funny look and I realize he might not remember my name. "My name is Willow."

"I know." He clears his throat then looks down at my tablet. I'm instantly grateful for the lessening of eye contact because it was strangely intense there for a moment. He looks back up a second later. "Well, Willow, I think there might be an issue with your tablet."

I look at him questioningly. "I haven't noticed any issues. "

He takes my tablet and connects it by a USB cord to his computer. "Well, most of the other runners are still only half way through their assignments."

"Do we all have the same number of assignments?" I ask curious.

"Yes you all received ten assignments." He checks the screen, which hasn't loaded yet and then looks back at me. "Look, you couldn't have finished all of your assignments yet."

I don't know why, but something about how he said that last part sets me off; especially since I know that I completed all ten assignments. "Well I did! It's not my fault the others are slow. I got the message stating that I've finished and that's why I'm here." I throw my hand up on my hip to add that extra emphasis.

He studies me for a second with a look that I can't quite place then he checks his screen again. He turns back to me a few seconds later with his mouth gaping open. He mouth's the word how.

I shrug my shoulders and add with a little attitude, "Am I dismissed then?"

He just looks at me with wide emerald eyes and says, "Um, I guess." He sounds uncertain but I don't sit around to wait for him to think on it further. I've got a library to check out. I turn on my heel and leave the office and Alec behind.

I don't have to look at my tablet to find the library again. I've already committed its location to memory. I round the corner and end up accidentally running into someone. I look up to find Connor standing there stunned. He dropped his tablet during my accidental attack so I bend down to help him grab it but end up bumping heads with him when he makes the same move. "Ouch." We both say in unison while rubbing our heads. I let Connor grab his own tablet this time as to avoid crushing our skulls again.

"Sorry." I say apologetically.

Connor looks frustrated and overwhelmed. At first I'm worried that it's aimed at my clumsiness but then he sets it straight. "It's okay. So what assignment are you on?"

"Oh, I'm done." I say but instead of feeling proud that my first day went so well, I actually feel kind of down. Now I have time to think and I don't feel like thinking.

"What? I'm only on number four. This is taking forever! As if I don't have enough issues with directions, my GPS keeps acting up. I swear that I've passed this same hall four times now trying to find the medical station. I think it's broken again."

I feel bad now that I just told him I was done. I definitely didn't want him to feel like he's doing anything wrong by how long it's taking him. "Hey, I can help you if you want. I know where the medical station is."

His dark eyes brighten just a bit. "Really? That would be great Willow. Thanks."

"No problem at all. I've got nothing to do." I say. After all, the library can wait.

I lead Connor to the medic station and then help him on several more assignments. We don't really talk much along the way but it's not awkward or anything. It would probably be with anyone else, but there's a type of comfort level between Connor and I. It's one that comes with having something in common: loss.

“We were only messing around, you don’t have to get your panties in a bunch!” A high pitch girl voice calls out from a room down the hall. Her giggling sounds like a Hyena.

“Yeah sorry, we were just having a little fun with you runner girl! What, you didn’t think it was funny sugar?” A guy adds, his voice dripping with sarcasm.

The Hyena girl giggles annoyingly again. I hear a sniffle sound coming from the room.

I look to Connor and he nods back to me. I don’t even have to say it out loud. We both start towards the room where the harassment is coming from. We don’t make it far before Claire, the one who sat next to me in class, comes barreling out of the room slamming the door behind her. Her hair is still in front of her face and it must have obstructed her vision because she plows right into Connor. The force of their collision pushes him back half of a step.

“Sorry.” Claire sniffs. She tries to move to work her way around us but Connor grabs her gently by the arms.

“Hey, what’s wrong? Did those people hurt you?” Connor asks seriously. His face is a mask of concern.

She looks up at him and behind all of that white blonde hair covering her face you can see her tear filled frosty blue eyes. Something in my chest pangs knowing that someone who looks so fragile and innocent is hurting.

“Did they hurt you?” Connor asks again a little stronger this time.

"No." She whispers then turns her head and starts wiping at her eyes.

"What happened?" I ask in a soothing voice. Maybe staying calm will help her open up.

She looks at me with a look of surprise. It's that look again that asks, are you really talking to me? I wonder what would make this beautiful, yet really strange, girl so skittish and self-conscious.

"It's okay, you can tell us." I say again gently.

Connor is still holding onto her arms so he takes this second to carefully let her go. He seems ready to catch her if she tries to dart though.

"They were playing a trick on me." She said.

"A trick?" Connor asks, his eyebrows rose in question.

She looks to him and then back at me. "Yes, they were messing with my GPS. They kept re-routing me here."

"How did they mess with your GPS?" I ask.

"Anything can be hacked." She says while wiping her eyes one last time. This time she looks at me with a bold certainty I wouldn't have thought she'd have. "They think I'm stupid; that I wouldn't know what they were doing. I am not stupid!"

I don't know Claire that well, but I like this side of her. She should show it more often instead of hiding behind all of that pretty hair. "Of course you are not stupid." I say matter of factly.

"How did you know that they were messing with you?" Connor asks pleasantly surprised by her short show of confidence too.

Claire looks at him and blushes again, looking down at her shoes. "I know a lot about computers and stuff. When I circled this block for the third time, I heard them laughing in the computer lab. I put two and two together and knew that they were messing with my map."

"So you went in there?" I ask. I really can't believe that she would confront them.

She looks thoughtful for a second then says, "Yes. It wasn't the brightest move. I was just so angry. My feet were aching from running circles and they were just sitting in there having a blast at my expense!"

Connor's eyebrows furrow and it doesn't take a genius to figure out what he's about to do. He side steps around Claire and stomps off down the hall.

It doesn't take me more than a few moments to realize I should probably follow him in there. "Stay here," I say to Claire and hurry to catch up to Connor.

Connor skips the pleasantries and immediately turns the door handle. It's unlocked and he marches right in; I follow behind him.

The teens inside the room turn to look at us in bewilderment. I count six of them, all guys, hanging around. In a normal room that many people would result in overcrowding but this isn't a normal room. I take in the layout of it with my mouth hanging open in awe. This isn't a simple bunk bed set up like my dad and I have. No, this is a plush layout that has to be at least five hundred square feet of semi-luxurious furnishings. Two queen-sized beds are set up on opposite sides of the room. They have decorated blankets and throw pillows, which are starkly different than our grey and white linens. In the middle of the room is a mock living area set up with a couch and a chaise lounge. There is even an intricately designed ornate rug on the floor. A large desk with a full sized computer is set up against the wall. Instead of plain white walls these walls are painted in soothing earth tones. A few framed oil paintings of natural landscapes are set up around the room in such a way that they look like windows to the outside. It's quite beautiful and much more fancy than my room or even my old house. How in the world does a person get a room like this? In comparison, this room makes my room look like a prison cell.

One of the boys steps towards us with his hands raised. He looks like a Ken doll with bleached blonde hair and big hazel eyes. His muscles look too proportionate to have come from real hard labor. Instead they probably are the result of months spent with an expensive personal trainer. "Hey man, we were just having a little fun," he says. I can tell from the sound of his voice that he was the one talking to Claire earlier.

I look to Connor to try and gauge his reaction. His eyebrows furrow and his eyes get all beady looking. It's kind of scary if you ask me. "Look pal, don't you have anything better to be doing than to be messing with this poor girl? Some of us have to work around here." Connor says nearly spitting in his face.

The guy he is talking to says, "I'm not your pal, the

name's Zack." He says pal with a disgusted look like he wouldn't touch Connor with a ten-foot pole. Then with a mischievous grin on his face he turns to the others. "Hey fellas, this guy here wants to know if we have anything better to do." He hikes his thumb back behind him pointing at Connor. They all laugh in unison like it's the funniest joke in the world.

I hear that hyena laugh and see a tall blonde who looks like a life sized Barbie doll, come out from the bathroom. I catch a glimpse of the bathroom before the door closes behind her. From what I can see, there is a garden tub and a double vanity in there. A small amount of envy creeps up at their luxuries and I try to squash it quickly. The girl must have seen my stare though because she speaks up in a haughty tone, "What? See something you like?"

My cheeks burn with fury at her calling me out. "No." I say and give her my best rolling of the eyes.

She sticks her hand on her hips then looks me up and down with her big baby blue eyes. "I saw you eyeing our place, you must be one of the less fortunate ones." Her voice drips with a false sense of pity.

"First, I'm not less fortunate, I'm Willow. Second, green's not really my color so no, I wasn't ogling your place." My chest aches when I remember how often my mom used to tell us that green doesn't look good on us when we were kids and saw others getting more than we had.

She doesn't respond, instead she lets out another hyena laugh. Wow, how can someone who tries to look so perfect on the outside have such an atrocious laugh? I let out a small giggle at that and she gives me the nastiest look that only makes me giggle more.

Zack smirks at me then turns back around to Connor. "In answer to your question, no, we don't have anything better to do. Well, unless you count twiddling our thumbs or taking a nap. But hey, now that you mention it, maybe twiddling our thumbs does seem more fun about now. Whatcha think fellas?" They laugh at his banter again and my frown deepens.

Rage is bubbling up deep inside of me at this guy's blazé attitude. "Seriously," I pipe up. "You have nothing else to do? No job? No school? There has to be something you guys are good at other than messing up someone's day here!" I know, it doesn't deserve an Oscar, but that's all I've got. I keep my eyes focused on him holding his gaze. I notice that he has the same hair color and the same shaped eyes as the Barbie hyena girl. I assume they are related.

Zack sizes me up before answering. "Yeah, we go to school, but only in the morning today. Tomorrow we start our Select classes. Now as to jobs, no, of course not! Well, now that you mention it, you may be able to count what we're doing now as a job. Teaching you both the art of technological hacking. May do you good someday." He looks back and forth from Connor to me then settles his eyes on me. "And as for you, I can give some private lessons if you ask really nice sugar." He reaches his hand out as if he was going to grab one of my curls and I swat it back down with a smack. He laughs. I don't have a mirror, but

I can bet that my face is the color of cherry pie right about now. I'm fuming!

"Now, if you'll be on your way, we're late for our appointment." He says the last part with a note of sarcasm.

As he starts to shoo us out I catch a glimpse of a photo above the girl's bed. The girl and Zack are in it. They are a bit younger and standing next to a woman who I'm assuming is their mom. I try to look a little closer because something's caught my attention. It's strange, in the photo both children seem to have the same golden brown eyes as their mother. Maybe it's just the lighting or shadows.

Before I can get a better look, Zack blocks my view. Then, in the blink an eye, he's ushered us out the door and has slammed it in our faces. I blink a few times trying to clear the cobwebs out of my head. "Come on, let's get out of here," Connor says.

Claire is still standing in the hall where we last left her. She looks like she's trying to figure us out. "Did you both just defend my honor in there?" Her eyebrows are furrowed in thought.

"Well, we didn't do that great of a job, but I think they got the point. Not that they took it to heart or anything." Connor replies.

"They're just being jerks." I say.

Claire studies us with her icy blue eyes then gives a small smile. "Thanks guys. Nobody has ever really done anything like that for me before. Usually people just act like I don't exist. Sometimes I think I must have a secret layer of camouflage because people often look right through me.

I'm not noticeable I guess. " Her smile drops.

Connor surprises me by saying under his breath, "I doubt that."

Claire must not have heard him since she didn't blush at his compliment. I add, "Well that's what friends should do for each other."

"We're friends?" She says the word like it's foreign and I instantly feel horrible that this poor girl has had to feel this alone in the world.

"If you want to be. I think we can use a support group in here. Especially if we have to deal with people like that." I point back with my thumb towards Zack's room.

She cocks her head at me and studies me for a second then says, "Yeah, I think I'd like that." She smiles which lights her face up in a new, beautiful way. Connor and I catch it like it's contagious and find ourselves grinning too.

I spend the rest of the afternoon helping Connor, and mainly Claire, finish up their assignments. It doesn't take too long because conveniently, Connor and Claire's routes correlate with each other. Surprisingly, they don't ask me how I can get from point A to point B without looking at the map.

We get done around 5:30; thirty minutes before our tablets say that supper is to be served. We go together to pick up Connor's little sister Lillie from class, then head over to the cafeteria to secure our places in line.

We sit together at dinner eating our mush. I look

around for my dad but don't see him so I assume he got a different dinner shift tonight. I do get to meet Connor's guardian, Sarah, whom I soon realize is only responsible for Lillie. Apparently Connor was allowed to sleep on a cot in their room last night however, effective tonight he will be moved to his permanent room. Apparently teens who don't have parents bunk up together in a mass dorm style room. Connor's body language tells me that he is very much not happy about this arrangement. I don't blame him because with his new schedule and separate room, he will rarely see his little sister. Sarah assures him though that she is in good hands.

I also find out during dinner that Claire stays in one of those dorm rooms for female teens. Each dorms hold up to ten same sex teens. Claire has seven roommates in hers. Most of them are from the orphanage she grew up in. None of them really talk to her though. They all think she's strange. She doesn't mention how she ended up in an orphanage but we can pretty much assume that she lost her parents to the virus.

After dinner we part ways for the night. I head back to my room to wait for my dad. I pass the time by taking a nice hot shower, which apparently I can only do three times a week per water and energy conservation restrictions. It feels good though to get clean. I hop into bed afterwards. I hadn't realized just how tiring today was and I find myself falling asleep soon enough.

"Hey honey." My dad kisses me on the forehead.

I awake from a dreamless sleep and look at my

tablet to see that it's only 10:00 pm. I haven't been asleep for very long. "Hey dad. Are you just now getting home?" I ask, stretching my arms above my head.

My dad looks exhausted and really, really filthy. I don't even want to ponder the dirt he's covered in. "Yeah. I didn't get to eat until nine. It's been a long day." He runs his hand through his greying hair. "How was your day?"

"It was good. Why are they making you work such long shifts?" I ask. We had started at nine this morning. That means he worked for at least twelve hours today. That seems rather long to me.

"The work has to get done." He studies me as if trying to figure out if he should tell me something. Instead of telling me what was on his mind he says, "Try to get some sleep honey."

I don't let him get away that easily. "Dad, what's up?" I rub the small amount of sleep out of my eyes that had formed during my nap.

He brushes back the hair from my forehead and steps back a little. I have to sit up to see him better since the safety railing is now partially blocking my view. He paces the room for a second then starts. "You know honey that your mother and I tried to keep you kids sheltered from the mess that's been going on in our country over the past few years."

I nod.

"I figure that you are old enough and mature enough now to know what's going on." He smiles at me and has a proud look in his eye. "You know that we have never had that much money."

I know that much. We learned in school about economics. There used to be a middle class in our country but for the past decade, or longer even, there has only been two classes: the rich and the poor.

"The government knew that this virus was getting out of hand a few years ago. At that time the plans for a way to stop it began. We were warned that we would eventually have to go into these shelters. Everyone was allowed the opportunity to pay for their space in advance. The prices were outrageous and completely unattainable for anyone other than the wealthiest families." A pent up look of frustrated anger shows on his face. "They told us that those who could not afford to pay for their spaces would still be admitted in, however, they would have to earn their keep. Most of us have no problem with that. We've been working hard just to stay afloat all of our lives, but Willow, I didn't know that they were going to make the children work for their spaces too!" His face turns red with his frustration. "They didn't tell us that! Did they treat you bad?" He comes up closer to the bed again and studies me to make sure he can't see any physical sign of damage.

I shake my head confused, "No Dad, they didn't. It was fine."

He looks at me intensely, "You can tell me the truth honey. Were they mean? How long did you have to work today?"

"I only worked five hours and it was easy work doing deliveries. Nobody was mean...Well, that's not exactly true."

My dad's eyes started to show the beginning signs of rage so I quickly continued to settle his fears. "The people at work are nice. We just ran into some spoiled brats who were trying to cause trouble." He calms down at this but still remains interested. "You know it makes sense though now. They have a much nicer place than ours. They are the same age too but they didn't have to work."

"Yes, their parents probably paid for their spot. I heard rumors that the paid rooms were very nice. Just because they don't work doesn't mean they have any right to treat you badly. Do I need to go talk to them?"

I give my dad a sincere smile. His love shows through in his offer to stick up for me. "No, I already spoke to them. They weren't really being mean to me but they were picking on another girl. I went in there and confronted them. I don't think it did much good but they had no right to bully someone just because they were bored."

That look of pride flashes across my dad's face again. "You did the right thing honey. I'm proud of you for standing up to those bullies. Most people wouldn't, especially when it's not their fight."

"Well you didn't teach me to be most people." I sit up taller and grin.

"No I didn't. I love you honey. You let me know if you ever need me to go beat down any snobs for you. Not that I don't think you can't handle your own. It's sometimes good to have reinforcements."

"Yeah, I've got those. I made two friends today." My dad looks interested so I continue. "Connor and Claire.

They are both in my class and they are runners too."

"That's awesome. You stick close to each other. It's important for you to have someone that has your back in here. I've heard some uproar from some of the other adult workers. They aren't too happy at the way they're being treated, especially with some of their children being forced to work. Also, I think a lot of it has to do with many lower class families getting declined entry. The wounds are wide open right now, so it might come to nothing after some time passes. I just want you to know ahead of time how some people are feeling so that you don't get surprised by any disgruntled behavior around here. Continue to stay close to your friends and make sure to report to me if anything odd comes up or if you feel mistreated in any way. Will you do that for me honey?"

"Of course." I wonder to myself what he means by disgruntled behavior but I don't continue to ponder it too much because I can tell that the day is catching up to my dad. His eyes look tired and his posture went slack. "Hey dad, why don't you go take a shower and get some rest."

He nods his head. "What? I stink that bad?"

"Yep!" I say pinching my nose with my fingers and waving the 'odor' away with my other hand.

My dad gets me in that one tickle spot right under my arm, my Achilles heel. I break out in giggles. He leans in like he wants to give me a hug but then remembers he's filthy and pats my head instead. "I love you. Get some sleep."

"You too dad." I reply and lie back down on my bed.

"Night." My dad turns and starts to head to the bathroom but I grab his arm before he leaves my bedside.

"Wait dad?" I ask nervously.

He turns back, "Yes?"

"Can I ask you a question?" I chew on my nails waiting for his response.

"Shoot." He says while making a fake gun sign with his thumb and index finger. My dad can be a big dork when he wants to.

"Who is ELE?" I don't know why it's been on my brain tonight but I feel like I need to know more about what's going on out there in the world.

He studies me for a long second then says, "I'm sorry that I didn't tell you before. I wanted to protect you but I can see that now you're becoming a mature and strong woman, just like your mother." His voice catches but he carries on. "You can handle the truth. ELE stands for Extinction Level Event."

I let out a loud breath. I really don't like the sound of that.

He continues, "An Extinction Level Event is exactly what it sounds like. This is where our planet was headed with the rapid speed that the virus was killing off the human race at." He stares at me as if trying to gauge my reaction.

I nod and say, "I understand."

He gives me a slight smile and then says, "I've known about Project ELE for a while and while I hate that it tore our family in half, I do understand why it was necessary." His face turns grim.

I blink away the tears that start forming in my eyes as I think of all of the people that have died and all of the people outside the safety of our shelters. "Thank you dad." I say sincerely. He looks at me confused and then I continue. "Thank you for protecting me as long as you could. I mean protecting my innocence. I don't think I could have handled that news before all of this."

He looks surprised that I would make such a mature statement. "I love you so much." Is all he says.

"I love you too dad." I sit up and give him a hug despite his apparent stink. "Night."

"Good night." He says and then turns to head once again to the bathroom. This time I don't stop him.

A minute later I hear the shower running. I think to myself about how much my life has changed in such a short period of time. It has only been eight days since my family left our house and headed towards the shelter lines and it has been two days since my family was torn apart. So much happened so fast that I can't help but wonder what changes life will bring me in the future. I don't get a chance to think about it for long because the running water lulls me into a dreamless sleep.

FIVE

Boring routine, that's what the next month is like.

School, work, dinner and bed. We barely have any free time. It didn't come as a surprise that neither Connor, Claire or I got accepted into the Select classes. I don't mind that much because I actually enjoy the mindless activity of running errands in the afternoon. Connor sometimes complains about it though, and by sometimes I mean all the time!

"Look, the pool. Yet another amenity we haven't gotten to use." Connor slouches as we walk by the heavily chlorinated corridor. His grumbling voice expresses his frustration.

"I wonder why they even built these places if we never get to use them." Claire interjects. She usually doesn't complain but sometimes Connor's moods can be contagious. We can't really blame him. My guess is that he's ADHD or something by his consistent nervous fidgeting and inability to remain still for longer than twenty seconds.

I look down at my tablet to check the time and someone rams me in the shoulder knocking me back a step. "Ugh!" I call out and turn around quickly to confront the hit and run offender. "Excuse you!"

Standing there in a red bikini with a towel hanging over her shoulder is Hyena girl. She get's a pinched up expression on her face like she smelled something foul and says, "You need to watch where you're going!"

I look at her incredulously, "Me? I don't think so. You rammed into me with your bony little shoulder." I don't know where that type of attitude came from but there is something about this girl that brings out the worst in me. Claire and Connor come and stand at my flanks to loan me their moral support.

"My shoulders are not bony!" She wines and then looks to one of her swim trunk clad, bare chested 'crew' members for reassurance. To my greatest pleasure nobody acknowledges her petty need for a confidence boost.

"Candy, you did run into her." Zack calls out from behind her. He walks up to me until he's crossed into my personal zone and then some. I blush and take a step back. He seems to take pride in the fact that he's making me uncomfortable. I can't help but feel awkward since I can't even name the last time I saw a man with his shirt off. Not that I think Zack is much of a man but it's still weird nonetheless. "Like what you see?" He asks full of cocky confidence. His only clothing is red swim trunks that sit loosely on his hips and a pair of swimming goggles, which are hanging from his wrist. His muscles almost look painted on and I wonder if he adds makeup to his abs to make them stand out more.

"Hmm," I look him up and down appraisingly and

find satisfaction when I see a slight blush spread on his falsely tanned cheeks. I shrug my shoulders and say "Not really."

A livid look passes across his eyes and for a second I get an uncomfortable feeling in the pit of my stomach. Just like that it vanishes and an amused look takes its place. "Well, I'm sure people of your...social status, don't have many interactions with those of the opposite sex. It's okay to feel nervous around me." A look of utter disgust pops onto my face. He laughs and the Hyena girl, who I now know as Candy, joins in on the hackling.

"You should join us." Candy says. "Oh wait, you can't! You have to work!" She cracks herself up so much that she snorts like a pig. I can't help the giggle that releases after that. She stops and glares at me with her hands on her bony hips.

"Well, if you do ever get a day off, you should hang with us." Zack stares at my nametag, which is located on my chest; quite convenient for him. "You can bring your friends too, Willow." I cringe at the way my name sounds on his lips.

"Thanks but no thanks." I say as I turn and walk in the opposite direction. I feel better after I put some distance between us and shake off the slime that they lathered on.

"Ewe! He was totally undressing you with his eyes." Claire says with an appropriate amount of distaste.

"Yeah, I feel totally scandalized." I say while wiping my sweaty palms on my scrubs. Intense conversations like that make me nervous but I feel good that I held my own.

"I should go and pulverize that rich boy's face!" Connor looks like he might just do it so I wave him off.

"Nah, they aren't worth it." I smile at him and pat his back reassuringly. I watch as his face calms down. Over the past month Connor has taken on the protective big brother role over Claire and me with zeal. Well sometimes I wonder if it's more than a big brother role with Claire, but I won't mention that.

I look at the timer on my tablet. "Crap! We are going to have to run. One minute and thirty seconds!" We all take off running down the winding hallways towards Headquarters. We barrel through the Admin office doors a minute late. Everyone turns and looks at us. Well, everyone except Alec. He appears to be intensely focused on his computer and he doesn't acknowledge that we came in late. Phew! I already got a tardy last week when I was late for class; I don't need a second one.

Alec looks up a moment later and his emerald eyes seem to settle on me. I shift side to side nervously while chanting in my head: You didn't notice. You don't want to give me a tardy. I guess my Jedi mind tricks worked because he stands up and addresses us as a group. "Good afternoon everyone. We will only be having a short meeting today as I have a lot to do. I have some good news though. We have finally gotten approval to allow you a free day once a week. These days will be staggered throughout the team and should be handed out next week. Now it's important that you know that you can lose your free day if there are any performance issues, reprimands or excessive tardies." I swear his eyes settle on me again for just a second and I hold my breath until he moves on. "With that said, get to work." We all turn to leave and he moves back to his desk.

I pull up my assignment list for today. Looking at the screen I do a double take. When I realize that what I'm seeing is accurate I stomp over to Alec's desk. Waving my tablet in my hand I ask, "There must be some mistake."

Alec looks up at me and continues typing as he talks, which sort of impresses me but mostly annoys me. "I'm sorry, what exactly are you referring to?"

"I'm referring to the twenty-five assignments that you've given me." I huff out but add a "sir," at the end.

He cringes at the 'sir' part but then replies, "There was no mistake." He looks back at his computer and continues typing rapidly.

I've noticed an unexplained edge between Alec and I over the past month so I usually try to steer clear of him when I can. Not today though, I won't be dismissed that easily. "No!" It slips out before I can think better of it.

He stops mid type and stands up from his chair facing me. "Excuse me?" He places both of his hands on his desk and leans forward so that his green eyes are within inches of my face.

I stand my ground. I'm not going to back down. "This is more than double my usual assignment count and double the workload of any other runner. That isn't fair."

He raises his eyebrow and with a gleam in his eye he says, "Life isn't fair, Willow."

I always figured that Alec wouldn't remember my

name since I've never heard him speak it out loud. I don't let my astonishment or the interesting tingle I felt when he said my name deter me.

"So you are punishing me for working fast?" I ask fuming.

"This is not a punishment. You have a time frame that you work and we are simply filling that time frame."

"Well then I will just slow down and work at the same speed as everyone else." I throw my hands up in the air to further show my dissatisfaction.

He cocks his head sideways. "Look, I know that you finish your work early and then help your friends. You don't think that things like that go unnoticed do you? Like I said, this is an hourly job not an assignments based job. You will do what is asked of you."

I roll my eyes and huff out a disgruntled "Whatever!" Then I take my tablet and my first delivery parcel and head out the door. I swear I heard him yell out something about insubordination but I didn't stick around to listen. What's he going to do, fire me?

Just to spite him I work faster than I ever have and still finish thirty minutes ahead of everyone else. I walk in through the door and hand him my tablet so he can upload the signatures for the deliveries I made. I catch a glimpse of myself in a mirror to the right of his desk. Some curls have fallen loose from my ponytail and my cheeks look pink from exertion.

Alec looks at me appraisingly and if I didn't know better I would think that look showed a hint of admiration and perhaps something else. He plugs my tablet in, types some stuff on his keyboard then unplugs the tablet and hands it back to me. "You can go ahead and leave now that you're done."

I've never been allowed to leave earlier than the end of my shift so I look at him for an explanation. When one doesn't come I turn and walk out.

That night after dinner I lie down to try and get some shuteye but have a hard time falling asleep. I replay the conversation we had and worry that perhaps I will have a reprimand tomorrow. I was honestly surprised that he didn't give me one today when I returned, nor did he even mention anything. It's no surprise that once I fall asleep I slip into dreams of Alec with his bright green eyes and jet-black hair.

I was still a little nervous when I walked into work the next day with Connor and Claire. I looked at Alec expecting him to rehash yesterday's events but he didn't. Instead he smiled at me. Heat flamed my cheeks when my brain conjured up last nights dream. I pushed it far to the back of my mind and looked down at my tablet. My assignment list was reduced down to fifteen. I look up at Alec who stares at me for a fraction of a second and then releases us for work without hosting his usual pep rally meeting.

Today I got my assignments done in my usual speedy time frame and reverted to helping Connor and Claire with theirs. Having gone back to a normal routine, the day went by fast, as did the remainder of the week. Every morning we checked our tablets in restless anticipation of our first free day. We've been crossing our fingers that we will get the same day off. The odds look to be in our favor since everyone has received their free day this week except for us. Hopefully with tomorrow being Sunday, which is also a no-school day, we will finally get our day of rest!

SIX

I was excited when I woke up this morning and saw on my tablet that today is in fact my first free day.

My dad wasn't so lucky. He still has to work. We both head over to breakfast together and down our cold oatmeal before my dad has to report for his shift. Not sure what else to do with my time, I stay seated at the table and make arrangements for Connor and Claire to meet me up with me. While I wait I browse the amenities app on my tablet trying to get an idea of what we should do.

Someone clears their throat next to the table and I look up to find Alec standing beside me. "Oh, um, hey." I stutter. I'm still not quite sure how to address Alec. I mean, he is my boss and all, so our conversations tend to be a bit awkward.

"You mind if I sit?" Alec asks.

I shake my head no, even though I do kind of mind.

He sits in the seat across from me. Alec tipis his fingers and leans forward. "Look, I know it's kind of awkward and all, what, with me being your boss, but I was hoping maybe we could hang out sometime?" His question catches me totally off guard and my jaw drops open. I watch as he grimaces and shifts in his seat, looking exceedingly uncomfortable.

"Yeah," I squeak a little uncomfortably. What should I say? No? I clear my voice. "I mean sure, that would be cool." His green eyes light up just a little. What the heck I think to myself. "Um, I've got some friends meeting me here soon; well, you know Claire and Connor. We were planning on doing something today, not sure what, but you're welcome to tag along if you'd like." Tag along? Does your boss 'tag along?' I mentally kick myself and look to the floor.

Shockingly he agrees, "Yeah, hey that sounds great. You know, I have to be quite honest with you. This sucks."

"Excuse me?" I ask a little hurt by his words. We've hung out for less than a minute and he already thinks it's lame.

"No, wait, that's not what I meant. What I meant to say is my job sucks." Okay, awkward, I think. "I mean, some people might think being in charge is cool, especially at my age, but in all honesty, it's just flat out lonely. People respect you and all, but they don't want to necessarily hang out and be friends. It makes me feel old even though we are all in the same age group."

Connor and Claire walk up behind Alec and stop mid-step. Alec continues to talk about loneliness and pours his heart out while they approach the table cautiously. Claire jabs Connor lightly in the ribs and gestures her head towards Alec. They both squelch a laugh and I try widening my eyes at them letting them know to chill out.

Connor gets a huge grin on his face and begins doing a silent version of the running man behind Alec's back. I look to Alec who seems to be oblivious of their presence behind him. Claire puts her hand over her mouth squelching her laughter.

She waves her hands at Connor to get him to stop and looks back over at me. She then proceeds to act like she's taking a seat and tipis her hands in front of her mimicking Alec. Connor nearly loses it and steps back away from us, hand over his mouth.

"It's just with my dad being who he is and all, it can be tough, you know?" My attention focuses back on Alec and I nod my head in understanding trying very hard to keep a straight face but not feeling like I'm succeeding. I honestly didn't hear half of what he just said because Connor started dancing in place again. "You know what's really interesting Willow?" Alec asks with a raised eyebrow.

I try harder to concentrate on him and not on what my friends are doing. "No, what?" I ask.

Alec lets a small grin appear on his face. His voice raises a few decibels, "It's interesting that Connor and Claire think I can't see what they're doing behind my back. Yes, that's interesting."

Connor stops mid running man and Claire closes her mocking mouth immediately.

"Oh hey guys! I didn't know you were standing there." Alec says in mock surprise placing his hand over his heart.

I bury my head in my hands. Oh my gosh, can it

get any more awkward?

"How--" Connor begins to ask but Alec doesn't give him the opportunity.

"See that metal tray dispenser right there?" He points to an area right behind me. " Yeah, I could totally see you the whole time."

A crimson color spreads across their faces as the realization dawns on them. Alec shakes his head, "It's cool. I would have done the same thing." He gives a small chuckle as Connor and Claire try and pull their heads out of their butts. "Really, it's all good." Alec says trying to reassure them again.

I bust up laughing at the calamity displayed before me. All heads turn to me, but I can't help it. That had to be one of the most ridiculous things I have ever seen. It doesn't take but a moment before everyone is laughing with me. Connor and Alec exchange some kind of macho male handshake. Then both of my friends join us at the table.

"So what are we going to do today?" Claire asks.

"I vote to go swimming." Connor chimes in.

"No." Claire and I both say simultaneously. This is our first time to hang out with our boss. I'm thinking that bikini's and swim trunks aren't really appropriate in this situation. Plus, I didn't get to shave my legs this morning so that idea is definitely vetoed.

Connor looks mildly disappointed. He suggests a second option, "We could see a flick at the theater."

Everyone looks at each other and we shrug at the

so-so idea.

Alec checks something on his tablet then says. "Well, if you are into Historical films we can go check it out. Today they are playing back to back documentaries of World War I, World War II and World War III."

"Oh that sounds like a blast." I say sarcastically.

"I don't hear any genius suggestions from either of you." Connor says a little sourly.

"I guess that leaves shopping or bowling. Since we get paid crap money we might as well check out the bowling alley." I open my eyes wide and hold my breath when I remember who is sitting at our table.

Connor and Claire give me that look that says, 'dude, pull your foot out of your mouth.'

"I mean, um..." I start to say but Alec waves me off.

"Look, I know you all don't get paid squat. I make only a little more than you do. I understand." He looks around at all of us who still look semi uncomfortable. "Let's pretend for today that I'm not your boss. That I'm just another kid like you trying to have fun."

"Kid." Connor harrumphs.

Alec turns to where he's facing Connor better and asks, "Just how old do you think I am?"

Claire says under her breath, "Old."

Alec raises his eyebrows to Connor.

Connor finally responds. "I guess like twenty or so." He cringes a little worried that he may be treading on the wrong turf with his boss.

"Ha! I'm only seventeen." Alec says.

"You're not even a legal adult?" Claire asks then adds curiously, "How did you get this job then?"

"Like I said in our first meeting. I've been helping out at my dad's business since I was fourteen. I pick up fast and I was managing shifts by the age of sixteen. It was only natural that my dad gave me a shift when he was assigned his position as lead administrator." Alec says. "Anyhow, I may be mature when it comes to work, but I still know how to have fun."

I blush when his green eyes settle on me.

"Sounds good. Let's go check out the bowling alley then." I say and stand up. Anything to get out of the strange eye contact thing that Alec was doing to me.

Everyone follows suit and we take the elevator to the fourth floor to check it out. I've never been bowling before but I've seen it done on television and in movies. It looks like fun. The elevator lets out in front of the pool area and my nose fills with that strong smell of chlorine. I look in the windows and notice it's extremely crowded today. I guess a lot of people are off this Sunday.

We follow the hallway down until we hear the sounds of balls hitting pins and crowds cheering. Twenty lanes are lit up in neon colors. We go to check in at the registration booth where a skinny teenager with a liberal peppering of freckles on his face tells us that all of the lanes are full. He adds us to the waiting list without asking, which is running about an hour long. I look around to the others for suggestions.

"We can wait," Alec says. "I don't mind."

Everyone else shrugs so I take that as a sign to go and find a table. I find one near the back and take a seat. Everyone else follows except Alec who has been intercepted by someone playing the guess who game. Newly manicured French tip nails are attached to the long skinny fingers covering his eyes.

"Guess who?" A girl calls out from behind him. I can't see her but when she lets out a hideous giggle I 'guess who' immediately.

"Ugh! It's Candy." I sigh but remain in my seat.

"Perhaps if we stay completely still and don't move an inch she won't see us." Claire says jokingly.

"I don't think she's worried about us seeing her. She seems to have her paws all over Alec." Connor laughs and watches the scene with pure amusement.

Alec doesn't seem too happy to be temporarily blinded so he just removes the hands and turns around. "Oh, hey Candy." He says blandly.

"Hi ya Alec! What are you doing on this fine Sunday?" She says in a sort of southern drawl that sounds completely fake.

"I'm hanging out with some friends." He looks back and gestures at us.

Crap, we've been spotted. I think to myself.

"Those are your friends?" She asks with repulsion.

Alec surprises me when he says, "Yeah, you got a problem with that?"

I hate to admit it but I love the shocked look Candy get's on her face.

"Well, I was just thinking that since you finally had a day off you would want to hang out with me or the guys." She rubs her index finger down his chest in a gesture that makes me want to puke.

To my delight, Alec removes her finger from his chest. "We don't really hang out anymore so I figured it was time to make some new friends."

Her mouth drops open for the slightest second then she closes it abruptly. She makes some annoyingly high-pitched shrieking sound and turns on her heal to stomp off.

Alec comes over to the table and looks at me curiously. "Wow, I haven't seen you smile like that, ever."

I quickly wipe the expression off my face, not realizing what I was doing.

"It looks good on you." He says and I look away shyly.

"So what was up with you and Barbie?" Connor asks.

"We went to school together. Her brother and I were on the same football team. That was back before we started predominantly doing our home schooling." Alec answers.

"Well it looked like she has the hots for you man." Connor playfully punches Alec on the shoulder.

"I guess so. We hung out a few times, but she's not really my type." Alec looks over to me ever so briefly and I feel a strange fluttering sensation in the pit of my stomach.

Claire looks over her shoulder and says, "Great, here comes her whole posse. Maybe we should just head out."

"Good idea." I would like nothing better than to keep my distance from Candy and especially from her brother Zack. He gives me the creeps.

We pass by them without saying anything. I feel Zack's stare as if it's burning my flesh but I look directly ahead and pretend that I don't see him. I do feel Alec stiffen ever so slightly next to me. I hadn't realized he was walking so close to me before then but I can tell that something put him on edge.

The tension in our group doesn't relax until we are back in the hall.

"So that idea seems to be botched. What's our next course of action?"

"We could go to the library." I offer.

Connor and Claire look at me like I'm nuts but Alec says, "That sounds great. I've been wanting to check to see if there are any good books in there."

I smile up at him. Alec continues to pleasantly surprise me. He's not the cold hard boss I thought he was.

We head down a flight of stairs to the Library. When we walk through the double doors my eyes are immediately focused on the countless books lining the walls. All four of us waste no time diving into the shelves. Thankfully they're categorized by subject area.

"Hey guys," I say. "Come check this out. There's a whole section related to this mountain." The bookcase is labeled with a sign stating: Local Selections. I pick a random book from the shelves and flip through it. Boring!

All it has in it are blueprints to the sewage systems and a bunch of information that I could care less about. Before I reshelf it, I look at the sewage map again. Something about it strikes a cord in my brain but I can't put my finger on it. I close it a moment later and move on to the other books. To my disappointment, I continually come across one boring instructional manual after another. Where's the murder mysteries or the science fiction? I look around at the other sections in the small library but don't see anything of interest. They range from indoor farming to, world history and the history of F.E.M.A. Not one single non-fiction book to be had in here.

I huff my breath sending my hair billowing from my face. With my back against the wall, I slide to the floor in an act of defeat. In less than an hour we have ran through the only activities that this shelter has to offer. There's got to be something else to do in this place. Connor, Claire and Alec all shelve the books they were looking at and come sit at my side.

"I don't know guys," I start. "I'm not sure what I expected to find, but this stinks. There isn't any fiction and the one non-fiction section that could be interesting doesn't really contain anything about this mountain that's useful. I guess we will have to find some other place to pass the time. Something to keep our mind off…things."

Connor and Claire nod their heads in unison.

Alec on the other hand seems lost in thought.

"I mean, there's got to be something fun to do here besides wallowing in self-pity or twiddling our thumbs.

This place is huge. There must be some trouble to be had." I furrow my brow in frustration. It's really not like me to be looking for something that will get me in trouble, but hey, give me a little credit. I need something to help me unwind. These last few weeks have been completely crazy. I sort through the visual of the map in my head looking for another activity to enjoy in the shelter. Then it hits me. "Guys, I think I've got it!"

Both Claire and Connor turn and look at me expectantly. Alec finally returns from 'lala' land and gives me his full attention.

I get up quickly and find the book I had recently reshelved. "Here, look at this." I open the manual on Sewage Systems and find the map. I lay it across the floor so we can all see. Taking my tablet out, I pull the general map up and set it by its side. I point my finger at the Sewage map. "You see here?" I ask excited that I've now figured out what struck that chord when I was staring at the map. "This is the map of the Sewage System. These tunnels run parallel to the halls, which I guess makes sense. If you look at the map of the facility that we use to make runs and this map simultaneously, you can see that these passageways not only connect to everything on the original map, but there are also some passageways leading to places that aren't named or mentioned. If you look really closely it looks like there is a whole other floor beneath the storage area." I look up from the map to see my friends staring at me like I'm nuts.

"You totally lost me." Connor says.

"Yep, me too. What exactly are you getting at?" Alec asks.

I laugh. It's hard sometimes for me to verbalize what my brain is processing so instead I put it in laymen's terms. "Guys," I say pause for dramatic effect. "I don't think these are sewage tunnels per say; I think these are hidden passageways." I look up to gauge their expressions.

Claire has a curious gleam in her eye but Connor busts out laughing hysterically.

"Secret passage ways!" I stare at him straight faced until he calms down.

"Hey it could happen. I heard a rumor about a spring somewhere down there that feeds into the mountain. That's how our water is being pumped in. There must be some way down to it. What Willow says doesn't sound too far fetched." Alec looks to me and I show him a grateful smile.

Connor's face turns a little red at having been shut down but he quickly gets over it. "Well, I guess there's only one way to find out."

"Let's go check it out," Claire squeals. She gets up super-fast and reaches her hand out to me. I take it and she pulls me to my feet. She's got some good strength for a girl so small.

Alec and Connor meet us on the upright and I reshelve the book. "Wait," says Connor. "We'll need that to know where we're going." He reaches for the book I'm shelving.

I gently stop his hand. "Remember Connor?

Photographic memory." I point to my head for emphasis.

A look of realization dawns on Alec's face. "So that's how you do it."

We all break out in a laugh at Alec being clued in to how I manage to get my work done so quickly. The librarian turns around and yells at us to be quiet. I put my fingers over my lips and we slip out the door but not before the librarian gives us a dirty look.

When we get into the hall Alec is the first to break the silence. "Guys, I'm not sure about this. It's labeled sewage system for a reason. We can't be crawling around in that stuff!" My eyes drop as I realize what he's saying. "But," Alec begins again with newfound hope. "I think I may know how we can still do this." All of us turn to Alec and give him our full attention. Alec pulls out his tablet and opens a map I hadn't seen before. "Perks of the job," he says answering my unasked question.

Connor and Claire inch closer to Alec and me as he punches in different options on his tablet. He pulls up a map of the lower level and it expands into a more detailed translation; one I hadn't seen before. I take a mental picture of the gigantic space that takes up an entire level as Alec begins explaining. "This is where all the supplies are kept for the different jobs in the facility. The sanitation department has rubber boots and other gear that would allow us to go into these tunnels. I'm not sure what's down there but we should be ready for the unexpected if you ask me."

We all nod our head in unison.

"So," I pause trying to gather my thoughts. "Once

we get down there, how will we know where the stuff is that we would need? I mean, it's got to be a pretty big area to take up an entire floor. And, what if we get caught? "

A small smile escapes Alec's lips. "In answer to your questions Willow: a) I don't know how we'll know what stuff is where; and b) we won't get caught if no one sees us." A small gleam catches his eye as a mischievous grin escapes me. I guess that was confirmation enough for Alec that I'm game. He turns to Connor and Claire, "You guys in?" He asks simply.

They look at each other and then nod their heads. We look like a bunch of Cheshire cats grinning the way we are. We've been working our butts off; now it's time to play.

"Wait," Alec says. "Before we go, we've got to figure out what to do with the tablets."

I furrow my brow. "What do you mean 'do with our tablets?' We take them with us of course." I say like it's the most obvious thing in the world.

He lets out a small sigh. "Seriously, you haven't figured it out yet?"

"Figured out what," Claire interjects.

"Figured out that the tablets track your every move." Alec says. He continues, "Willow, how on earth did you think I would know that you help Claire and Connor when you run? Hmm?" He asks me. He doesn't wait for my response before he starts tapping into his tablet. A map pulls up of the facility with a bunch of red dots that are moving slowly across the screen. "Now, I only have access to the runners under my direction, but there's a large map in headquarters that has all of the residents of the entire facility being monitored simultaneously. Yeah, kind of creepy, I know." He puts his tablet back in his satchel that he carries and waits while we all brainstorm.

Out of nowhere I hear this guttural laugh coming from Claire. We all stare at her like she's lost her mind. She puts her hands on her knees and continues to laugh for a moment longer until she settles down enough to speak. "Sorry," she says between breaths. "Okay, I think I have an idea." She looks around her to make sure the coast is clear then huddles closer. "So, Alec, you say that they track us by our tablets so we can't really leave them anywhere right? I mean, that would look pretty obvious if we sit in the same spot for several hours." Alec nods his head and she continues, "So what if I could guarantee that we'd leave them somewhere and they would move around throughout the day?"

Alec furrows his brows, "I'm listening."

"Okay," says Claire. "What if we found a way to tape them to the bottom of something that gets moved around all day." We all nod our heads waiting for the punch line. "So, I say we put them on the bottom of say, a maid cart, or the cafeteria tray carts?"

Connor begins jumping, "Claire, that rocks!" He pulls her into an excited hug and keeps jumping. Claire's body stiffens and her hands remain at her sides. Connor must sense this because he stops mid bounce. He clears his throat. "Sorry 'bout that. Just got excited." He looks down at his foot and I try and stifle a small laugh.

"So anyway," I say trying to change the subject. "Claire, I think you're onto something. Alec what do you think?" We all look to Alec for final approval.

"I think it's go time." He says with a smile on his face. "Okay, so here's the plan. I'm going to go into the office and grab a roll of heavy-duty tape and meet you all back here. Then we'll each go our separate ways, tape up our tablets and then meet by the elevators in the commons area. Sound like a plan?" We all nod our heads in agreement.

"Wait," I interject. "I mean, it sounds like a fail-safe plan, but how are we going to find our tablets when it's all said and done?" I hate to sound like a killjoy but it's a valid question.

"Good question, Willow." Alec responds. "All I have to do is retrieve mine first and then I can pull up each of your tablets locations. Maid carts and tray carts don't move that fast; I'm pretty sure we can manage to track them down. We all good with that?" Alec asks everyone.

"How are you going to find yours?" I ask.

He smiles at me. I feel a flutter in my stomach. "I'm going to be earning extra credit by working on my only day off. I'll just tape it to the underside of my desk."

"Clever." Connor says.

We all nod our heads in unison. "Okay, hands in." Alec puts his hand out in the middle of the circle. We each stick our hands out and put them on top of the other. "Okay, on the count of three. One, two, three..."

I'm not sure what we're supposed to do so I just stand there. We look at Alec a bit awkwardly, "Were we supposed to say something?" I ask Alec.

He just rolls his eyes and removes his hand. "Oh, never mind. Let's meet back up in half an hour." We agree and disperse to find our secret hiding spots.

Thirty minutes later we've stashed our tablets and are waiting by the elevator in the commons area; all of us except Claire that is. "I wonder what's taking her so long," I say tapping my foot.

A few moments later Claire rounds the corner out of breath. "Sorry guys, the maid was trying to chase me down. She thought I was trying to steal her small shampoo bottles."

I let out a short laugh and push the down button on the elevator.

"Here goes nothing." I say to no one in particular.

We all pile in and Alec pushes the button at the bottom labeled 'S'. The elevator doors close and we jerk at the motion. The ride down seems to take forever. I'm not sure if it's just a long way down or if the elevator is just slow. My ears begin to pop at our decent so I'm guessing it's the former. After a good minute the elevator settles and the door opens. We shuffle off and the doors close.

Before us is a vast room at least ten stories high illuminated by dim track lighting. There are humongous wooden crates lined up for as far as the eye can see. Each crate is large enough to hold our entire group inside then some. I count four different rows in the warehouse and immediately feel our plan fizzle. How are we going to be able to find what we need? "There has to be over one hundred crates in here. There's just no way--" I begin.

Claire cuts me off. "Well, there must be some organizational method or a map. They wouldn't just store crates like this where the contents are impossible to locate." Without another word Claire begins searching the area near the elevator doors. "Ah-ha," I hear her say from around the corner. "Found it!"

We all shuffle around the corner to find a piece of paper haphazardly taped to the right of the elevator. There is a label for each crate briefly telling of the department for which they belong. Claire takes her finger and begins searching for Sanitation. Her finger stops on one of the sections at the far end of the warehouse. "Here," she says. "I wish we could take this map with us. It's going to be hard to find."

"That would be my job," I say taking in a mental snapshot of the map. "Follow me." My friends pause and look at me questionably but once again I point to my head and without saying anything else they nod their heads.

It takes us a good five minutes to find the correct boxes. Not because they're hard for me to locate, but because of this area being so big. "If I'm right, they should be right...up...here." We stop in front of a stack of boxes.

Alec finds a latch on the side of the box and pulls the boarded door down. It lands with a loud thump as he lets it drop the last few feet to the ground. We all freeze at the sound. It doesn't look like anyone's in here, but with as vast as this place is we can never be sure. A few moments pass as we listen for any footsteps or voices. I breathe a small sigh of relief and watch as small bits of wood dust settle on the floor. Alec is the first to step into the crate. He finds a string and pulls on it. A light clicks on the ceiling of the crate and illuminates its contents. Shelves have been built on either side of the crate holding different sized cardboard boxes. Thankfully, these boxes are labeled. We all pile into it and begin searching for things we may need.

"I've got gloves," I hear Claire say.

"Here's some boots," Alec says as he wrestles a box to the floor.

"And here's some goggles?" Connor says like it's a question. "Not sure we'll need them but here they are," he says justifying his comment.

"Oh, here's some waders." I read the label on the box out loud.

We each drag our boxes out of the crate and open them together. I pull out several pairs of waders from mine and find they are a 'one size fits all,' which basically means I'll look like I'm drowning in them. Oh well, I think to myself. It's not like I'm going for fashionista of the month or anything. We pull out four of everything and then put away the boxes.

I look through the items and find the boots. Those are also a 'one size fits all.' They look like clown shoes if you ask me. They are so big that they can fit over our tennis shoes.

"Sweet! Look what I found," Connor exclaims from inside the crate. He brings out a small box placing it at my feet.

"What is it?" I ask.

He pries it open and pulls out a-- clothespin?

"Connor, why would we need clothespins? We have laundry facilities upstairs."

Connor gives a small laugh and jumps up. He opens the clothespin and says, "So we don't have to smell the poo!" He opens the wooden pin and holds it over the bridge of his nose. "See," He says in a nasal voice before he lets go of the clothespin all together. "Ta-ahhh! Owww!" His eyes are watering as he quickly pulls it off his nose.

We break out in hysterical laughter as he rubs the bridge of his now-red schnozzle. He glares at us and says, "That freaking hurt!" He crosses his arms over his chest to show us his displeasure with our laughter.

"I say bring those pins along Connor. We can always use them as a weapon against the sewer rats!" Claire jokes and puts her arm around Connor in a playful, conciliatory gesture. He blushes. All of the frustration is gone from his expression and he just looks at Claire with big dopey, infatuated eyes.

"Or the alligators. We can pin their mouths shut!" Alec jests.

The sweet look on Connor's face gives way to an annoyed grimace. "Very funny guys."

Claire's laugh diffuses the tension and Connor eventually joins in with the rest of us.

"Oh! There's still one more thing we need," says Claire. "Flashlights." We all give her a mmhmm and begin searching the contents. Thankfully, stuffed in the corner, there is a small box labeled flashlights.

"Let's just hope they have batteries," I mumble to myself.

We each grab a pair of gloves, waders, boots, goggles and a flashlight and start changing. Once I get mine on I turn to the others. I almost pee myself at the sight of them. I immediately begin laughing hysterically unable to control myself.

We look absolutely ridiculous. Our goggles are way too big for our face, and the waders in and of themselves are a sight to be seen with the way they hike up to our armpits and hang from suspenders.

We gain control over ourselves and start closing things up, boots squeaking as we waddle about.

I feel like a penguin hobbling around with these clown shoes on. I stop mid stride, "Wait. Why exactly are we wearing all this gear now? Can't we take it off? At least the boots, until we get there?" I reach down and take off the boots leaving my shoes on underneath and the others follow suite.

"Okay," Alec begins. "I guess we need to figure out where the sewer lines start, or at least where we can gain access to them."

All three of them turn to look at me. "What?" I say. "Oh, yeah, photographic memory." As if I need to remind myself.

I look around at where we are. "Well, if memory serves me right, and it usually does, there's some sort of entrance a few feet to the left of the rear elevator. I'm not sure what kind of entrance it is, but it had the lines on the blueprint like it was a door of some sort."

"Alright then, let's get this show on the road," Connor says with a little too much enthusiasm.

It doesn't take us long before we can see the elevator shaft about twenty feet ahead of us. Claire stops suddenly and holds out her hand to quiet us, not that we were making much noise in the first place. "Do you hear that?" Claire whispers.

We all stop and look around listening to the silence. Then I hear it, a small clanking sound coming from the direction of the elevators.

"We need to hide, and fast," Alec whispers in a panic. He ushers us all in behind a large grouping of boxes near the rear wall. We get as far back as we can and kneel on the ground. We are all huddled close together.

I'm leaning against Alec and my nose is so close to his neck that I can smell his aftershave. It smells like mint and spices. Alec holds his finger up to his lips to quiet us.

I notice that the boxes are all labeled with the number three. I cringe, hoping that the odd number isn't some sort of omen. My heart starts pounding and I pray that I don't have another one of those panic attacks.

We hear the sound of the elevator coming to a stop and the doors open. Instantly I hear Candy's trademark laugh as her and her minions step off the elevator. I squeeze back further into our corner trying to become one with the box behind us.

Alec must sense my anxiousness because I feel his hand enclose mine. I freeze not knowing what to do. Heat rushes to my cheeks. I've never really held a boys hand before, at least not a boy that I'm not related to. It feels comfortable and safe. It also feels--I don't know, different.

I'm pulled back to the situation at hand when I hear several pairs of footsteps staggering around on the hard cement floor. "Dude, she is totally wasted," a male voice says.

"I ammm not," I hear Candy say accenting the 't'. She sounds completely out of it, drunk even. I hear a heavy thud on the floor and one of the people mutters a slew of cuss words.

"Help her up man, she keeps falling." This guy doesn't sound that sober either. Their steps move closer to where we are and I try and scoot back more in hopes of becoming invisible. I feel Alec's arms wrap around me. My heart flutters but for a different reason this time. He's the only thing keeping me grounded right now. With the way things are sounding out there, God only knows what would happen if they found us. They seem pretty wasted, but I have no doubt that Candy will tattle on us in an instant. Not that they should be down here in the first place, but who would get in trouble in that situation, the rich kids or us?

"Did you find the--stuff?" Candy asks slurring the words together. She lets out a loud laugh and I cringe.

"Oh man, she is so out of it," one of the guys says. "Here you take her so I can try and find the box." The footsteps stop only a few feet from us. I can see them clearly now and hold my breath. If they were to turn around, we would be spotted for sure. There are three of them: Candy, Zack, and some other guy who is holding Candy up. I don't know his name, but I remember seeing him before in Zack's room.

The guy hands Candy over to Zack who has to stagger back a few steps as he adjusts to the added weight of his sister. "Hurry up man; she's getting heavy."

The guy holds his tablet and presses a few buttons. "K, it says medical supplies should be on the next row, about four boxes down. It'll have a red cross label on the side." Zack repositions Candy and they begin walking away.

I listen to their heavy footsteps as they move further and further away. I suddenly feel light headed and realize I hadn't breathed. I let out a swoosh of breath, feeling remarkably safer now that they aren't so close.

"I'm going to see if the coast is clear," Alec whispers a minute later. "Just stay here." Alec squeezes my shoulders and gets up from behind me. The sudden loss of his touch makes me feel cold. He was the only thing keeping me from going into panic mode.

I watch as Alec peeks around the corner. He stays there for a moment then comes back towards us. "Okay, they're far enough away now that they won't be able to see us if we're quiet. Let's just go quickly so they don't find out we're here." Alec tells us in a hushed whisper. We all nod our heads and slowly get up. Alec goes to the corner again and makes sure the coast is still clear.

He ushers us forward with his hand and leads us out into the open. I walk quickly and quietly feeling utterly exposed. I really don't want to find out what would happen if they saw us or what type of reprimand we would receive if we get caught down here.

We manage to get past the elevators and to the area where the blueprints said a door should be. I don't find a door but I do find a large metal grate located on the back wall just feet from where I'm standing. I quietly walk towards it pointing to it so the others will see. This has to be it! It's about four feet in diameter so it's definitely large enough for the normal human to move through it. I run my fingers along the edges of the grate trying to find a way to open it. Disappointment elopes me as I figure out you'd need a screwdriver to get it open. I put my head in my hand frustrated with the situation. We got this far only to be stopped by a few simple screws.

I feel a tap on my shoulder and look back to find Connor standing there holding out a swiss-army-knife. He whispers, "May I?"

I nod my head and smile as he goes to work. He works quickly and quietly handing me each screw as he takes them out. Two minutes and eight screws later, Connor starts to remove the grate. It makes a small scraping sound. He immediately stops and we listen to see if they heard us. We breathe a sigh of relief when we hear no sign of Candy or her minions.

With the exception of a few more squeaks, Connor manages to shimmy the grate off fairly quietly. The crawl space is large enough to crawl through comfortably so I silently volunteer to go first. I put on my boots and get on my hands and knees. I crawl in awkwardly and the others follow behind.

The concrete tubes are cold and hard against my knees. I move forward far enough to allow everyone room to get inside and then I wait. Connor is the last to crawl in. After he's inside he grabs the grate off the floor and sets it up against the wall. It makes a small thud and I inwardly cringe. Connor snaps around and waves his hand for me to hurry up and go. I crawl through the shaft as quickly as I can. The further we move away from the opening the darker the tunnels get. We don't want to chance turning on the flashlights just yet so I move along through the dark, using nothing but my memory as a guide. Soon I come up on a turn and am grateful, as I know it will give us the cover we so desperately need.

Once we're all huddled together around the corner I call them in together for a quick meeting. Connor turns on a flashlight from the back and illuminates our group. My eyes feel a bit blinded by the white light but it's nice not to be wrapped in absolute darkness. "Okay, so right now we're in a shaft that leads to the sewers. There's going to be a lot of twists and turns and uphill/downhill climbs before we're going to get there. Just stay with me okay? I know exactly where I'm going." I nod my head and turn back around not waiting for confirmation from my friends. The last thing I need is someone to doubt me, which could make me doubt myself. Lord only knows where we'd end up then.

Crawling around in the tunnels makes for an interesting challenge. The light from the flashlight bounces up and down against the concrete walls with Connor's movements. I don't know how he's holding it while crawling, but I'm grateful for the light even though it's bouncing all over the place. With all the gear on we end up squeaking and making all kinds of racket. My knees and hands are sore from bearing the weight of my body. Thankfully we don't have much further to go. We round the last uphill turn and almost run smack dab into a large metal plate. "Well, I guess this is it," I say. We are finally in a spot that gives us all standing room so we slowly get up. If I didn't know better, I'd say you could hear the creaking of our knees as we stood.

Alec looks at me bewildered. "I still can't believe you just did that from memory. I wouldn't have been able to do that in a thousand years!" I give him a small laugh.

"Seriously, Willow. You really do rock," Connor says. Claire gives an agreeing smile and inwardly, I feel like a million bucks.

"Okay, so I guess we'd better get ready. This is probably going to be pretty nasty." We all pull our goggles on and Connor moves up to the front to help get the metal plate off. Alec moves past me to help Connor who hands Claire the flashlight. She points it at them. Connor's knife comes in handy again as he pulls out more screws. He sets them on the ground and he and Alec start moving the plate away.

My eyes transfix on Alec's arms as the strain of the heavy plate becomes apparent. His muscles tense as they work to lower it to the ground. I didn't realize how muscular and strong Alec was.

"Willow." Alec calls my name.

I immediately snap out of my trance and feel embarrassed. They've set the plate on the floor and he's motioning for me to lead us again. I wonder if he noticed me staring. I clear my throat. "Okay, let's move." I inwardly laugh as my voice sounds flustered.

We have to crouch to walk through the opening but we get to stand back up on the other side. I look around and notice that we are standing on a large platform.

Claire moves to the ledge and illuminates the nine-foot drop down to the sewer tunnel with her flashlight.

Without hesitation, Alec jumps down gracefully followed by Connor.

Claire and I inch up towards the edge. Both of us take our goggles off to get a better view. "Isn't there a ladder or something," I say to no one in particular. Alec comes towards me and reaches out his hands. "Here, I'll catch you. Just jump."

I stare at him blankly. "Just jump?" Ha, it's that easy.

He pulls his goggles off too and then nods his head.

I can't believe I'm going to do this. I squeeze my eyes shut and take the plunge. I feel a slight free-fall feeling in my stomach before a pair of hands wrap around my waist. My fall is broken and I'm lowered slowly to the ground. I open my eyes to find Alec's hands still around my waist. "You okay?" he asks.

I nod my head, afraid to talk for fear my voice might break. Butterflies are dancing in my stomach and my pulse is speeding up. I imagine that I can feel the warmth of his hands around my waist but logically I know that it's impossible for his body heat to transfer through the thick rubber lining of my waders.

We stare at each other for a second and then, Alec wakes up from whatever trance he was in. He removes his hands from my waist.

I clear my throat and turn away from Alec so he doesn't see the red flushing my face. I watch as Connor helps Claire down in the same way. I can see the baby pink blush fill her cheeks from having physical contact with Connor. The tunnel is fixated with a slight awkwardness that runs thick in the air.

I grab my flashlight out and turn it on. Connor picks his up from the ground too. We look around at the 'sewage tunnel' in front of us and stare at it for a few seconds realizing that this tunnel is missing one thing: sewage. Back home when I was younger, I would go to the sewage tunnels near the creek by our house. They were about the size of the ones we're in right now, but that's where the similarities stop. The ones by my house always had dirty water running out from somewhere. They also had this distinct smell that would intensify the further in you went. This tunnel just smells slightly musty, like nothing really.

I look to the others who seem just as confused as

I am. "This isn't like any sewer I've ever seen," I say aloud. The others furrow their brows and nod in agreement.

"Maybe if we walk further in, things will start to change," says Alec. Leave it to Alec to make sense of a confusing situation.

"Well, Willow, lead the way," Claire says ushering me forward.

Girls in the front and guys in the back; that's how we walk down the long, never-ending tunnel. Strangely, the scenery never changes; it's just cement tunnels, clean as a whistle. I keep listening for dripping water, or some sounds that a typical sewer would make, but come up short. No rats, no sewage, nothing.

As we walk, Claire leans in and whispers to me, "I think he likes you."

I nervously peak behind me to make sure the guys didn't hear. "Who?" I ask her.

She gets a mischievous grin on her face. "Alec, that's who. Don't tell me you haven't noticed."

I gawk at her. "Uh, no he doesn't. Besides, I see how Connor looks at you. Now, he's the one that's got it bad!" She smacks me on the shoulder playfully and we giggle.

I turn back to look at the guys and find that we have definitely sparked their attention.

"Something funny ladies?" Alec calls from behind us.

We try and stifle our laughs. "Nope, we're good." I call back to him. Claire elbows me in the arm and I return the favor.

We walk for another ten minutes or so. Claire and I tease each other back and forth, "Does too." "Does not." The guys just roll their eyes at us.

Claire stops suddenly, staring ahead like a deer caught in headlights, not moving. "Do you hear that?"

We all look around exchanging glances of confusion. "Are you hearing things again Claire?" I jab at her.

She doesn't blink an eye. "No, listen. It's like water rippling or dripping; I'm not sure which. Don't you hear it?"

I look to the guys. We shake our heads in unison. "Uh, no Claire, we don't hear anything."

We walk a few yards forward and then the faint sound of something ahead penetrates my ears. Like Claire said, it sounds like water dripping.

"I hear it now," I say. We make our steps lighter as we edge closer to the source of the noise.

It seems dimmer all of a sudden and I look up to see that Connor's flashlight went out. "Good thing we brought extra batteries," He says.

I shine my light on Connor as he digs through his bag to get more batteries. I stifle a chuckle at Connor's appearance. He looks goofy since he's the only one still wearing the goggles.

Alec moves to pull out his flashlight but I say, "No, lets save the other two flashlights for later. Obviously they kill batteries quickly so we should have backups."

Alec nods.

Connor's light flickers back on as he snaps the

battery cover back in place. We start moving again. This time Alec is by my side as we walk. The further we go the louder the dripping sound becomes. In fact it doesn't sound like just one drip but several drips of water hitting different surfaces. If you listen just right and open your imagination up you can nearly hear a melody playing out by the inconsistent drips.

We keep walking and I realize that I'm no longer leading us by my memory because the recorded map of the tunnels has already ended. I wonder why the map stopped if the tunnels keep going. I can tell we are moving uphill by the burn and strain my calves are feeling. The dripping sound starts to get muffled as we move upwards. We walk higher up for a few more minutes until our flashlights hit a brick wall up ahead.

"Ah, lame!" Connor calls back from behind us. He rips off his goggles and throws them on the ground.

Disappointment washes over me as I stare at the brick and mortar that blocks our path signaling the end of our journey.

"Hey, it's okay. This was still fun." Alec rubs his hand on my back in a comforting gesture.

I look up at him and realize that we are standing only a breath apart. Alec looks radiant in the dim light and I can see that he really means what he said. He did have fun. I still feel let down that we didn't find something amazing in here but I have to admit that the sense of adventure was still worth it. It was something to do and I got to do it with Alec; a guy I probably never would have hung out with in another life.

"Yeah, it was fun." I say in a whisper as I stare up at his glowing green eyes that seem to be pulling me hypnotically toward him.

"Ahum!" Connor clears his throat loud enough to break my daze. We turn in his direction to see him standing over Claire who has her ear pressed to the ground.

When we walk back over to them she sits up and says, "It's down there. Listen." She puts her ear back to the ground and we all get down following suit.

I groan when I move to my knees. It feels like they are covered in a thousand bruises.

"Shh!" Claire says.

I put my hands up and whisper, "sorry."

"Listen." She gestures for me to put my ear to the ground. I comply this time and I hear the dripping sound. We are right above it! I look up at her with wide eyes.

"How can we get down there?" Alec sits up and asks.

"I don't know but there has to be a way. Let's retrace our steps." We all get up. This time we pull out all four flashlights and bounce them all around the tunnel walls as we walk slowly.

"Got it!" Alec calls out a minute later. I run a few feet ahead to where he is. His flashlight is illuminating a circular metal grate on the floor. It's less than three feet in diameter. We must have walked right past it earlier. We can hear the dripping much clearer from the holes in it.

"Hey Connor, want to give me a hand with this?" Alec asks.

Connor runs up and sees what we're looking at. "Score!" He says with excitement. He pulls out his knife yet again and starts working on the screws. This grate takes a while longer to pry loose. He has to pull out over twenty screws. Once they are all out both he and Alec work to remove the cover.

We all stand shoulder to shoulder around the now open hole in the ground. We shine our flashlights down into the pit and find another nine-foot drop to a new tunnel. We look back up at each other and silently ask the question of who should go first. Connor volunteers by raising his hand and waiving it around excitedly.

"Wait, if we drop down there, how are we going to get back up?" I ask.

"Good question," Alec answers. "I think we need to plan this through a bit better. Plus, I think it has to be getting close to dinner time."

My stomach growls loudly in response to the thought of dinner. We got so caught up in what we were doing that we didn't even stop to eat our granola bars.

Claire nods her head in agreement. "I think that's wise. We should head back and perhaps try again next Sunday..." She looks up at Alec and asks, "Wait, do you think we will get another day off together next Sunday?"

Alec smiles and says, "I schedule the time off so I don't see why not." We all smile at his answer.

"We could probably find some sort of make shift ladder to bring with us next time." I add.

Connor looks really disappointed but then says, "I

guess if we are all going to be sensible then we ought to head back." He places the metal grate over the hole but leaves the screws off. Hopefully nobody will come down here and find it tampered with. For good measure he puts the screws in his pockets so they aren't as noticeable.

We turn and start heading back the way we came. Claire calls out, "Wait!" We all turn back to her. She's still standing by the grate and I'm wondering if she changed her mind about taking on this adventure later. She grins really big and pulls at her giant rubber waders. "I say we leave these here. Just in case we need them next time."

We all start laughing as if we all just remembered how ridiculous we look. "Good idea Claire bear." Connor says. We all stop laughing just long enough to give him a strange look over his new found nick name for Claire. I look over to see her icy blue eyes smiling up at him. I guess she likes it.

I'm the first to start stripping off all the unnecessary gear. "Yep, no use in bringing all this back with us." Alec stares at me and I suddenly feel self-conscious taking off the rubber wader pants. I have my scrubs on below it but it still seems a little weird. He recognizes that I must feel awkward because he averts his eyes and then starts taking off his gear.

A few minutes later we have a giant pile of gear, minus the flashlights, stacked in a neat pile. "We should probably hide this stuff. I mean, I'm not sure how often people come down here but there's no reason to raise a red flag."

"Yeah that sounds good." Alec says. He and Connor pull the grate off again. We shove our stuff clumsily down the hole then re-cover it again.

"Let's go." I lead them out of the tunnels. We get stuck at the platform where we jumped from earlier. I guess we should have thought of the same how are we going to get back up plan before we made this jump..

We shine our lights around looking for something to aid us in climbing up. I know the guys can lift us up but how are they going to get up there.

After finding nada, we decide that Connor will give Alec a boost up and then he will go in search of a rope. Connor gets down on all fours and Alec steps onto his back like he's a human step stool. Connor lets out a grunt as Alec's weight hits him. Alec still has to jump even with the boost Connor gave him. He jumps, then quickly grabs a hold of the ledge and slowly starts pulling himself up. For a second he struggles and I wonder if he's going to fall but eventually he makes his way up.

"I'll be right back." He says mostly to me once he's safely on the platform. He leaves and we wait.

Thirty minutes passes by as we twiddle our thumbs at the bottom of the platform. "I should have gone with him." I say. "I don't know if he will remember his way back or not."

"I'm sure he'll be fine." Connor says. He pulls out one of the granola bars we packed and opens it up. We all take a small piece of it and chow down gratefully. My stomach still feels hungry.

Two more granola bars and another thirty minutes later Alec still hasn't returned. Both Claire and Connor are sitting on the floor leaning against the platform wall. They look on the verge of falling asleep. I pace back and forth as a worrisome nausea grows in my stomach. I think of the possibilities of Alec being lost out there. Or worse, maybe he got caught.

"I need to go." I look at Connor who is nodding off. "Help me up." I shake his arm to wake him.

"Huh?" He says then clears his vision.

"Help me up." I say pointing to the top of the platform. "I'm going to go find him."

"Um, okay." He stands up slowly. I guess today's adventure took a lot of energy out of him. Or it could be the lack of protein. "How do you want to do this? Do you want to stand on my back like Alec did or do you want to get on my shoulders?"

I gauge the nine-foot distance and try to remember my tree climbing skills from way back in the day. I'm not sure if I have enough upper body strength so I opt for the shoulders.

"Okay then." He leans down really low to the ground. "You stand on my shoulders and then slowly I will raise you up. Just stay close to the wall and use it to balance yourself."

"Okay." I say nervously as I stand on his shoulders. I'm a little more than a foot off the ground and he hasn't even started to stand yet. I'm already feeling wobbly. "Just go slowly please."

He complies and moves slowly off his knees. He inches up to where he's halfway standing. "Can you grab the ledge?" He asks through grunted teeth as my hand gets closer to the top.

"Almost there." Claire calls in support from behind me.

The ledge is just above me so I inch up on my tippy toes and grab ahold of it. Connor stumbles in that second and I start to wobble. "Crap!" I feel like I'm about to fall so I make a last ditch effort to grab at the ledge that is now just above me. I miss and start falling sideways slightly. Connor's hands grip onto my feet and it slows my fall for a second but then gravity takes its ultimate toll and pulls me down to the cold hard concrete with Connor on my tail. It feels like slow motion as I reach my left arm out in front of me to break my fall. No use, it snaps under the weight of my body. I feel my ankle twisting as Connor falls awkwardly on top of me and it all ends with a teeth chattering slam of my head into the concrete. Stars burst in my eyes and the air is knocked out of me as the world goes black.

"Willow!" I hear my name being called over and over again through the thick fog. I ignore it because this darkness is a comforting bliss. "Willow!" They call again. With each call of my name I feel more and more pain. It starts with a light prickle in my ankle, then moves to a radiating pain in my skull. When the fire comes and washes over my arm, it comes with a high pitch wailing sound. The cry calls out to me over and over until I open my eyes to find Connor and Claire leaning over me.

"Oh my gosh, Willow, are you okay? Speak to me!" Claire runs to my side.

I try to answer her over the loud moans in the background and it's not until I reach for my voice that I realize the cries are coming from inside me. My arm is still twisted in the wrong angle and I can see from the horror in her eyes that it must look as bad as it feels.

Tears are flowing freely down my face and I feel the sweat breaking out on my forehead as I become more and more conscious of my injuries. "It hurts." I cry. A thousand shooting stars fly across my vision as I try to move my arm to my side. I wail again in pain.

"We have to help her." Claire calls to Connor who looks like he's frozen in place. Not knowing what to do.

I writhe around on the ground crying out. My head feels like it's going to explode with every movement I make. An intense nausea makes my stomach roll.

"What the?!" I hear someone land on the ground next to me and then those green eyes are staring at me full of concern. He pushes the sweat-drenched hair from my face. "What happened?" He calls back to the others but doesn't move his eyes from mine.

I lock onto those eyes and imagine that somehow they can heal me, take the pain away from me.

"She fell." Claire cries hysterically.

He looks down at me, worry and fear display on his expression as he reads the pain in my eyes, the pain in my cries. "I'm going to get you help, Willow." He turns to look at Connor who is still frozen. In the absence of those green eyes I feel the pain again. I cry out and he flinches. "Look Connor, you need to help Claire up first." He addresses Claire. "Claire, you let down the ladder I brought and Connor and I will hoist Willow up."

"Okay." She says panicked. They move away from us to start going to work. A few minutes later her flashlight is beaming down at us from above.

Alec's eyes return to me and I feel that peace again, that reprieve from pain. Even though it's probably psychological I hold onto it. He strokes my hair back comfortingly. "I'm going to have to move you now. It's going to hurt, but I have to get you out of here." He says.

I nod and continue to stare at him through my blurred eyes. His emerald eyes look kind of like a water painting to me through all of the tears.

"Okay Connor, come help me." He calls out.

A second later Connor's at my side. "I'm so sorry Willow, I'm so sorry." He sounds so sad and pitiful but I don't look at him. I just focus on Alec's eyes to get me through. "Is o-ka-y." I grunt out.

"We need to move now Connor. She needs to get to the clinic quickly. You climb up. I'm going to hand her off to you at the top." Alec says.

"Yes." Connor hastily leaves my side and climbs the ladder. Alec looks back into my eyes and says, "Do you think you can hold onto me with your right arm?"

I think about it for a second which makes my head hurt. It feels like I'm swimming through fog but eventually

I agree. He nods then hoists me up into his arms. I cry out in pain and he flinches. "I'm sorry, you are going to be okay babe."

I don't think anything of the intimate reference, my brain is not working right anyhow. It's turning to mush as the shooting stars play across my vision.

Alec stands up holding me cradled to his chest. I put my right arm around him. "I know it hurts but you need to hang on okay? Don't close your eyes."

My eyelids flutter and I feel like closing them.

He jostles me a little which sends the pain shooting back up my left arm and down in my leg. "Can you do that for me?" He asks intently.

"Yes." I say in a throaty voice that doesn't sound like mine. He starts to climb. He uses only one arm and in the other he carries me. It takes him a while to move up a few rungs in the ladder. In fact due to the pain I'm writhing in, those few moments seem like an eternity. My right arm starts losing its grip as my body starts to shut down, blacking out from the pain again.

"No, you need to stay awake. I need your help Willow!" He calls loudly into my ear. It startles me and I work to pull myself away from the blackness. I tighten my one armed grip on him again. He moves up a few more rungs and then I feel myself being hoisted up onto the platform by Connor. Alec pulls himself up a minute later and then takes me in his arms once again. This time he doesn't ask me to hold on. I sink my head into his chest and I let the blackness take me off to a land that has no pain.

SEVEN

The steady rhythm of beeps pulls me out of a drug-induced sleep.

I see the light behind my eyelids before I open them. My eyes cringe as I slowly squint more and more. The stark white walls make me feel cold and I shiver. My head feels thick and heavy.

"Honey." My dad is at my side in an instant pushing my unruly curls out of my face.

I try to process everything through my brain as I notice the sterile medical equipment and the monitors. I look down at my right arm where there is an IV sticking out my hand. I try to move but it hurts.

"Don't push it. Just rest honey, you're safe." My dad says. I turn towards his voice and find him in a yellow hospital outfit complete with a clear face mask. I try blinking my eyes a few times to clear the cobwebs.

My left arm is throbbing and I look down to find a bright white cast covering the lower half of it. It's held up in a navy blue sling. My left leg is elevated in another sling above the bed. It looks like half my body is broken. Everything starts flooding back.

"Where am I?" I say in a dry throaty voice that

cracks half way through. My dad grabs a cup with a straw from a metal tray table next to me. He puts it up to my lips and I greedily take in the thirst quenching water. It feels luxurious as it slides down my sandpaper dry throat. I look up at my dad waiting for an explanation.

"You're in the hospital honey. Don't you remember what happened?" He asks me worriedly.

I do and my heart starts to beat as I wonder what kind of trouble we are in. Did they find out where we were? I opt to play dumb so I shake my head.

"Your friends said that you were trying to climb some cement steps behind the pool area and slipped. Had a pretty nasty fall. It's a wonder you didn't break more bones."

Yes, lucky indeed, I think to myself. It's not like I like the fact that my friends told my dad a bold face lie but what other choice did they have? It still doesn't explain why my dad is dressed the way he is. How would I be contagious if I just broke some bones?

"What time is it?" I ask, my head pounds with each word I spit out.

My dad furrows his brow then a look of understanding passes over him. "Time, you ask?"

I nod my head.

"Well…" He glances at his watch. "It's five till six."

"In the morning?" I ask.

My dad nods his head in confirmation. In that moment I begin to notice, behind his mask, the purple bags that have formed under his eyes as well as his 'way beyond five o'clock shadow' growing on his face.

"Wow, I didn't realize I'd been out for that many hours." I say. It doesn't seem like any time has passed really.

"Hours?" my dad questions. "Honey, you've been out for days…four to be exact."

"Four days!" My voice cracks at the attempt of yelling. My dad simply nods his head. I lay my head back on the pillow trying to let this sink in and groan from the pain that radiates through my skull. I reach my hand back to rub the spot that hurts the worse and feel a goose egg sized knot there. Yikes, I really must have slammed it into the ground. It's a wonder I don't have amnesia or something worse.

"Do you feel okay, would you like me to get the nurse?" He hovers over me for a second until I wave him off.

"Well I feel like I got hit by a semi truck, but I don't need the nurse. I was just surprised that four days went by without my knowing it."

"Yes, I was so scared Willow. The doctors assured me that you would be okay, but still." His face grows serious. "You have to be more careful. I couldn't handle it if I lost you too." His eyes start to tear up and mine begin mimicking his.

"So dad, why are you wearing all that getup? It's not like breaking bones is contagious or anything." My dad lets out a small laugh, apparently relieved that I changed the subject.

"Well, with all the scrapes you got when you fell, you contracted something called MRSA."

I give him a confused look. "What's MRSA?"

"MRSA is a type of staph infection you can get from having multiple abrasions." He doesn't wait for me to respond before he goes on. "They did a routine test when you went in for surgery for your arm. You broke it in two places. The test came back positive for MRSA, that's why you're hooked up to an IV right now. For the antibiotics, and also the pain medicine. Because they caught it early, they are hoping they can kill the MRSA in a few weeks or so. Now your bones are going to take a bit longer to heal." I just stare at my dad trying to let it all sink in, multiple broken bones and MRSA. He must realize how I'm feeling because his face lightens up and he changes the subject. "So, now that you're up, there's been something I've wanted to ask you."

I wipe at my eyes with my one good hand and look at him.

"Who's Alec?"

The mention of his name makes the hairs on the back of my neck stand on end. "Alec?" I question, my voice cracking, even though I know darn well who he's talking about.

"Mmmhmm," my dad says. I look at him with a semi-confused expression so he continues. "The reason I ask is that he seems to be mighty concerned about your wellbeing. And when I say mighty concerned, I mean almost territorial. He's been up here visiting during all his free time."

I know I'm blushing, I can feel it. "Alec's just a

friend dad. A friend from work," I stutter. Woot, ten points to Willow for a quick comeback answer! I don't know why, but it feels weird talking to my dad about Alec. Even more bizarre to hear his name come from my dad's lips. We've never really had 'the talk' or any conversation related to boys. I mean when you're holed up inside a house with your family for the first part of your high school career, there really isn't a need.

"So, he's just a friend...from work," my dad questions again.

"Dad," I say trying to feign annoyance.

He raises his hands in an act of innocence and sits back down.

As if on cue someone raps softly against the door. I half expect to find the nurse coming in to give me meds or something but my mouth drops open at the sight of Alec, at six in the morning. Now I see what my dad is talking about when he extenuated the word all before, as in all his free time.

My heart starts fluttering when he looks my direction. Swoon! Is it just my imagination, but does Alec look exceptionally hot this morning, even through the ridiculous mask? He has some stubble growing on his chin, which makes him look a little older than seventeen. He's wearing dark green scrubs that make his emerald eyes stand out. He looks happy to see me but worried at the same time.

"Alec," I begin, not sure what to say.

Instead of saying anything to me he acknowledges

my father first. "Hello Mr. Mosby. It's good to see you again."

My dad cracks a smile, "Indeed." An awkward pause follows as my dad looks to Alec, back to me and back at Alec again. "Oh, right. I'm going to get a cup of coffee. Can I get either of you anything?" My dad asks rubbing his hands on his pants.

Alec and I shake our heads.

"Okay then," my dad says getting up from his chair. He steps into the hallway and turns back towards me. "I'll be out here if you need anything," he says leaving the door slightly ajar. He peaks his head back in a second later, "Anything at all."

"Thanks dad," I say waving goodbye to him. The door never meets the hinge, I'm guessing my dad meant for it not to. Awkward.

Alec crosses the room towards me and puts his hands in his pockets. "So," he says while balancing back on his heels. "I'm glad to see you up, I mean not up, awake is what I meant," he stammers.

His response cracks me up. I've never seen him so flustered, it's kind of endearing. "Hey," I say reaching for his arm. "It's all good. Look, I'm fine. Just a little banged up is all. And, I have you to thank." I drop my eyes, and my hand realizing how intimate my voice just sounded. My cheeks turn an unnatural shade of red. I'm not sure at what point things got awkward between us, but the tension is so thick you could cut it with a knife.

"I would say you are a lot more than a little banged

up." He scans my many casts and slings then adds, "I was really freaked out!" His eyes show more worry then they lighten up and he stares down at my lips. "I'm just glad you're okay, that's all."

We stare at each other for several seconds somehow speaking unnecessary words with our eyes. My heart begins fluttering as Alec leans in like he wants to kiss my cheek. Could he be aiming at my lips? I've never kissed a boy and my heart goes wild with the thought. The only thing separating us is a foot of air and that stupid mask.

My dad peaks his head in the door at the same instant and Alec launches himself away from the bed.

"Oh, hey dad," I say with an unnaturally high pitched voice. I don't even have time to process what just happened.

"Alec, Willow," my dad says curtly before sitting back down in his appointed seat with his newly filled cup of coffee. "Oh, don't mind me you two, just pretend I'm not here."

Oh. My. Gosh. If I could crawl in a hole right now I so would. My cheeks are filled with an intense heat.

"So," Alec interjects looking all too calm. "Don't worry about work; looks like you'll be needing to take it easy for a while. But hey, if you feel like you're up for doing something but can't be a runner yet, I could really use some help in the office. You know, filing papers and that sort of thing." Alec swallows hard and I can tell he's trying to keep his cool.

My dad takes a loud slurp of his coffee and turns

the page of a magazine. "Oh wow, look at that. There's a quiz here on how to keep a boyfriend. Yep, I'm gonna have to take that one."

I try and stifle a laugh. I think this is my dad's way of saying visiting hours are over.

As if on cue, Alec looks at his wrist, where a watch would go if he had one. "Would you look at that, I've got to get to work," he says. "I guess I'll be seeing you around Willow." He asks it in a more question type of statement.

"Yeah, that sounds good. Thanks for stopping by; it means a lot. Tell Connor and Claire I'm doing fine, okay?"

"Will do," he says.

"Have a good day Mr. Mosby." Alec turns on his heel and walks out the door.

EIGHT

Alec, Connor and Claire visit me often during the next three weeks.

The doctors said I have to stay in the hospital until the last of my surgeries are completed. The MRSA was gone by the two week mark. They've already done two minor surgeries on my arm since I broke it in several different places. They have a final surgery scheduled later this week to finish their repair work.

My leg is healing up. It turns out it was just a major sprain, no broken bones. They've done a few CT scans of my head and said that there's no damage there. The doctor made a joke about me having a very nice brain and I laughed accordingly even though it kind of creeped me out. I really don't like hospitals or all of these scans, tests and surgeries. They make me feel too vulnerable and weak.

The plus side of my stay is that every day before work and after work Alec comes to see me. It drives my dad insane but makes me smile. Connor and Claire come several times a week too, always together. Connor always brings a deck of cards to entertain. One time, when I had all three of them here, we had a ridiculous competition to see who could eat the most pudding cups in under a minute. Connor won by two. The nurse came in a few seconds later and got to see the aftermath. Needless to say I am now limited to two visitors at a time and my pudding privileges have been revoked.

My dad was given a small reprieve from work when I first injured myself, but he had to go back after the first week. So most days it's just me, the television which only plays old re-runs, the remote control, and a nice stack of schoolwork. I am so sick of soap opera reruns that I could scream.

When the day finally comes for my release I nearly hop out of the bed. "Now, don't you be jostling your arm around like that, you hear? Or you'll be back here faster than a drunken girl in stilettoes." I let out a nasally laugh. My nurse has got to be one of the funniest ladies I've ever met. She gives me bottle of pain pills and my discharge orders. The orders state that I need to stay off my leg as much as possible and that I can't return to normal work duties for another three weeks.

I get home about ten minutes later after hobbling most of the way. It only takes twenty more minutes for me to realize that I can't stay in here for another three weeks. I'll go insane.

Alec made sure to remind me on every visit that his offer still stood to help him in the office when I got out. I pull out my tablet and do a quick one finger text to my dad telling him that I'm going in to work. He doesn't like the idea and makes sure to voice his opinion in all caps.

I send him a return message stating that I love him then throw my tablet back into my satchel bag and strap it around my waist. I'm so grateful that Claire brought my tablet to me the following day after I broke my arm. That was one less thing I had to explain to my dad…why my tablet would have been found on the underside of a maid cart.

It takes me fifteen minutes to make the trip to headquarters. Usually I can make it in less than five, but I have to stop several times to rest and catch my breath. Since when did I turn into such an old lady? Alec jumps up from his desk and runs over to me to hold the door open so I can limp through it.

"Hey there super trooper!" Alec grins and his green eyes light up.

"Hey." I say a bit out of breath. I try to blow the hair out from my eyes and catch a glimpse of myself in the reflection of a picture frame. I look like a hot mess! The hair in front of my face is slightly drenched in sweat and my curls are sticking out this way and that. Alec reaches his hand up to push my hair out of my face but he drops it quickly when he looks around the office. Some people have glanced up to stare at us from their desks.

Alec clears his throat, "Okay, you can help me in the back with some filing." He points to a door across the room. I gage the distance and while it's only a few yards away it might as well be miles. I can't believe how low my energy level is.

Alec walks ahead, punches a code into the door

lock and opens it. I move slowly and painfully. When I push past him into the room-which holds a small desk, two chairs and seven metal filing cabinets- I plop down into the first chair I see. I lean back trying to catch my breath like I just ran a marathon.

Alec chuckles as he steps inside and lets the door shut behind him. "Maybe we should get you a wheelchair."

I give him a don't test me look which just makes his grin grow larger. I roll my eyes and scratch at my left arm. "This cast is so itchy, I can't wait to get it off next week!" I wine.

"I know they are horrible. I've broken many bones before." His grin turns into a sweeter smile. He walks over to the desk and grabs a black permanent marker from the drawer. He sits next to me. "May I?"

I look at him confused and nod slightly. My breath catches again, not because of exertion but because Alec is touching me. He gently pulls the sling strap over my head and slides it off my arm. He places it on the floor and then moves my arm to rest it across his legs. I raise my eyebrow when he uncaps the marker and smiles up at me. Good cow, it feels like he's undressing me!

"This plain white cast is just too drab. It doesn't fit you at all." He starts drawing something on it then adds, "Hey, no peaking."

I turn and look straight ahead at nothing. I wonder if he can hear my heart beating fast. I use my right hand to try and straighten out some of my unruly curls. Alec stops drawing for a minute and pushes some of my hair behind my ear for me. I look at him and realize just how close we are. My breath hitches and my eyes wander down towards his lips. I've never kissed anyone before and I wonder in that instant what it would be like. He traces my lips too with his eyes but then looks away just as quickly. My cheeks heat up and I turn back to stare at the blank wall while he continues doodling on my cast.

My stomach does its fluttering thing and I try to will the butterflies to stop flapping their wings while I contemplate how things got so awkward between Alec and me. We've always had a bit of tension between us; but lately, every time we see each other, the air is charged with electricity. I find myself torn between wanting to go back to the way things were when we could joke around as friends, and wanting desperately to explore that electricity even if there's a risk of shock involved.

"Done!" Alec breaks the silence. He puts his hand in mine and lifts my arm up so I can see the cast.

I look first at the way our fingers are intertwined perfectly together and then force myself to break my gaze away to look at his artwork. "Wow!" I say as I stare at my newly transformed cast. "I didn't know you could draw like this!" I look up at his eyes and he looks pleased that I like it so much. I look back down to study the details of his drawing. He's sketched an entire mountain scape onto my cast with a Sharpie. It's complete with a setting sun, small pine trees and a glistening lake. "Wow." I say again. The details are so clear and vivid even though it's all in black and white.

He blushes this time and says, "I'm glad you like it." He looks down at our hands but doesn't pull his away yet. "Are you still in pain?"

I look up into his eyes, which have grown serious. I shrug. "Nah, they got me on the feel good medicine so I barely feel the pain."

"Why did you try to climb that? Why didn't you just wait for me?"

I can tell by the way he looks that he's been contemplating this question for a while. I have questioned myself as well. "I thought you might have gotten lost or worse. I thought something might have happened to you."

"I was fine, it just took me a while to find a ladder, that was all." He looks away for a moment. "I have never been more scared in my life than I was when I saw you lying there like that. Like a broken doll. So perfect, yet so broken." He takes a deep breath as if conjuring the scene up into his memory.

I pull his chin back up to see my eyes. "Look, I'm fine now."

His green eyes harden slightly. "If I'd have just been there."

"Hey it's not your fault!" I demand. "I made the choice and nobody could have foreseen that accident." I continue to stare at him for a few more seconds until his eyes soften up a bit. "And see, I'm almost as good as new." I flash him my pearly whites. "Maybe better, even."

His eyes pause and linger on my lips. The awkwardness is starting again. My hand feels feverish in his. My blood is coursing through my veins and I swear I can hear my heartbeat as I gage the ever so slight distance between our lips.

The electricity is so thick in the air that my nerves tingle and goose bumps rise on my arms. I look into his eyes and see that they have a bit of a dazed look. He starts leaning closer to me and I stay perfectly still, not sure what to do. A second later his lips touch mine ever so gently.

I gasp a slight breath in surprise. I've never been kissed before! I don't know what to do. He takes my intake of air as an unwelcoming sign and pulls away quickly.

He pulls his hand from mine and says, "I'm sorry Willow." He stands up and paces the room. "I didn't mean to make you uncomfortable." He pushes his hand through his dark hair making it look all messy and incredibly hot.

I stare at him with wide doe eyes. My mouth is gaping open as I try to find words to say. What do I say? Sorry, I got nervous? Let's try that again? Can I get a do-over? Instead I close my mouth and stare down at my hands for a moment. I look at the drawing on my cast and that's when I decide to muster the energy and the courage to stand up and go to him. I don't know what I'm doing and I probably look ridiculous limping towards Alec, but I'm determined.

He looks up at me surprised and a little embarrassed. When I speak now my voice comes out in a throaty whisper. "Please, try it again."

He stares at me long and hard as if trying to decipher a difficult puzzle. I inch my lips closer to him and that's all it takes for him to close the gap. His lips are on mine in that instant and fireworks are exploding in my brain. He kisses me hard with our mouths closed and a dizzy sensation overtakes me. My knees nearly go weak but he puts his hand on my lower back pulling me closer into him.

The sound of someone pressing the code into the door jars us from our stupor and in a flash Alec lets me go and I nearly sink to my knees. It's crazy how intense the feeling of separation is, I swear I can still feel his lips on mine when the door opens.

"So this is where you will file the papers." Alec opens a filing cabinet a few feet from me. I nod clumsily and avoid turning to look at the door.

"Hello father." Alec says to someone behind me. I don't dare turn around to meet Mr. Blake's gaze for fear that he will be able to see a big ol' glowing sign across my forehead that states: I'VE BEEN MAKING OUT WITH YOUR SON.

My cheeks are still flush, my lips swollen and my blood is still pumping warm and hot in my veins when I hear his dad behind me.

"Hello Alec. What is going on in here?" There is a stone like hardness in his voice with zero tenderness that you would hear in a usual father-son conversation.

Alec looks at me and then behind me. He clears his throat before saying, "Since this young lady is injured and has a doctors note for light duty, I figured that I would put her to work taking care of some of these files."

An uncomfortable silence passes and I wonder what type of stare down Mr. Blake is giving Alec. "That's fine, but I need you both to vacate this room for a few moments."

"No problem." Alec says. He picks up his tablet from his pouch then punches in some numbers. "Willow you may take your fifteen minute break at this time." For good measure he adds, "Don't be late."

My eyes widen in surprise and I give Alec a funny smile then say, "Yes sir." I wipe all expressions from my face as I turn around and see Mr. Blake standing there inspecting me like I'm some type of lab rat. He looks thinner than he did on the first day I met him, but he still has that air of superiority and intimidation about him. "Good to see you again Mr. Blake." I say nodding my head before I limp out of the room. He doesn't acknowledge me in the least.

I nearly run into someone when I get out into the office. I look up to see a man in a white lab coat who looks mildly annoyed as he walks past me. He looks strangely familiar. He's at least a full foot taller than me with greying hair and a goatee. I place him a few seconds later as Dr. Hastings, the man from the assembly announcement; the one who is in charge of this whole facility. I wonder what he's doing here. Much like Mr. Blake he doesn't acknowledge me as I limp past.

I walk out into the hall and take a drink from the water fountain. I bend down and splash some of the cool water on my face to clear the fuzziness that is still present from my earlier make out session. I touch my lips when I stand back up. My first kiss and wow was it a kiss! I wonder if they're always this intense?

When I turn around I see Alec in the empty hall behind me. His face is grinning and he puts his hands in his pockets. "Hey."

The blush makes its way to my cheeks again when I meet his green eyes. "Hey." I say back while trying to wipe all of the spare water off my face. "By the way, you didn't tell me you had acting skills."

He takes a fake bow and says, "Yep, I've gotten used to putting on a performance for the old man." His face takes on a serious expression.

"What do you think Dr. Hastings was doing with your dad?" I move away from the water fountain to stand by Alec again.

He shrugs his shoulders. "Hmm, I don't know. I mean I know that my father is on the F.E.M.A. board. I figure they are grabbing a file or something. There are a few cabinets with some heavy-duty locks on them. There must be some top-secret stuff in those."

"Hmmm." I bite my lower lip while contemplating what might be in those cabinets. I look up to see Alec staring at me. His eyes have that same glossy look that they had right before he kissed me. My stomach flutters and I secretly hope he will do it again, even if his dad's in the next room. I see his desire pass through in his expression but he shakes it off. Why must Alec be so sensible? Surely he could lose his job or get in trouble for making out with one of his employees, but I think he should just throw caution to the wind!

I guess my disappointment must show because Alec chuckles. "You are really beautiful Willow." He says sincerely.

"Yes she is!" Claire says in a chirpy voice and comes up from behind Alec. "I'm so glad you're feeling better Willow!" She seems mighty bubbly today.

Honestly I'm amazed at how different this Claire is to the timid fragile girl that used to hide behind her hair. Connor comes up behind her and pokes her in the ribs and she giggles. I wonder if Connor might have a lot to do with that fact.

Connor smiles at me. He has a few packages in his left hand so I'm guessing he's in the middle of his shift. "Yep, it's good to see you up and moving around. Is the boss making you work on the same day you got out of the hospital?" He shares some type of weird handshake high five, combo thing with Alec.

"Nope, I stared at the white walls of my room for all of ten minutes before I decided I had to evacuate. I've felt like a caged animal over the past several weeks being stuck in a room day in and day out. A girl has to have some fun you know." I blush when I think about how much fun I just had kissing Alec, blushing even more when I realize how badly I want to do it again.

"Speaking of caged animals, when are we gonna go on another adventure?" Connor asks.

"I don't think that's a good idea, especially after the debacle that happened last time." Alec lifts my left arm up gently as if the cast doesn't stick out like a sore thumb already.

"Hey, a few broken bones isn't going to stop this girl!" I say yanking my arm back. "Ouch!" My pain meds must be wearing off because my arm is killing me.

"You okay?" Alec asks worried.

I nod my head and cradle my arm to my body. "Yeah, I think I need to take my medicine. Anyhow, what I was trying to say is that as soon as this cast is off I'm ready! We have got to go back and check out what is down there."

"Yay!" Claire says excitedly. "Wow, that drawing on your cast looks pretty rockin'!" She moves closer to examine it.

"Alec drew it." I say proudly, looking up at Alec who seems like he may need more convincing about our side adventures. I figure he won't be so worried when I'm all healed and back to normal.

"Dude, that's cool!" Connor looks at it. "You should keep that after they cut it off you."

"Yeah, maybe I'll frame it and put it above my bed." I say jokingly and everyone laughs including Alec. I'm grateful that he's lightening up a bit in regards to my injuries.

The door to the office opens and Mr. Blake and Dr. Hastings step out.

"So, after you are done with that run, you will need to stop back by the office. I have a few extra assignments for the two of you." Alec addresses Connor and Claire who both take the hint, nod their heads and walk away quickly.

"I'm checking back in from my break sir." I say to Alec. He gives me a look that says he didn't know I could act as well.

"Are you done in the filing room sir?" Alec asks his dad.

"Yes. Get back to work." That's all Mr. Blake says before walking away along with Dr. Hastings who is holding a file in his hand. I stare at it for a few seconds curiously. My eye catches the word immunization but that's all.

When they are out of hearing range Alec says, "Mr. Blake can be a bit of a jerk wad sometimes."

I smile up at him sympathetically trying to make him feel a little less let down by the non-existent father/son emotions. "Yep."

He grins in return and we both head back inside to work.

NINE

The next several weeks consist of the same thing, day in and day out; with the exception of all the stolen kisses Alec and I sneak.

I go to school with Connor and Claire, and then I go to "work." It can't really be called work though. Alec has me filing but he makes sure I don't get much done.

Today I get my cast off. I'm not too excited about that, because it means I'll need to go back to running soon. On the upside, it also means on our next day off we'll be able to explore the "sewer system" further. Alec's been trying to talk me out of it every time I bring it up but I give him 'the look' and he quickly changes the subject.

"Alec, you really don't have to take off work. I can get there on my own you know." Alec is insisting that he go with me to get my cast off. Deep down though, I really do want him to go, I just don't want to come across as needy.

He playfully tugs at my hair inching closer. He closes the door to the office with his foot and a lump forms in my throat. He takes hold of my cheek in his hand and puts his lips to my ear. His breathing on my neck sends shivers down to my toes. "I'm pretty sure you can get there on your own. It's just that…" He nibbles at my ear. "…I will pretty much make any excuse to spend more time with you." The huskiness of his voice makes me melt. He takes a step back furthering his distance and speaks as if what just happened didn't. "So, are you ready to go."

I take a deep breath and put my hair behind my ears. I will myself not to speak for fear of sounding like a mouse and nod my head. It's been a couple of weeks but our relationship, at least that's what I'm calling it, still seems brand new.

He opens the doors and we make the short journey to the doctor's office. In the elevator his lips find mine in a greedy manor, and when it dings, he composes himself like nothing happened leaving me speechless and breathless.

I sign in on the clipboard at the front desk and we sit down to wait. I pick up a magazine and flip through it. I find a crossword puzzle and fold back the page. "Okay, smarty-pants. Let's see how you are at crosswords!" I say a little too smug. "Alright, seven down: To go astray or diverge. It's eight letters." I tap the pen I got from the sign in sheet on my chin. I look over to Alec who has a funny expression on his face. "What," I challenge, letting a small laugh come through.

"Oh, nothing. I just like watching you while you're thinking. You get these cute little lines between your eyes."

I roll my eyes, "Oh really, do I? Okay, smarty-pants what's the answer," I ask, knowing full well he won't know it.

"Aberrate," he says simply.

I raise my eyebrows at him in response. "Lucky

guess," I say as I write it in. "Okay, next one, and this one is going to be really hard." I scan the side column looking for one no one would ever get. "Ah, here we go. You ready?" I don't wait for him to respond before starting. "A morbid fear of sounds or the fear of your own voice. Fifteen letters, starts with an 'A'." There, I think, that should keep him busy.

"Acousticophobia." He says cockily.

"What!" I yell a little too loudly. I soften my tone when other people start looking at me. "How on earth did you know that?"

Alec just shrugs his shoulders.

I scribble in the answer. "Either you're the smartest person I've ever met, or you're pulling my leg. Which is it? And I expect an honest answer!"

Alec tries to keep from laughing but he's not doing a good job.

"What?" I say as his laughter becomes contagious. I playfully slap him on the arm. "Tell me!" I say.

"Okay, okay, you don't have to get all violent on me!" Alec tells me playfully. "I spent a lot of time in the waiting room the first several days you were in the hospital. Got tired of watching reruns of boring old soap operas so I did all the crosswords."

"Willow Mosby," a voice from the other side of the room calls. I glance up to see a plump nurse looking around the room.

"Here," I say holding up my hand.

Before I can stand up, Alec puts his hand on mine.

"You want me to go with you? You know, to hold your hand and stuff?"

I don't really need to give it much thought. "Yeah, sure, if you want to." I catch a gleam in his eye. Of course he wants to.

I lead the way over to the nurse and she puts us in a small room off to the right. She lays my chart down on the table and turns to leave. "The doctor will be with you in a minute," she says as she turns and walks out, shutting the door behind her.

I take a quick glance around the room and get really nervous when I see this mean saw looking thing hanging on the wall. "You don't think that's for me, do you Alec?" I turn to him as my anxiety increases ten-fold.

Alec sees this as a sign to comfort me. He takes my hand gently from my lap and wraps it in his. I slump into him finding immediate comfort.

It doesn't take long before the doctor comes in. He's wearing the typical white lab coat. He has white hair that is sticking up all over the place and bottle-cap glasses. He looks at me over the rim, "And you must be Willow. I'm Dr. Pain. Please, don't think I'm being funny, that's my real name. Got the birth certificate to prove it."

I try to let out a small laugh, but my mouth won't let me. I squeeze Alec's hand a bit harder and he rubs the side with his thumb in a comforting gesture.

The doctor begins shuffling around the room gathering tools and cloth and that dreaded saw readied to be used. I can't seem to take my eyes off the blade. The doctor wheels the tray over to where I'm sitting and pulls the rolling chair over as well.

"Now, just trust me, this won't hurt a bit," the doctor tells me.

Yeah, trust a doctor named Dr. Pain. Not going to happen.

He reaches for my arm and I reluctantly give it to him. "Oh," he exclaims when he sees the small mural painted on my cast. "You want me to cut around this for you? It would be such a waste of good art."

I nod my head and try to smile. "Yes, it's very special to me," I reply. My heart is picking up speed and I work to keep from going into a panic attack.

The second I hear the saw blade turn on I close my eyes and put my head in Alec's chest.

"Now don't move, okay?" The doctor asks me, shouting above the noise. A sound of cutting wood penetrates my ears and my brain is screaming, danger, step back! I try not to flinch as I hear the plaster cracking on my arm. It doesn't take more than ten seconds before I feel the cool air hit my arm for the first time in what seems like months. I look down at my pale weak arm that hasn't made an appearance in a while. It's really skinny compared to my other arm and looks kind of funny.

The doctor turns off the saw and hangs it back up out of the way. I bend my wrist cautiously, thankful there's no pain. It just feels weird. I turn my arm slightly and see a small bruise that has almost dissipated as well as a three inch long scar. That must have been where I had the surgery.

"Just make sure you take it easy for the next few days. I'm going to give you a sling to wear while you adjust to not having the cast on. After that, you'll be good to go." The doctor hands me my empty cast and leaves the room with the door still propped open. He returns a second later with another navy sling. He helps me put it on then leaves.

"Well, I guess we can go," Alec says while helping me up. I clutch the cast as we leave. He puts his arm around my waist. As we walk away I wonder about us. Are we in a relationship? I don't ask though. For right now, I feel good with how things are. I don't need a label to tell me how I'm starting to feel about him.

TEN

As usual school's a bore. For the next few days all I can think about is finding where that storm drain thing leads.

We've been talking about it every chance we get. Alec has set our next day off together on Saturday, which is tomorrow. I know I'm going to have a hard time sleeping tonight!

I lie in my bed going over the maps in my head. It's hard to think about the maps when Alec's perfect face keeps flooding my thoughts. I keep trying to figure out what we are. Are we together? Boyfriend, girlfriend? I'm too afraid to ask such a silly question so I figure I'll just let it ride, hoping he brings it up in conversation.

I eventually fall asleep sometime after two a.m. I hear my dad come in sometime in the night but I'm too tired to greet him. I feel so awful for how much they're working him.

My tablet wakes me up at six a.m. the following morning. There's a new group message to us from Alec. Meet me by the lower elevators in twenty minutes, is all it says.

I wipe the sleep from my eyes and drag myself into

the bathroom. I brush my teeth, put on my blue scrubs and pull my hair back in a ponytail. I grab my tablet and slip out of the door. No need to wake my dad who will have to get up in a half hour anyway.

The hall lights are still dimmed; apparently they conserve electricity in the night hours this way. They'll come on full force at seven.

I run into Claire on the elevator down. "So, you and Connor, huh?" I ask jabbing her lightly in the ribs. I've noticed their looks during class and even caught them holding hands one time. They don't say anything about it so I figured, now is as good a time as any to ask her.

A blush spreads over her pale face as she looks down at her shoes.

"Hey, it's all good," I say trying to reassure her. "Connor's a really nice guy."

She finally smiles and looks up at me. "Yeah, he really is. I think I might be falling for him, but it scares me. Everyone I've ever loved in this world has either left me or died. I feel like my heart is too far out there right now… like maybe I should pull back." She takes a second. "Oh, Willow, I'm sorry. I didn't mean to sound so depressing this morning!" She has a pleading look on her face.

I put my hand softly on her shoulder. Sometimes I forget how alone Claire is. She finally told me a little more about her parents when I was in the hospital. Her mom had died from the virus and her dad went into a heavy state of depression. He had to give her up because he couldn't properly care for her. She often thought that a part of his depression had to do with how much Claire had resembled her mother.

"Claire, look at me." She does. "Connor's not that type of guy, okay. He's not going to leave. And you can be assured that I'm not going to leave you either! You're my best friend." I have never said that to Claire before, but it's true.

A sparkle gleams in her eyes. "You mean, I have a bestie now? I've never been able to use that word and 'I have' in the same sentence before."

I laugh at her use of the word bestie. The elevator dings and Claire takes me in a crushing hug. I hug her back as the elevator doors open.

Connor and Alec stare with mouths dropped open. "That's hot," says Connor and apparently Alec agrees, nodding his head.

"Oh, shut up!" I say playfully. Claire and I get out of the elevator.

"So," Connor says while rubbing his hands. "What's the plan?"

Alec grabs his satchel and opens it up. We all peer inside and see flashlights, power bars, and an assortment of other things I guess we might find useful, and a pack of gum. Way to plan ahead Alec, I think. "I have the supplies we'll need for the day. Now, we just need to take care of our tablets." Alec hands us each a small roll of duct tape. "Okay, let's get rid of these and meet back here in ten."

I take my duct tape and set off to find a maid cart.

Alec and I meet up on our way back from hiding our tablets. He gives me a small wink and that's all it takes to get the butterflies in my stomach moving. Just the proximity of being so close to him makes my heart soar.

We round the corner back towards the elevators and find Connor and Claire in a rather passionate embrace. I stop abruptly and turn my head. Alec does a little coughing thing and they both jump so high their feet leave the ground.

Claire puts her hand on her heart. "Oh my gosh, you guys scared me!"

"Sorry about that," I mutter.

"Well," says Alec breaking the awkward silence. "I think it's about time to go, yes?" We all hop in the elevator and Connor pushes the 'S' button for Storage. The door opens and we all hobble out taking a moment to make sure nobody is around.

When we feel the coast is clear we slink over to the grate. Connor goes to work, like before, taking out the individual screws and handing them to me. I take it I'm the official screw holder-er, if that's even a word. Connor slides the grate off a little bit at a time making some slight squeaking noises as he goes.

We take turns crawling in as before with me being the point man, or woman, I guess. Connor slides the grate back on and we begin our journey to the 'sewer systems'. You would think with all the twists, turns, and pathway changes, one would get lost, but that's so not the case with me. It feels like second nature already.

It takes us a while but we eventually make the last turn and stop next to the final grate.

Connor removes it and Alec puts his hand on mine. "Let Connor and me go first. Then we'll help you ladies down." The guys have a rope ladder in their bag but they are trying to avoid having to take it out until we are on our return trip.

I hate being seen as a weak link, but I'm not about to break another limb. He already helped me successfully down the first jump from the platform, the one where all heck broke loose before.

We nod our heads at the boys and they begin to jump down. Claire goes first and Connor helps her down. I'm next. I jimmy my way as close to the edge as humanly possible and stop. Alec has his hands lifted up towards me putting my anxieties at rest. I scoot down backwards like a small child and take the leap of faith. Alec catches me immediately and slowly lowers me down to the floor. He leans in to my ear and whispers, "I'll never let you go, Willow."

Goose bumps run up and down my arms like freight trains. "Thanks." I manage to say without swooning.

"Dude, it's another freaking tunnel." Connor complains. "This one better lead somewhere."

We shine our flashlights around the tunnel trying to see ahead of us. I catch sight of all of our gear from the last trip in the corner and chuckle. It was pretty useless.

"I'll take the lead on this one." Alec says and heads to the front. Since there is no recorded map of these tunnels, my memory isn't useful for navigation. I fall in place behind Alec and the others follow single file as the tunnel becomes increasingly narrow.

"There it is again." Claire says.

I stop and try to listen to what she hears and when I focus really hard I manage to hear the steady dripping sound. "It must be coming from up ahead." I say.

We start walking forward and I can nearly feel the moisture in the air the further we go into the cold, dark tunnels. The tunnel takes a turn and we end up in an even narrower one that gets increasingly shorter in height as we walk. We go from standing full up, to crouching down and eventually we have to get on all fours to crawl. All of us put our flashlights away to better crawl except for Connor who is in the back as usual. He's holding onto the flashlight in his mouth. It casts eerie shadows that bounce off the tunnel walls.

"I guess your big mouth finally came in handy." Alec jokes as we crawl. Connor can't answer which makes Alec's anecdote that much funnier.

I'm grateful for the lightening of the mood because this tiny tunnel is making my insides go crazy. My stomach starts to clench and my heart races. I've never been claustrophobic but something about the way the flashlight bobs up and down against the tunnel walls and the cool damp air makes me feel nervous. The further we crawl the louder the dripping sounds become and the smaller the tunnel seems to get.

"Ah crap." Alec calls from ahead of me.

I realize what he's complaining about when my hand lands in shallow water and the first knee of my scrubs gets soaked. "Well, no turning back." I say.

Alec stops and grabs his flashlight to get a better look. The ceiling of the tunnel is wet in some places and dripping water. Up ahead there is another turn. "Interesting. I wonder where all of this water is coming from." He says.

None of us answer because we don't know. In my head I just pray this water is clean water and not sewage. It doesn't stink so I think we're good.

He starts crawling again and when we make it to the turn we enter a new tunnel that is getting increasingly taller as we crawl. Eventually we are able to stand up again and I breathe a sigh of relief. The nervous feeling starts relenting as I stretch my aching, soaked knees.

We all are able to turn our flashlights on again which makes the tunnels look a lot less eerie. We walk forward and take one last turn. "Oh my gosh!" The air whooshes out of me and I stop dead causing Claire to run into my back.

"Hey don't just stop...Whoa!" Claire says upon looking around the cavern.

Connor makes a whistle sound showing his amazement. We all stand quietly for a few moments just illuminating the area in front of us with our four flashlights.

It's unbelievable. I have never seen a place like this in real life before. We are standing at the entrance of a gigantic cavern the size of two football fields. Stalactites drop down from the ceiling in thousands of inconsistent sizes and lengths. Five or six of them are so long that they reach all the way down to the ground. The most amazing thing about the cavern is that it's filled with a lake or spring or whatever you would call this body of majestic looking sea-blue water. The dry or actually semi damp ground only extends twenty feet into the cavern before the water starts. We walk further in to the water's edge and shine our lights against its surface. The water is clear and seems to get deeper the further out it goes.

"Cool." Connor whispers.

"I know." Claire whispers too.

"Why is everyone whispering?" I ask quietly.

"Perhaps subconsciously we are trying to keep from scaring the bats awake." Alec says in his full voice.

Everyone giggles but I shiver. I never liked the idea of bats or anything with fanged teeth. Creepy!

"I wish we brought our swim suits." Connor says. I turn around to look at him. He's sitting on the ground taking off his shoes.

"Wait, you aren't gonna go swimming in your underoos are you?" I ask nervously. I'm not prudish about seeing a guy in his boxers but I certainly don't want to dress down to my white underwear and bra in front of Alec.

"Only if you want me to." Connor jokes sarcastically and Claire slaps him on the back of the head. I stifle a giggle while Connor rubs his wound. "Ow!" He says in a whiney voice.

Claire laughs and says, "Man up Connor. I didn't hit you that hard."

That sets Alec into a laugh and Connor gives him the 'don't knock me when I'm down' stare. Alec stops laughing.

Connor rolls his pants legs up and touches his toe to the water. "Freezing!" He says then tests it a little further. I see him visibly shiver as his whole foot steps into the water.

I lean over and touch it with my hand. It isn't necessarily freezing but it's mighty cold. I would say it's either in the high sixties or low seventies in temperature.

Claire trots over barefoot and walks into the water close to Connor. "Oh my." She says. Connor puts his hand around her as she shivers.

I look to Alec and shrug. We both start taking off our shoes and socks. I roll up my scrubs to mid thigh and step in. It feels even colder on my feet then it did on my hands. I stand there for a moment allowing my body to adjust to the temperature.

Alec comes to my side. We stand there for a few more minutes and then I start inching forward.

"Be careful babe." Alec says.

The term of endearment warms my heart and I feel more courageous to move forward. I grab ahold of his hand and he matches my step. We walk forward slowly. We keep our flashlights shining on the water in front of us. For the most part, the water seems clear all the way down to the bottom. We are able to walk twenty feet into the water before it reaches knee level. When we get to a stopping point we all just stand there in silence shining our flashlights around the cavern and enjoying the beauty of this secret place.

"I wonder how many people know this place is down here." I say.

"Most likely only a chosen few since it's not marked on any of the maps." Alec answers.

"Yeah, but somebody must know. After all there is a manmade tunnel leading to it." Claire offers.

"Well it's our place now." Connor says and mimes the action of sticking a flag into the ground like the astronauts did when they made it to Mars so many years ago.

"Yep! This can be our secret hangout." Claire says sounding youthful like a kid.

Connor gives her a loving look and it makes me smile. I like to see people who have been through a lot find happiness. Alec must like it too because he squeezes my hand just so.

My stomach growls loudly and I blush.

"Guess that's the alarm for lunchtime." Alec says playfully. He pokes me in the ribs, which tickles. I giggle and splash him a bit with my foot. "Watch it!" He says and then makes a move to splash me with his hand but I run from him back to dry ground.

He chases me, both of us sloshing through knee-deep water laughing like kids. A second later my feet are up out of the water and he's got me in his arms. He swings me around like I'm lighter than a feather and I laugh as my world spins. A moment later he sets me down on dry ground and I wait for my brain to catch up with the rest of my body. When the dizziness settles I lean into him.

Connor and Claire are talking and have already made their way to dry ground and are rummaging through our supplies in search of the Powerbars. I look up at Alec and my heart is like butter, melting in the gaze of his emerald green eyes. He leans in kissing me gently on the lips.

Then he whispers in my ear, "Lunchtime." He turns me around and we start walking to where Connor and Claire have set up a mock picnic.

"This isn't much of spread is it?" I ask Claire who's looking up at me with appraising eyes. I guess they saw the kiss too.

"Well there are honey flavored Powerbars and cinnamon raisin. So at least you have a little bit of variety." She replies with a silly grin. I imagine she's singing that 'kissing in a tree' song in her head.

"We need to bring our swimsuits next time." Connor says between bites of his Powerbar.

"So I guess we've found us a new hang out spot." Alec says.

"Yep and it's only for us!" Claire says.

"Yep, this is our place!" I say in confirmation.

We finish off our Powerbars and spend another hour exploring the shallow waters and talking about a whole bunch of nothing before we head back for the afternoon. This has to have been one of the best days I've had in a while.

ELEVEN

After finding the cave and spending time with Alec, going back to school this morning sucks.

Not to mention it's Monday. This class doesn't make it any better either. The only thing I can think about is getting back in that cave and exploring…that and Alec. The teacher just drones on and on about who knows what. This week we have full day classes since there is standardized testing on Friday and Saturday. This full schedule is killer. In an attempt to get us to study for the tests they have excused us all from work until Friday afternoon, which means I don't get to see much of Alec.

Thankfully, with Connor and Claire in my class it's bearable. Our teacher must be blind or deaf to not hear us texting each other back and forth. She left our tablets unlocked so we can take notes but of course we are using our freedom for something much more worthy. We get to our fourth round of twenty questions when it's time to break for lunch.

We all hustle down to the cafeteria for our lunch; Connor, Claire and I take a seat at our usual table. After a few months of being here, clicks and bonds have formed and everyone pretty much knows who their circle of friends is. There are a few loners, but most everyone has at least one ally.

"Yum, more mush," I say dropping the mush back on my tray from my spoon.

"Tastes good to me," Connor says with a mouthful.

I inwardly laugh at Connor. You could probably feed the guy kitchen scraps and he wouldn't care. There's a tap on my shoulder and I turn around to find one of the older, day runners standing behind me.

"Are you Willow Mosby?" She asks all official-like.

I nod my head. "Yeah, that's me."

"This is for you," she says while handing me a small envelope. Then she's off to her next assignment. I take the envelope and turn back to the table. Connor and Claire are staring at me.

"Well, aren't you going to open it?" Claire asks a little too excitedly.

I'm curious too so I begin to break the seal on the envelope. Inside is a small index-type card. Scrawled in black pen it says:

Willow, will you be my girlfriend? Check one:

☐ yes
☐ no
☐ maybe

Love, Alec

My cheeks blush a dark shade of crimson while my heart leaps out of my chest.

"So, what does it say?" Claire asks, feigning to hide

the excitement in her voice. She pushes her hair out of her face to get a better look.

Do I tell her? Um, yes. “It’s from Alec,” I say. “He wants to know if I’ll be his girlfriend.” I cringe wondering if that sounds corny.

I look up to find Claire beaming. “Willow! That’s so sweet! What are you going to tell him?”

I don’t have to think very hard about this one. I get a pen out of my bag and check yes. “Well, of course I’m going to say yes!” Claire and I squeal like a bunch of schoolgirls, which technically we are.

Connor makes a joking squeal of a sound to join in and flaps his hands up and down hysterically. We just roll our eyes and both playfully push him at the same time.

I spot the runner that delivered me the envelope and flag her down. I give it to her and ask her to take it back to Alec. She looks a bit confused at first but nods her head and leaves, taking the envelope with her.

The afternoon drones on in class and all I do is daydream about Alec. My tablet vibrates alerting me to a message. I put it on my lap figuring it’s probably Claire or Connor.

To my amazement it’s Alec!

Alec: I got your note.

I smile really big.

Me: I got yours first

I check back up to find the teacher still talking about Lord knows what.

My tablet vibrates again.

Alec: I miss you.

My heart soars.

Me: Miss you too.

I text back thinking how absolutely corny we sound. I don't care though. This is my first boyfriend and I'm allowed to be a little cheesy.

Alec: Are you doing anything this Friday after school? I'd like to take you on a date.

I stifle a ginormous grin that's threatening to surface. Friday is my birthday, but I haven't told anyone yet. That's right, my sweet sixteen. A hit of sadness hits me when I think about my last birthday. My mom had told me that we could start planning my sweet sixteen party. She would tell me stories about hers as we had clipping parties. We clipped pictures of dresses from magazines, pictures of food, cakes and more. We were making a collage before everything in my world seemed to fall apart.

Alec: If you're busy...

Alec's text pulls me from my thoughts.

Me: Well, Mr. Blake, I think I have to work.

A few seconds go by and he replies.

Alec: Hmmm, looks like Ms. Mosby isn't on the schedule anymore and neither am I. Strange coincidence, I know.

I giggle and hit reply.

Me: Well then, Mr. Blake. I guess I am free then. Where are we going?

My tablet vibrates.

Alec: I'm not telling; it's a surprise.

Eek, I love surprises!

I'm brought back to the present when Ms. Thomas barks my name. "Willow, what's the answer?"

I look like a deer caught in headlights. "Ummm, can you repeat the question?"

Ms. Thomas cocks her head. "I asked, what is the twenty-eighth amendment of the constitution about?"

Phew, I know this one…thankfully. I straighten up in my seat. "The twenty-eighth amendment is the amendment that closed our borders off, sealing us off from the rest of the world."

The teacher cocks her eyebrow at me. "Very good Willow, I'm so glad you were paying attention," she says sardonically.

I quickly type in "G2G," and send it back to Alec.

The rest of the week drags on slowly. The highlights of my days are seeing Alec for a few minutes at dinner. The intermittent moments between stolen kisses are what I live and breathe for. His sweet text messages sent to me at school make the anticipation of Friday bearable.

Apparently, Alec took all of us off the schedule. Luckily Connor was given the opportunity to spend a rare afternoon with his little sister Lillie. He invited Claire to join him, which means I get Alec all to myself. Not that I don't want them joining us, but…Happy Birthday to me!

TWELVE

By the time Friday rolls around I can barely sit still long enough to focus on my test.

I tap my fingers against the desk and check my tablet for the umpteenth time only to realize a few measly minutes have passed. Ms. Thomas gives me the evil eye. I wonder if she thinks my fidgeting is a case of testing jitters or if she thinks I'm trying to cheat. At least my restlessness takes the attention off Connor for once; I'm sure he's grateful for the break. Even with my lack of concentration I still think I do well on the test. It's kind of hard for me to fail a test with my photographic memory. I wonder if that would be considered a form of cheating. Not that it matters anyway, I learned all of this stuff last year when my mother was homeschooling me.

I over emphasize the final tap on my tablet screen, sending my completed test to Ms. Thomas. I look around the room and see that I'm the first person done.

Ms. Thomas looks up at me like I'm crazy. "Are you sure you don't want to go back and review your answers Ms. Mosby?"

"No, I'm good." I say and then look back down at

my tablet.

She makes an annoyed grunting sound which I simply ignore.

They have a video for us to watch after the test and mine starts up. I throw on my earphones to listen. It's an old video that I've seen a thousand times about the importance of education and college. It tours several of the country's finest institutions. I wonder if they will still be around after all of this is over. I can't even fathom the normalcy of going to an actual college or even a real live school. I wonder if anyone can after most of us have been holed up for a good part of our academic careers.

Right before school lets out Alec sends me a text.

Alec: Bring your swimsuit, no questions. Meet me by the first floor elevators at 3:30. Miss u!

I smile at his message. The first half is so boss-like, while the second is the Alec I've come to know personally. When he mixes the two it cracks me up.

Me: See u soon!

School is dismissed promptly at 2:15 and I'm the first one out the door. I give a small wave to Connor and Claire and I am on my way. I head to one of the small stores in the commons area and purchase a piece of purple ribbon and some lip gloss. It costs most of my money, but I don't care. The lady at the checkout smacks her gum as she scans my tablet. I watch my paycheck diminish to almost nothing and I'm out the door in less than a minute.

I rush back to our little apartment and hurriedly scramble into the bathroom. I pull my hair up into a ponytail and tie the ribbon around it. I find my bathing suit and put it on then squirm into my pink scrubs careful not to mess up my hair. I wash my face and pinch my cheeks a few times to develop some resemblance to blush. I apply the lip-gloss and run my lips together. Yep, they look kissable to me! I look down at my drab scrubs and sincerely wish I could change styles or something. As soon as I can afford a sewing kit I'm going to alter these bad boys. I've already seen Candy and her posse around in alternate versions of the scrubs. She even turned one version into shorts and a cute tank top. I figure if she doesn't get in trouble then it must be okay. I just want to take the sides in a bit, maybe alter the neckline. My mother taught me how to sew when I was younger. It would make her proud. I smile at my mother's memory which quickly turns into a frown. I shake it off and take a deep breath looking into the mirror. Not on your birthday, Willow I repeat to myself.

I take a quick peek at the clock and realize I have five minutes to spare. I sigh at my reflection. This isn't necessarily the sweet sixteen dress that I had imagined but it will have to do. I apply one more layer of lip gloss for safe measure, check my ribbon and I'm out the door.

I bump into my dad on the way out. "Oh, hey dad!"

"Hey Willow." He takes one look at my face and hair ribbon. "Where are you off to?"

Without skipping a beat I answer him. "Off to go hang with some friends." I cringe…I said friends, as in plural.

"Friends or friend?" My dad asks.

I knew I wouldn't get away with being vague. "I'm going to hang out with Alec." I give him the honesty he was looking for and it makes me feel good.

"Alec, hmm." He runs his hands through his greying hair. "He seems like a pretty decent guy."

I nod my head and say, "He is dad."

He studies me for a bit longer making me slightly uncomfortable. "Okay, well you have fun. I'm going to head in to get a bit of shut eye. I've got to work the night shift."

I hate how much they're making my dad work. I pull him into a brief hug then leave for the elevator.

"Be safe," he says as I walk away.

"I will, Dad. Love you." I breathe a sigh of relief and then realize, my dad didn't even remember my birthday. He's always been good at remembering and making a bigger than necessary deal on my birthday. I guess I can't blame him though; he has so much on his plate right now. He seemed too tired to even grill me about going on my date. Well that could have to do with the fact that I think deep down my dad likes and trusts my boyfriend. I'm very grateful for that because I can't imagine doing anything that would damage our father daughter relationship. We are quite possibly the only family we have left.

A lump forms in my throat and I push my feelings aside for the time being. It's my birthday and I'm going on my first real date.

I hop on the elevator feeling giddy from head to toe. The ride down seems like it takes forever. The elevator dings on the first floor opening up to Alec, standing there with a large and full backpack. As soon as he sees it's me he rushes into the elevator and clicks the door close button.

My heart skips a beat as the doors close.

Alec pulls me into an embrace and kisses me passionately on the lips. I return the favor letting my whole body get absorbed in his kiss. He pulls back far too soon with a wicked smile splaying across his lips. "Strawberry," he says as he licks his lips. "I like it."

I blush bright red. The elevator dings on the Storage floor and the doors open up into the vast room. Alec takes my tablet from me. "Hold the door, would you Willow?"

I nod my head, "Sure."

Alec climbs onto the side rails of the elevator and pushes up one of the cork ceiling tiles. He puts the tablets in them and closes it back off. I give him a smile of satisfaction, genius! "So, what's the plan?" I ask Alec a little breathlessly.

"You'll see," is all he says.

I kind of figured where we're going, what with the swimsuit and being here on the level marked for storage.

Alec takes my hand and squeezes it softly. "Ready?" I nod my head as we clamor off the elevator.

It takes us about twenty minutes or so of climbing through the different tunnels and grates until I find myself with wet knees crawling through the last round of tunnels. This time we set the rope ladders up at each drop before we jump down, since there would be nobody to help give Alec a boost back up.

We are starting to get much more efficient at making this journey. Alec even found a way to fasten the flashlight to the shoulder of his backpack so we can see better.

Excitement coerces through me when we reach our cave. The light hits the stalagmites. They are so beautiful. Alec climbs out of the tunnel and helps me down. Just his touch makes my heart dance with joy.

Alec and I walk over to the water's edge and he places the backpack down. Shining the light inside, he pulls out a lantern looking thing and goes to work setting it up. Within a few minutes a bright glow begins to illuminate the cavern. I turn off my flashlight thrilled I can now see panoramically. The area is simply breathtaking.

I feel Alec's arms wrap around me drawing me softly to him. "Happy Birthday," he says whispering in my ear.

A small smile escapes my lips and I turn to him. "How did you know it was my birthday?" I playfully question.

Alec jokingly laughs, "A man has his secrets." I hit him lightly on the arm.

"Secrets, schmecrits," I say taunting him.

He laughs and holds his hand out dropping something cool and metallic in my hand. "For you," he says.

I open up my hand to see what he gave me. "A paper clip necklace!" I exclaim!

Even in the dim light I see him blush. "I know it's not much, but you know there isn't a lot here that I can give you."

"No need to apologize," I tell him. "I think it's sweet and thoughtful. It is a homemade gift after all. I'm going to keep it forever."

He moves around me and 'fastens' the necklace to me. "Hey, it's one step up from a pasta necklace," he jokes.

I laugh. "Yes, you're right about that! But this way, I don't feel the need to eat it."

To my amazement, Alec has packed a little picnic for us. He sets out various cans of stuff around a small towel he must have brought from his place. "Are you hungry," he asks while placing some silverware on the blanket.

"Not really quite yet," I say. I'm a little too excited about this place to eat now, plus dinner's not officially supposed to be for another few hours.

"Good," Alec says. "Neither am I. So, what do you say we go do a little exploring, then go for a swim and we'll finish it off with our special 'lantern lit' dinner." He smiles at me and I know I'm a goner.

I nod my head. "Sure, that sounds fun!" He finishes unloading the backpack and gets his flashlight. I click mine on illuminating the space before me in a bright white glow. Alec takes my hand making it feel so warm and inviting and we're off.

We follow the areas that are around the large pool of water finding all kinds of things. There are these strange white bugs I have never seen before as well as white tadpoles. I haven't looked up to see if there are any bats because, truth be told, I'd rather not know if there are.

I reach my hand out to touch one of the stalagmites

that have grown up from the floor and Alec stops me. "Don't touch them, just look. The oils on your fingers could alter their growth." I pull my hand back. "And we don't want that," he reiterates. It's hard for me not to touch them though because I'm such a tactile person. The texture looks so cool and inviting.

"Willow, shut your flashlight off for a sec," Alec says. I give him a questioning look but turn my flashlight off squeezing his hand infinitesimally tighter. "Look, do you see over there, in the corner?"

I look to the corner and see a very subtle beam of light. So subtle, that you would have to know what you're looking for to be able to see it.

Alec turns his light back on and I follow suite. "Let's go check it out." He took the words right out of my mouth. We inch along careful not to step on any geologic marvels and make our way to the far corner. Although, when we get there, it isn't really a corner at all. It's a hidden pathway leading further into the infrastructure.

"Should we go in?" I ask Mr. Geology to make sure it's safe.

"Willow, is that really a question?" He smirks at me.

I return the smile with one of my own. This is so exciting! We inch into the narrow space between the cave walls gripping each other's hands a bit tighter as we make our way through. At one point the walls almost touch each other at the top so we have to get down and waddle like a duck to get by. The light begins to grow and grow until we don't have to really use our flashlights, except we do anyway.

We round the final turn and come to a cavern that looks very similar to the one we were just in. Similar, except for the small hole in the ceiling that is funneling in a small beam of light. The room is markedly warmer than the other room; my guess is because it has some heat from outside seeping in. There's another large pool of water in this room; it looks a lot more inviting though. My guess is the temperature of the water is significantly warmer.

As if reading my mind Alec says, "Looks like a good place for a swim. You game?"

I smile and follow him to the edge of the large pool of water. "Sure." We kick off our shoes and take off our socks. After that though I begin to feel self-conscious.

Alec must see the worry on my face, "I'll turn around while you get undressed." Without waiting for a response he turns around.

I wonder if that means I can't watch him… And so I do, because I can. While I wrestle with the drawstring that's tied around my waste I watch as Alec takes off his shirt. The muscles in his back flex and soften as he brings his arms back down. Yum, I think to myself. I finally manage to get my pants undone and I take off my shirt. I make sure my swimsuit is on right and tell Alec, "Okay, you can turn around now."

He smiles at me and I blush. He has never seen me with so little on but his eyes don't rake over my body like I would have expected. He stares into my eyes sweetly then comes to my side and takes my hand. He leads me to the water. I put my foot in and feel the warmth pour through my body. It's not as warm as a shower or bath, but it's soothing nonetheless.

Alec doesn't waste anytime diving into the water. His head pops up just under the light a few seconds later. He shakes his head as he comes up sending water spraying around him. The outside light hits it just right and his hair looks like it's glistening. "Man this feels good!" He exclaims.

I can tell he's a throw-caution-to-the-wind kind of guy as I tiptoe out towards him in the middle. Oh, enough with the pleasantries, I dive in right after him. The water is so clear under here that I can see his feet treading water up ahead. I pop up right next to him feeling the warm light bathe my skin. "It does feel good," I say as I push my wet hair out of my face. I look up through the natural skylight in the cavern. We both float on our backs staring up at the sun and the sky that is so far above us.

I forgot how much I missed the open sky. My heart warms and I feel suddenly like everything might turn out right after all. Some inkling of hope hits me and I think of my mom and my little brother. My heart tugs slightly but deep down I have the thought that they may make it after all. I mean, here I am in a cavern staring up at the sun, it could be totally possible that they are staring up at the same sun right now. That is, if my brother is still well and has not been overcome by the heat or the virus.

"A penny for your thoughts." Alec says quietly into my ear beside me.

I consider not answering but I say after a few

seconds, "I was just thinking of my family."

He pulls me into his arms. I rest my head on his shoulder and he treads water carrying both of our weight. "I bet they are out there Willow. They can't all just be gone, like that."

"I was just thinking that same thing." I say quietly still feeling a little sad. I look up and gaze into his eyes. "Wow, I've never noticed how beautiful your eyes are… they're the most unique shade of blue/green I've ever seen." I reach up briefly to stroke his cheek.

"Blue?" says Alec questionably. "That's strange; I don't remember having a blue hue to my eyes."

I inch closer. "Hmm," I say looking into his eyes. "They look blue to me, maybe it's just the way the light is hitting them."

"Yeah, it has to be the light because your left eye kind of looks a little green too. It's pretty cool looking though." Alec plants a light feathery kiss on my lips. "Happy Birthday Willow. I know this isn't much, but I hope it's enough." A sincere smile splays itself on my lips.

"Alec, this is more than enough. This has to be the best birthday I've ever had. Honestly." I want him to see how grateful I am to be spending my day with him, but I don't want him to see the hint of sadness that the void in my family has left me with. In order to not ruin the moment I slip through his arms and duck down into the water. Swimming further out, enjoying the sting of my muscles as I push them to their limits. I pretend that the warm water is melting away any sadness or worries. I bob back up a moment later taking in a gulp of air. I turn around to see Alec's head duck below the surface. I tread water waiting for him to come back up.

I feel something tickle my feet. I scramble away thinking it's a fish until Alec's head pops up. "Gotcha!" He says, voice full of playfulness.

I splash water at him and he feigns like he's hurt. I see a twinkle in his eye indicating 'game on' and away I go…Alec chasing me from behind.

We play for what seems like hours in the water. Playing games like we did when we were children including, Fish Out of Water and Marco Polo. He even gives in when I ask him to have an underwater tea party. We race each other using different strokes we know…even the butterfly, which I suck profusely at. I look like a dying fish.

By the time we're done I'm starving and can't wait to see what's for dinner.

Alec and I hike back around to the blanket with all the goodies on it and dive in. "Where'd you get all this food?" I ask Alec in between mouthfuls of canned chicken salad. The buttery crackers melt in my mouth. Yum!

"I got connections." Alec jokes.

"I bet! A perk of being a part of the upper class. The rich can get anything." I look up at him when he doesn't laugh and the grin on my face falters when I see Alec's expression. Oh crap.

"What's that supposed to mean?" Alec asks looking not so happy.

"Um." I stutter.

"Do you classify me in the same group as Zack and Candy?" He spits their names out like they taste bad.

"I don't Alec. I was just trying to joke." I say sincerely. "I know you're nothing like them."

He stares at me for a few seconds and then says, "Okay. I'm sorry I got kind of worked up but I couldn't stand it if that's what you thought of me. I may come from money but I work hard, I don't just sit around making other people's lives miserable like they do."

"I know. I'm sorry." I say biting my lip. I look down feeling miserable. I never meant to hurt his feelings.

He scoots closer to me and raises my chin with his hands until my eyes are level with his. "You know it's a good thing you are cute." He says with a boyish grin that changes into a questioning look. "Hey, did you poke your eye?"

I look at him confused. "I don't think so." I say.

"Hmm, your left eye has a red spot in it. Kind of like what happens when someone pops a blood vessel but instead it's on the brown part of your iris." His staring starts making me a little uncomfortable.

"Does it look that horrible?" I move back away from him and reach my hand up to my eye self-consciously.

"Hey, it doesn't look bad Willow. You have to be looking very closely to notice it." He pulls me back towards him and the look in his eyes makes my stomach do summersaults. "And nobody should be able to get as close to you as I do." He brushes a wet strand of hair from my face. "You are really beautiful Willow."

Awe! My self-consciousness melts with his words. He leans in and kisses me gently. My heart races and takes a few moments to calm down even after he's pulled away.

"Thank you Alec for this amazing day." I say as he goes back to eating his food.

"Anything for you." He says. "I wish I could have found some cake but this cookie will have to do." He pulls out a chocolate chip cookie and presents it to me. "Happy Birthday to you, happy birthday to you, happy birthday dear Willow, happy birthday to you." He sings dramatically.

I'm smiling so big that my face hurts. I accept the cookie from him and take a bite. It's stale like those pre-packaged cookies that sit on the shelf for months, but it satisfies my sweet tooth. I break off half and hand it to him. "For you."

"Why thank you." Alec says smiling. He takes a bite and a smudge of chocolate stains his lips. I wipe it away playfully and give him a quick peck on the cheek.

"So, today was my first time to celebrate my birthday with my boyfriend. It was the first time that we found this cave. The first time we saw the sun in a while. And it was our first fight!" I grin spiritedly at him.

"Wow, a lot of firsts." He says. "And I'm glad I was with you for them."

We talk some more while we finish our food and clean up. Alec tells me about some of his birthday memories. I feel bad when I find out that his mom had died a few years back. I hadn't known that about him. He moves on from the subject quickly though, not wanting to spoil the mood.

"We better head out." Alec says regretfully after a little while.

"Yeah, I guess. Maybe we can come back on our next day off. We could show this place to Connor and Claire." I say a little torn. I want to share this amazing place with our friends but I also want to keep it as Alec and my secret place.

"It's a date." Alec says.

"A double date." I say with a sly grin. We both laugh at that then head out.

The trip back seems to go by a lot faster than the trip in. Normally that's a good thing but in this case it just means I get that much less time with Alec.

We reach the opening and climb out carefully making sure that very little noise was made. We put the grate back on and head for the elevator. It dings and we hop on. I hold the door open button while Alec fishes for our tablets. He passes both of them to me and I release the elevator button and press the button for floor three. The elevator lifts us at its usual quick speed and when it opens up into the common area we step out into a silent hallway.

"It must be late." Alec says looking around. There isn't a single person out on the floor.

I hand him his tablet that I'm still holding and then slide the lock screen off mine. My stomach drops when I see twenty missed messages and the time. It's nine p.m. I pull up my list of messages and my eyes halt when I see the three red bolded message lines from the shelter officials.

The first notifies us of a mandatory assembly that began at seven-thirty p.m. The second one state's that I failed to check in and that I should bring my tablet to an official immediately. The third is written in all caps and says that I have twenty minutes to notify an official of my presence at the assembly or I would receive a permanent reprimand on my record. In smaller font it states that additional consequences can be assessed depending on the nature of the situation. I look at the time on the third message and see that I have exactly two minutes to bring my tablet to an official. My heart leaps into my throat and I look at Alec.

He must have identical messages because he grabs my hand and pulls me into the elevator immediately. He presses floor one and the elevator begins moving. "Look, when this opens you separate from me and go in through another entrance to the assembly. I don't care what you say, but lie. Tell them you didn't see the messages, your tablet was off, whatever you have to tell them. Just don't tell them where we were, okay?'

I nod and my palms starts sweating as the doors ding open. We run into the empty foyer and make our way towards headquarters. Alec runs past me to go in through an entrance further down and I take the first set of doors into the auditorium. My heart is leaping as I walk into the dim, gigantic assembly hall. A video is playing and I have no idea what's going on. Thankfully the video seems to be so enthralling that nobody notices me.

I make my way towards a female official who is standing a few rows in front of me. I speed walk and tap her on the shoulder. She turns around and doesn't seem too pleased to see me, especially since I'm interrupting the video presentation. I hand her my tablet and whisper a bit shakily. "I um, my tablet was off and I just turned it on and it had all of these messages and the last one said that I had to bring this to you."

The female official is a few inches taller than me and has a more masculine build to her. I feel extremely intimidated as she stares me down with beady hazel eyes. She looks down at my tablet and my heart races and presses a few things on the screen. She starts to hand it back to me but then asks, "Why did you not hand this to the official upon entering?"

My mind tries to come up with an excuse and I know that the pause in answering her is going to make me look guilty. I finally think of something. "I came in with my dad and we were with a really big group. Nobody asked me for it and I just figured that when they checked my dad's tablet that I would be counted present since we are together."

She studies me for a second and looks around me as if trying to find my dad. "I've been covering this entrance and I know I wouldn't have let you go by without seeing your tablet."

Crap! "Um, I didn't come in through this entrance. I came in further down there." I point to my left. There are at least fifteen rows with different officials to my left so I figure it's the best option. She looks at me and I just know that she's going to see right through me and know that I haven't been here. She's going to ask me why I would come all the way to her to check in. She looks in that direction and I see her looking in the direction of a tall lanky male official. She rolls her eyes and a slight ping of hope hits me. Maybe she doesn't like that official.

She returns her attention to me, her eyes squinting as if she's trying to figure me out. The crowd around us breaks out in a loud round of applause. She looks back at the screen and a look of pure disappointment covers her face. She looks back at me annoyed, pulls the screen up on my tablet, types a few things that I can't see onto the touch screen and then hands it to me. I grab it from her and she immediately walks away in search of another official. My guess is she's wanting to find out what just happened on the video.

My heart starts slowing down the further away she gets from me. If she was still suspicious she certainly wouldn't have handed the tablet back to me. I slide into a seat on the end of a row in the back and avoid making any eye contact with those in the neighboring seats. I don't pay attention to the video that's apparently talking about the heating process. Instead, I look down at my tablet. A green warning message is displayed across it stating: Class Three Reprimand. In smaller print I read the notification that as a consequence for a Class Three Reprimand I will be assigned community service for the next month, to commence on any free day I am given. Awe Man! There go all of my hopes of further exploring our caves for a while.

I read the general message under the reprimand,

which states the different classes. Apparently a class three is the lowest level and is considered a sort of deferred adjudication where it can be removed from my permanent record upon the completion of all community service. I read the other classes of reprimands and find that class two is a serious level of discipline which requires paying restitution, completing abundant community service and it will go on the permanent record which could affect a persons employment opportunities. A class one reprimand can result in actual prison time and in some cases could result in a person being exiled from the shelter. A shiver passes down my spine. I never knew that there was a prison in this shelter, it's not labeled anywhere on the maps. I also never knew that they would actually kick someone out of here. I mean, that could be a death sentence!

To get my mind off it, I start looking through the other seventeen messages on my tablet. There are seven messages from my dad asking where I am. They get more and more worried as they go on. I feel horrible that I put him through this. I had no idea that this assembly would be called but one of the number one rules in the shelter is to always carry your tablet. Obviously that rule is for this very purpose.

The other messages are from Connor and Claire just asking where I'm at and commenting on the video. It turns out the whole thing is about how the removal of the patches is working. The earth is heating up nicely, yada, yada, yada. They still estimate that we will need to remain in the shelter for another two years. Connor complains about that part the most. Especially since his parents are out there. I concur with that, I don't want to wait another two years to find out if my mom and little brother survived, but I obviously don't have much choice.

My tablet vibrates and a new message from Alec comes on the screen. "Are you okay?"

"Yes, I got a reprimand though." I type back.

"What?!" He texts which tells me that he must have gotten through the situation a lot better than I did.

"Yes, it's only a class three though." I say.

A few minutes pass and then he sends, "Okay, that doesn't look like it will be too bad. How many days did you get of community service?" He must have just searched through the shelter facts to find out what the different classes mean.

"I have to go on every free day for a month." I type.

"I'm so sorry babe. This is my fault." He sends.

My stomach flutters in a good way at his use of the word babe. I can't help smiling as I type. "Not your fault. This still was the best b-day ever."

"I still feel horrible but I will find a way to make it up to you." He types.

"You don't have to make up anything. I'll be fine. Looks like they are about to let out." I type as the lights come on in the auditorium. Everyone around me starts getting up and I follow suit.

I head back to my room immediately. When I get in I answer my dad's texts and let him know that I'm fine. I was just sitting with my friends. He seems relieved to hear back from me. He tells me that he has to go back into work but that he loves me. He sends another text with a picture of a birthday cake.

Dad: Happy Birthday Honey!

Me: Thanks!

My heart warms knowing my dad remembered after all. I need to find time to talk to my dad about what's been going on in my life. We used to be close and not telling him about everything seems unnatural. My dad has always been there to support me but lately we've had zero time together. I make a promise to myself that the next time we have alone time I will tell him about Alec and even about our cave.

I take a shower and change into my pajamas. It feels good when I lay down in my bed. I didn't realize how tired I was from our exploring and then the emotional stress of finding out we nearly missed the assembly. I was going to text Claire to see how her time with Connor and Lillie was but I find it hard to keep my eyes open. I decide it can wait till tomorrow and I succumb to the sleep that is calling my name so sweetly.

THIRTEEN

Seven a.m. comes far too early as my tablet vibrates me awake.

I yawn and stretch my arms over my head. I practically crawl into the bathroom mumbling about how I hate mornings along the way. I'm quiet though as to not wake my sleeping father. I turn on the sink and splash my face with cool water. As I towel dry it off I take a glimpse of myself in the mirror.

My eyes widen in horror as I take in that eye Alec was talking about. It is not just a small dot of red, it's like a quarter of my eye is red. What's even freakier is the dark green ring that circles my iris. I know that's never been there before!

I lean in close to the mirror and open my eyes wider to examine it. It looks creepy to me. The only time you see red irises are in those badly depicted vampire movies. I move my face around allowing the light to shine all around my eye. What the heck is wrong with me? With the green and red, my eye looks like Christmas time gone wrong. Deep down I want to run to the nearest doctor to get this thing looked at, but something is telling me not to. Just wait it out Willow, I tell myself.

I sneak back into the other room where my tablet is and bring it into the bathroom with me. I remembered seeing a small, funny looking dot on the top of the tablet. My guess is it's a camera. I search the icons for a camera app and find one. Ah, ha! I say to myself. I position the camera up to the mirror and get a close-up shot of my eye. I send it to Alec and ask him in the message.

Me: Is this how it looked yesterday?

I hit send and wait. With nothing else to do I braid my hair. As I am clasping the bottom with a rubber band my tablet vibrates.

Alec: I don't think so, but maybe it's the light. You might want to get that looked at.

Then a second later another message pops up.

Alec: Ah crap, I just cut myself. Got 2 run!

Me: K

I push the tablet aside. I'm trying to put two and two together and it doesn't make sense. I've seen what it looks like when you poke your eye and it…bleeds. Sabby did it once when he was about three with one of my pencils and it didn't look like this. It looked like it was bleeding, not perfect and symmetrical. It just doesn't add up.

Suddenly I'm overly self-conscious about it. I pull my hair back down out of the braid and arrange it in front of my face. In a fleeting moment, which I most definitely don't think through, I grab some scissors and cut some long bangs around my face. I cringe upon seeing long strands of my hair fall to the floor. No going back now. I guess my vanity is getting the best of me today. I work to try to even them out. In the end my bangs end up long enough to where if I wanted, they would nearly cover my eyes. I cut them in an angle though so they can swoop over my left eye. I figure there's no use in walking around fully blind when my right eye seems normal...for now.

I look in the mirror to examine the finished product. A long exasperated sigh escapes me. I keep telling myself in my head over and over that it's a new fashion statement. Tomorrow, everyone will do the same and cut bangs like mine. Yeah right, Willow, my annoying common sense chimes in.

I glance down at the clock and realize I only have a few minutes before I have to be down to breakfast. I scoop up the hair as best as I can, dispose of it in the trash and put back the scissors. I hurriedly get dressed, grab my tablet, and b-line for the cafeteria all the while careful not to wake my dad.

Self-consciously I drag my newly cut bangs in front of my eyes thinking man, if I only had my sunglasses this would be ten times easier. I could just feign a headache and be done with it.

I drag my tray over to Connor and Claire sitting it down with a thump.

"Wow," proclaims Connor. "Did someone wake up Emo this morning?"

Claire slaps Connor on the shoulder. "Hey, I like the bangs, it's totally cool!" She exclaims in what sounds like mock enthusiasm.

"Thanks," I mutter while keeping my head down.

The rest of breakfast is strangely quiet with Connor and Claire saying something every now and then to break up the awkward silences. Except what they say isn't making sense.

One time Connor blurts out, "I wonder why claire doesn't like show tunes." It sounds muffled…different.

And, one time Claire said to no one in particular, "Yeah, a nail salon would be nice," her voice sounding different too.

I can't put a finger on what's going on.

After breakfast we trek up to our classroom and take our seats. There are so many voices' talking it's hard to think straight. To my surprise I look around and notice that I can hear people talking but practically no one is moving their lips. It's so strangely bizarre and foreign that I put my head in my hands and cover my ears. The sounds are somewhat muffled, but not in the least bit gone.

I shake my head and look up grunting in frustration. I must have grunted pretty loud because all heads, including Ms. Thomas' turn in my direction. "Sorry," I mutter. "Bad headache." Yes, Willow. That'll explain your attitude and your new hairstyle.

Heads begin to turn away from me but I hear comments like: "freak, loner," and "looser," drifting from different people in the room. I can't understand why Ms. Thomas is letting them say these things.

I look to Ms. Thomas for help and hear her say in a muffled voice, "Teenagers, this job makes me sick. i don't even get my saturdays off anymore. this is so not worth it!"

I furrow my brow in utter frustration and look over to Connor and Claire. To my surprise they're facing forward like nothing is happening. I pull the text app on my tablet up and text a hurried group message to them.

Me: Did you just hear what Ms. Thomas said???

I hit send and watch as Connor and Claire get the messages.

They both look confused. I hear them say, "No," but again in those bizarre muffled voices. My tablet vibrates softly in my palms and they both respond with No.

I'm beginning to get freaked out. I look over to Claire who looks like she's doodling on her tablet. Suddenly, in the middle of class I hear her say, "Blah, blah, blah. This teacher can ramble! Seriously, why would she think we're listening? This has to be the most boring class ever!"

At this point my mouth drops to the floor. I look up at Ms. Thomas and she just continues on with the lesson! Is she deaf? I shrug my shoulders and decide to try it out, "Boring," I say loud enough for everyone to hear.

My face pales as Ms. Thomas stops mid-sentence and turns to face me, complete with beady eyes and a red face. I sink low into my seat. "What did you just say, Willow?" She says as she spits my name. Then I hear her say in a muffled voice, "You little twerp, you think I like doing this?"

My eyes go wide at this. Her mouth didn't move. I think it's at this moment I have come to accept that I'm going crazy. "Nothing," is all I can stand to mutter in response.

"That's what I thought," Ms. Thomas says while turning around, continuing the lesson.

I look over to Claire whose face is burning red. She gives me a look like, what gives, and I just shrug my shoulders. I keep my hand over my ears for the rest of the class until the bell rings.

I grab my tablet and hurry out the door eager to get away from the bizarre and personal comments no one should dare say aloud. As I walk towards the cafeteria I keep my head low realizing that the muffled dialogue I'm hearing is dramatically decreased when I do this. But, keeping my head low does have its consequences. I practically mow over several people with my tray on the way to our table. It's Über embarrassing.

Claire and Connor each slam their trays down and display a look of annoyance. I cringe and Claire begins, "Willow, what the hell is wrong with you?" Leave it to the normally calm natured girl to speak up first. She stares me down. Then in her muffled voice I hear her say, "She's acting so bizarre, maybe she's on drugs."

"I am not on drugs," I say to defend myself.

Claire's mouth falls open, "What did you just say?"

"I said I'm not on drugs," I repeat, confused by why she's asking me to repeat it.

"Willow, I didn't say that."

I give her a disgruntled look. "I just heard you!" Then it dawns on me, and a look so horrific must come over my face as I watch Connor and Claire's reaction to my epiphany. "Wait, Claire, think of a number between one and ten million. And Connor, think of a color, not a primary color, but one that is bizarre."

They look at each other and shrug their shoulders. "One-hundred-thousand," I hear Claire mutter softly.

"Macaroni and cheese yellow," I hear Connor say almost in unison with Claire's response.

"One-hundred-thousand and macaroni and cheese yellow." I say, watching for their reaction. Connor and Claire grip the sides of their chairs and look at me completely bewildered. They both look like they are on the verge of passing out. "Sit," I command. The last thing I want to do is invite more unwanted attention to myself.

"What the heck was that Willow?" Claire asks. Connor just continues staring at me with a blank expression.

"I don't know. It's like I woke up and now I can hear everything!" I exclaim.

"Everything, Everything?" Connor asks. The dumbfounded expression is still on his face. "Claire is hot." I hear Connor's muffled voice say.

"Yeah, I think she doesn't know just how beautiful she really is." I say looking at Claire. Connor's mouth drops open again and Claire's cheeks redden as she realizes what I must have heard in his mind.

"How do you turn it off?" Claire asks.

I shrug my shoulders. "I have no idea. I mean I can muffle it somewhat if I keep my head down and don't look at anyone."

"I think the better question is how did you turn it on?" Connor asks.

"I'm not sure how I turned it on." I'm starting to feel a little frustrated about my lack of knowledge when it comes to these new freak worthy skills.

"Why do you think this is happening now?" Claire's expression is thoughtful and curious.

"I. Don't. Know." I enunciate each word with frustration. I feel like an instant jerk when Claire's face falls. "I'm sorry, I just don't know any more than you do. I really need to see Alec." My head is starting to pound again so I rub my temples with my index fingers. I look up at Claire with watering eyes.

She looks at me and immediately gets up from the table and comes around to sit by my side. She rubs my back soothingly and says, "It's okay sweetie we'll figure this out." She pushes the hair from out of my face and I look up to hear her muffled voice say, "She looks sick." The second she registers my eyes she gasps. "What in the world?" A whole series of questions that I can't quite make out are running through her head.

I quickly look down and hold my hands to my ears. My head is pounding so hard now that I feel as if it's going to explode.

"Should we take her to the doctor?" Connor asks worried.

"No! Alec." I say through clenched teeth. My head is hurting and each word feels like a hammer hitting my temple. I keep my head down as Claire stands and helps me up from the table. I walk that way staring at Connor and Claire's white tennis shoes as they lead me out of the cafeteria. For the time being I can't hear any inner thoughts but I doubt I would really be able to concentrate anyhow with this pulsating headache.

I watch a pair of bare feet walk towards us. They are perfectly pedicured with hot pink nail polish that can only belong to one girl that I know. When I hear the hyena laugh I know that my guess was right on the money.

I look up to see Candy, Zack and their posse walking in our direction. I look away quickly but the voices have already started to flutter into my brain. Candy's muffled inside voice is just as annoying as her real one. "Pathetic. What does he see in her? And those bangs? Ick!"

I hear one of the other guys say something about Candy's rear end but surprisingly I can't hear a thing that Zack is thinking. I look up at him and he gives me a strange eerie look. I look down quickly only to see his tennis shoes stop directly in front of me.

"So where do you think you're going?" Zack asks.

I keep my head down and Connor speaks up for me. "She's not feeling well. I'm taking her to the nurse."

"Hmm, looks like someone had a little too much fun last night. So was it pain pills? Alcohol? What did you get into darling? Cause rumor has it you were late to the assembly." Zack says a little too coy-like.

How in the freak did he know that? I look up at him surprised. I strain my mind to hear what he's thinking but it's like I'm hitting a brick wall. The one time I could use this freaky gift thing and it doesn't work?

Claire yanks me to the side out of Zack's path and

then pulls me forward down the hall away from them. "Jerks!" She yells.

Candy laughs and so do some of the other guys.

Connor is at my other side and they both usher me into a nearby elevator. I look up to see Zack still staring at me intensely as the elevator doors close. A chill runs down my spine as I get the feeling that somehow he knows what's up with me.

The elevator pops open and we start walking towards the office in headquarters. When we reach the second floor area that is open to below with all of the different offices and shops, my head nearly pops off. Floods of voices fill my brain. It sounds like millions of people yelling in a language I can't understand it's so jumbled and garbled up I can't make out a single thing.

"Ohh!" I cry out as I grasp at my head and push my hands over my ears. It hurts so bad and I can't get it to stop. My knees buckle and I feel myself falling but Connor catches me before I hit the floor. He picks me up and runs with me away from the open air area into a much quieter hall.

"Go get Alec." Connor instructs Claire and I hear her running ahead of us. He finds an empty office and takes me inside.

He lies me down on the floor out of sight of the windows. "I think this office is empty. Are you sure I shouldn't get the nurse?" He asks looking at me worriedly.

I shake my head. I feel the tears running down my cheeks because while the headache isn't as debilitating as it was in the main headquarters area, it still hurts horribly.

"What happened?" Alec demands as he runs to my side and drops to the floor.

I keep my eyes shut because it's helping with the headache a bit. "It hurts." Is all I manage to say to him.

"We're going to the doctor." He says while starting to pull me into his arms.

I shake my head and more tears of frustration start to fall through my shut eyes.

"Look at me Willow." He pushes the hair back from my face and I start to open my eyes to look up at him. I blink away the tears and stare into his eyes. I can't help noticing the dark blue ring that is now outlining the outer area of his once solid emerald colored eyes. I stare into them for several seconds before I notice, all of a sudden, that the headache is completely gone. There is zero pain. I can even hear his inner voice now and it's the most beautiful thing I've heard in a while. "I can't let anything happen to you. I love you."

My heart flutters and my breath catches. I can hear him going through his mind about how worried he was that I was sick but I'm looking better now. Then he thinks about how beautiful I look even with my new bangs. He's intrigued by my eyes and thinks about the change he's noticed in his as well.

"Are you okay babe?" He asks.

I nod my head. "Yes, I think so."

"What happened?" He asks. He's stroking my hair back soothingly and it feels so good that if I were a cat I would purr.

"I have no idea."

"She doesn't know what's going on with her but some freaky stuff is happening here." Connor says. Claire nods in agreement.

"Like what?" Alec directs his question towards me.

I cringe worried that I'm going to sound like a nut job. "I really don't know but it's like I woke up and my eyes looked all crazy and I've been getting these headaches and I can hear what people think." I say it all in one quick breath.

"What people think?" Alec looks at me as if I made a joke that he didn't quite get.

"She's not messing around man, she really can hear thoughts. I'm telling you, freaky stuff here!" Connor interrupts, looking completely frazzled.

I sit up now, allowing Alec to still cradle me somewhat in his arms. I need him to believe me, so I lean in and whisper ever so softly in his ear, "I love you too." I lean my forehead against his for a second as if my brain can transmit to his brain what I'm feeling and what I'm going through. I pull back and look into his eyes and can see instantly that he believes me.

"Wow." Is all he says out loud, but inside he says, "I love you," again and again. He studies my eyes and I hear his inner voice, which tells me that he doesn't find them creepy, but interesting instead.

"A-hum." Connor breaks up our intimate moment. "Gross, that's like my sister." I hear him saying inside his head.

"So sweet!." Claire says inside her head.

She playfully shoves Connor for interrupting our moment then she gets right to business. "Is your head feeling better?"

I nod and then move off of Alec's lap and sit cross-legged on the ground. We are now all sitting in a small circle.

"That's interesting. I guess you have the magic touch Alec." She jokes but I look at Alec as if something clicked.

"Yeah, it was like the instant I looked into your eyes my headache went away." I say looking at Alec.

He has a strange expression and I hear him say inside his head, "No it 's not possible."

"What's not possible?" I ask.

He looks at me wide eyed and then inside his head I hear him say, "I don't know how keen I am that you can read my mind."

I smile up at him. "I don't know how to turn it off yet."

"Okay, well we will have to figure that out. Anyhow, a few weird things have been happening to me today too. I cut myself shaving this morning. I saw myself bleeding and everything. I immediately washed my face off with water and then when I looked up again in the mirror the cut was gone. Like it just vanished." He says.

"Hmm, maybe it wasn't as bad as you thought it was man." Connor says attempting to lighten the mood.

"I said that to myself this morning too. However, a few hours later I got a nasty paper cut while filing some paperwork. I ran to the restroom and cleaned off all the blood only to find that there was no cut or any type of laceration on my hand anywhere." Alec looks at me and pulls some of the hair back from his forehead. He points to a spot at the top right corner near his hairline. "The freakiest thing of all is this!"

I look at him confused. "There's nothing there."

"Exactly! I've had a scar there since I was five years old. I fell out of a tree, or actually I was pushed out of a tree when my friend got mad that I beat him to the top. I scraped my head on one of the branches on the way down and had to get ten stitches to close it up. I've always had that scar…until today." He pushes the pant leg up on his left leg. "And right here, there was a large burn from where I stupidly wore shorts while riding a dirt bike when I was thirteen. My leg had rubbed up against the exhaust pipe and it singed the skin right off." He points to his inner calf. "I have no scars anywhere. They are all gone!"

He rakes his hand through his hair. "I just don't understand. It's scaring the crap out of me." I hear his inner voice mutter.

I reach over and take his hand in mine rubbing my thumb across his in a comforting gesture. I bite my bottom lip trying to sift through all this newly discovered information.

Claire's been sitting pretty despondent but finally speaks up. "I don't know what's going on but whatever it is has to be connected to something you," she says while pointing to me, "and Alec have done that Connor and I haven't."

I nod my head in agreement, she has a point. I furrow my brow trying to take it all in. Hesitantly, I notice I'm not hearing anyone's thoughts. That's odd. "Claire," I begin. "Think of something, like your favorite flavor of ice cream."

"Um, okay," she says aloud.

I listen expecting to hear something but come up blank.

"So…?" she implores.

I shrug my shoulders, "I didn't hear anything." I'm not sure if I feel relief or what. My tablet goes off and I let go of Alec's hand so I can check it.

" Oh, I probably ought to check into work." I hear Claire say in her head.

"I'm still hungry." Connor says inside his. He rubs his belly and I barely contain my laugh.

"That's so weird. I can hear you all again." I say looking at each of them.

I look to Alec and he says inside, "This is pure crazi… " I grab his hand and his thoughts are instantly cut off. I let go of his hand again. "What is she do… " I grab his hand again.

"Um, are you feeling okay Willow?" Alec raises one of his eyebrows in serious question.

"Yeah, it's just that for some reason, when I hold your hand I can't hear anyone's thoughts but when I let go, I can hear them again. It's like you are buffering them when we make physical contact."

I move closer to Claire and grab a hold of her hand. "Um, awkward.." She says in her head, while Connor mutters, "That's hot, " in his.

"So it only works when I'm holding your hand." I'm staring at Alec now and he looks just as intrigued as me.

"That's really interesting." He says rubbing his temples as if that could somehow give him all of the answers to what's going on right now.

I look down at my tablet and the calendar reminder is on the screen stating that I have to report to the assembly hall for community service immediately. "I wonder why I don't have work today." I look to Alec.

"As a gift for having such high test scores in our shelter they've given all of the students a second free day. I couldn't find a way to schedule you all to have the same two free days this time." Alec says looking apologetic.

"Not that it would matter anyhow since I have to do community service for the next month." I sigh heavily.

Claire and Connor look excited. "How long will we be getting two free days?"

"It's indefinite as of right now so don't worry." He smiles a sexy smile.

"Good. Well I have to go, I only have three minutes left, but we will talk more later." I can hear mutters of them feeling sorry for me.

Alec's is the worst because in his head he wishes he had the community service. He blames himself that I'm stuck with it. I lean in to kiss him goodbye and as if I put in the best earplugs ever made, the entire world goes quiet. It's just Alec and me sharing a goose bump, tummy fluttering, swoon worthy kiss.

I pull back and the world goes haywire again inside my head but this time I feel energized and healthy. I no longer feel a pounding headache or the overwhelming exhaustion. I tell everyone goodbye and head out of the room with a spring in my step. I walk, or more so run through the halls towards the assembly room. When I reach the main outer area where the assembly hall is located I try to open the main doors but find them locked. I walk along the hall that surrounds the exterior of the enormous circular assembly room, trying to find a door that's unlocked. I try several but have no luck. I keep walking the perimeter and find myself nearing the end of a large, empty hallway where there is a final set of metal double doors. I presume this is the entrance for the assembly speakers and staff.

A chill runs up my spine when I hear footsteps behind me. I open my mind to try to hear the thoughts of whoever is approaching but all I hear is dead silence. My heart starts racing as I realize just how deserted this area of the hall is. I turn around slowly to find Zack a few feet behind me.

"Hey sugar." He calls to me.

Nausea rolls in my stomach and something about this situation tells me I should get out of it. I remain facing him but start backing away. He chuckles and moves towards me.

"Um, hey Zack." I say trying to keep the nervousness out of my voice. I stare at him long and hard trying to find a way to read his mind. I need to know what his intentions are and am frustrated to find myself hitting a brick wall when it comes to reading him.

"So, I'm thinking you and I need to talk." He says in a sly voice.

He's bridged the gap between us. I step backwards quickly and feel the cool hard surface of the wall hit my spine. I look to the side and realize that I just backed myself into a corner only a few feet away from the door. "Maybe later, I'm late." I say. This time I can't hide the quiver in my voice.

Zack steps even closer to me now, invading my personal space. He places both of his arms on the wall on either side of my head caging me in. My heart starts beating at rapid speeds and my brain is telling me to run. He leans ever so close, to where his eyes are now only inches from mine.

He stares at me with this strange intensity that I've never seen before. I don't know if it's the lighting or if it's just me, but it almost appears that the alternating colors of green, brown and yellow that make up his hazel eyes are swirling. "Kiss me." He says in a quietly demanding voice.

My mind goes a little hazy and my eyelids droop. Something in me makes me move ever so closer to him. I look down at his lips and start closing my eyes. I don't feel the same butterflies in my stomach that I get when I'm anticipating kissing Alec. Alec!

I shut my eyes tight and shake my head. What was I thinking? My muscles tense up as I recoil from him.

I move my head back even further against the wall as if trying to make myself one with it. "What the freak? Hell no!" I say loudly.

He looks shocked and I take that instant to push him away and speed towards the door. He catches my arm and pulls me back.

"What did you just say?" He asks in complete shock.

"I said hell no! What are you thinking Zack? Let me go!" I yell at him while struggling to pull my arm free from his hold. He only grips my arm tighter and I cringe in pain. Realizing that he's hurting me, he releases his grip. Well maybe he's not a total psycho if he's not trying to hurt me. I think to myself but something is really wrong with him.

He pulls me closer to him again. He's got a hold of both of my arms now but he's not squeezing them tight enough to make it hurt. He puts his eyes even closer to mine and tries again. "I said KISS me!" He says each word with such a force that I feel compelled to listen to him. That same sensation goes through me and I start leaning in towards him, my eyes start to close and then bam, I snap out of it again! I turn my head from him.

He squeezes my arms tightly and then backs away from me laughing strangely. "What is wrong with you?"

"What is wrong with me? What is wrong with you? Do girls actually kiss you when you do that? I mean, you can't just go up to someone that you've been a punk to and expect them to promptly obey you when you tell them to kiss you." I look at him incredulously. My cheeks heat and my brain reels over the possible reasons as to why I nearly obeyed him. I love Alec. Why in the world would I actually have contemplated kissing Zack, even for a second? I take some deep breaths. I don't want to show Zack just how much he ruffled my feathers.

He moves closer to me and studies me again. I try to back up and find myself up against the same wall. Stupid wall!

He pushes my bangs out of my eyes and stares at them with a strange intensity. I find myself somehow frozen for a second but I come to my senses and slap his hand away allowing my bangs to fall back in front of my eyes again.

"Something is going on with you." He says accusingly. There is no hint that he's guessing; he knows something is up.

"What do you mean?" I ask trying to play dumb but my heartbeat has sped up again and I can hear it in my ears. I would pay a million pennies for this guy's thoughts. Why can't I hear him?

"I mean, your eyes are different and something is going on with you. You wouldn't listen to me. How did you do that?" Zack asks.

"I don't get it Zack, what are you trying to ask? Not everyone has to listen to you." I'm now thoroughly annoyed and a little freaked out.

"Excuse me." A man clears his throat behind me. "Is there a problem here?" He asks.

I turn around to see an older gentleman in his late forties with greying hair and pale green scrubs standing at the now open doorway to the assembly room.

I take the opportunity to say, "Yes, I'm Willow Mosby. I'm reporting to community service and this man is bothering me." I point to Zack who gives me a smug look. I wouldn't be so smug if I just got caught harassing someone.

The old man comes up to where we are standing and gives Zack a stern look. "Are you bothering this young lady?"

Zack looks into the man's eyes, which instantly glaze over. "No I'm not bothering her. We were just talking." Zack looks at me with a slick smile.

The man turns towards me and shakes his head just a bit. "It sounds like you two were just having a nice chat. Now you need to come inside. You are late for our service rotation. We will have to add an additional week due to this, which will make it five weeks total of community service for you young lady."

Zack puts his hand on his shoulder and the man turns around again. His eyes glaze over as Zack talks to him. "No, she's not late. Also, today is the last day of her community service. She will have satisfied all terms of it after today. Do you understand?"

The man nods his head. Zack lets go of him and the man turns back to me. "I bet you are glad to be finished with your community service today. It's time to go in. You of course don't want to be late."

"Yes sir." I say incredulously to him. I look back at Zack with wide eyes.

He turns to walk in the opposite direction down the hall. "We'll talk more later sugar." He waves his hand at me and continues walking away.

That may have been the strangest fifteen minutes of my life. I follow the old man into the auditorium to complete my first and last day of community service.

To my complete surprise, Alec is leaning against the banister looking mighty fine as my community service shift comes to an end. My head is pounding after having to listen to people's thoughts hour after hour. It wasn't too long after being away from Alec that my mind became susceptible to people's thoughts again. I couldn't figure out how to turn it off. Sadly, I've notice when people have idle time; it gives them more time to think, which means a bigger headache for me.

I waste no time jumping into Alec's arms. He wraps them around me in a comforting hug and plants a soft kiss on my lips. I let out a soft moan as all my aches and pains slip quickly away. My body feels refreshed. It feels like I've had a day at the spa, not a day hunched over picking up trash. Alec kisses me softly on the nape of my neck, before placing me gently back down on my feet.

"You are my saving grace, you know that?" I ask Alec.

A smile fills his face as he stares at me. "Glad to be of service ma'am." He acts like he's tipping his hat to me and I laugh. "I figured you'd need me after an afternoon like this," he says as he sweeps his arm gesturing to the others that are leaving.

"You have no idea." I reply. We start walking back towards the commons area. I gratefully hold Alec's hand as we walk, relishing in the much needed silence. "So, what did you do today?" I ask Alec.

Alec and I eat a perfectly normal dinner together. We part ways a little while later. After a very nice goodnight kiss I head to my room for the night.

Time to check the mirror! I've been wanting to do it all day to see if my eye has gotten any better. I lean in close to the mirror and brush my bangs out of my left eye.

Geeze! It's not getting better at all, its only getting worse! The green ring still circles my iris but it looks more pronounced. The red spot is still there and now there's a little bit of dark blue to the right of my pupil.

Urgh! What in the world is going on with me? Before I lay down for the night I tell myself that if it's not better in a few days, I will go to the doctor.

FOURTEEN

My work schedule on Sunday is so busy that I barely get to see Alec at all.

They gave me a heavy workload today probably because most everyone is off except me and three other runners.

When five o'clock rolls around I gladly hand my tablet over to Alec to download my delivery signatures. We are the last two in the office so I sit on top of his desk next to him as he finishes the last of his work. I watch him typing furiously on the keyboard. I don't pay attention to the words being entered on the screen, instead I take the time to study him in a way that you can't do when someone's looking at you. Well, at least not without totally creeping him out.

His hair is so dark that it nearly looks black on most days. Today, when I look at it just the right way I can see the deep brown and chestnut colors that stand out underneath the light. I also notice that his eyebrows furrow in and his eyes squint ever so slightly when he's concentrating. It's endearing.

I inch myself closer so I can see more of his eyes.

The deep emerald green that he once had is now completely replaced with the most unique shade of navy blue that I've ever seen. It starts out dark, almost black around the outer part of his eye and then fades into a lighter, yet still navy shade of blue as it leads into his pupils. Both of his eyes are completely changed and I wonder why only one of mine has changed.

Alec turns and catches me staring. He doesn't say anything though. He shuts the computer off and stands up from his chair. He leans in to where I'm sitting on his desk and studies me.

"What are you doing?" I know I'm blushing and it's possible that I should feel self-conscious but nothing about Alec's stare makes me feel unsure of myself. If anything the look that he's giving me makes me feel beautiful and more confident.

"I figured if you got to study me for an uninterrupted five minutes then I should get to do the same to you." He smiles.

"Oh, you saw that?" I push some of my hair behind my ear.

He nods his head but continues to appraise me.

My body feels warm and flush and the butterflies are dancing around again in my stomach. The silence is killing me so I decide to break it. "So, what exactly are you studying?"

"Hmm, an exquisite specimen really." He says in his best official scientific voice.

I crack a smile at his corniness.

"Yes, her teeth are perfectly white. Her unruly waves have a color that is quite unique, it reminds me of a mix between caramel and toasted coconut."

I giggle. "I'm sure it doesn't taste as good as either of those."

He pushes his hand through my hair and continues. "Her eyes are almond shaped and one is the most beautiful brown I've ever seen."

I put my hand up to my left eye knowing that it must look horrible and freakish.

He pulls my hand away and sets it gently on my lap. He pushes my bangs aside and says, "And the other one is the most amazing mixture of colors that she seems to think is odd but I think it's stunning." He kisses me on my cheek then finishes. "I will conclude my findings with one final appraising statement. Willow Mosby, you are the most breathtakingly beautiful creature that I've ever set eyes on."

I forget to breath, instead I stare at him stunned yet feeling so loved and more beautiful than I've ever felt before. He pulls me into his arms in a passionate kiss. I stand up and lean into him. I feel as if we aren't close enough. I feel a lightheaded dizziness wash over me as our lips part.

He kisses me on the bridge of my nose and then says, "We better get you something to eat. You've been working your tail off."

"Sounds good to me." I look up and give him a peck on the cheek before we head out of the office.

Alec puts his arm around me and pulls me closer to him as we walk.

"Have you seen Connor or Claire today?" I ask.

He nods his head. "Yeah, I saw them earlier. They were on their way to you-know-where," he says in a hushed voice since there are a lot of people moving about in the hallway.

"Ah, I wonder if they found the other part of the cave." I say in a hushed whisper.

"I don't know how I feel about that." Alec says in thought.

I have the same mixed feelings. That place was so special and I selfishly wanted to keep it just Alec and my place. I push that feeling aside knowing that my friends deserve to know about the cave too. "I hear you but if they haven't found it, we should definitely show them next time we are there."

"You're right babe. They would totally love it." Alec says as we enter the cafeteria and jump in line.

After we get our food we end up finding Connor and Claire sitting at our usual spot. They aren't even touching their food but are talking in hushed whispers. Claire spots me and practically jumps out of her seat to her feet.

I stop, taken back by her audacity. Claire is such a shy, 'in the background' kind of person. I don't know if I've ever seen her jumpy…or is it excited? I can't tell. "Hey Claire, what's up?" I barely get the words out of my mouth before I'm dragged by my free hand over to sit next to her.

Claire squeals with delight. "Guess where we went today?" Claire asks trying but feigning to hide her buoyancy.

I sit quickly, ready for her to dish it out.

"We went back to the cave today and found the most amazing place!"

I share a knowing look with Alec. Not wanting to rain on her parade, I let her continue while acting mildly surprised. "Really? What was it?"

Claire looks so excited that she just might explode in a few seconds. "We found another cave, it was so cool! It had a big underground spring, but it was a lot warmer. We could even see the sky!" She looks at me in amazed anticipation then continues. "The sunlight came in from above us through this little hole. It was so amazing! I can't believe we actually saw the real sky! It's seems like forever since we've seen outside! I wish you were there!" She takes a deep breath, winded from talking so fast. She then gives me a frown extenuating her last point.

I nod my head in response trying to look interested. I hope she doesn't get mad when I tell her Alec and I have already been there. Claire drones on while I eat. I nod my head every now and then to show her I'm listening. But when I see Candy sitting in a nearby table I can't help but shift my thought focus to Zack.

His actions yesterday were so unsettling and I can't put a finger on the extent of my anxious feelings yet. There are too many unanswered questions with Zack. Does he know about my newfound abilities? How on earth did he make that man change his mind about my community service? I think back to the picture I saw so long ago in his room. His eyes are different now than they were in that picture. Could that be correlated to the changes Alec and I are seeing in ours?

My head starts aching again as Claire continues on about the cave. I rub my temples, then I run my hands up over my head bringing my bangs up with it. I should probably tell her we were at the cave earlier, I think to myself. I look up at Claire who has suddenly stopped talking. I soon realize that I must have lifted my mental guard because suddenly I can hear her thoughts. I should stop listening in, but my curiosity wins.

"Wow, her eyes look crazy weird now. Is there a hazel spot in them now? Yes, it's right there! I wonder if she knows…should I tell her?"

"Hazel? What do you mean hazel?" I ask interrupting Claire's inner monologue.

"Oh, man. I totally forgot you can do that!"

I look away in embarrassment. "Sorry Claire. I'm trying to work on that."

She pulls her arm around me. "Willow! I know you can't help it." She puts her face right in front of mine and talks to me like she would a small child. "It must stink having to hear everyone's thoughts, well, it's probably cool sometimes. Well, I don't know... Just know it's okay. You're my best friend, and well, if I had to choose one person that could do that, I'd choose you." The sentiment in her voice is almost tangible. I smile at her.

"Thanks Claire bear." I say back to her. Her face beams. I guess she likes the nickname Connor gave her.

Suddenly, I remember what Claire just said. My eye has hazel in it now? I look around for a mirrored surface and find my spoon. I pick it up and move into the light just enough so I can see a semi-clear reflection. I move my bangs out of the way and gasp at my reflection. There's a definite trace of hazel in my eye now. It lines the outer edge of my left eye just outside of the red portion. I look at my other eye and it still reflects the normal brown it's always been. I compare the two a few more times before looking back at the table.

Everyone stares back at me, expressions all blank. What do you say when freaky things are going on with your friend anyhow?

Alec breaks protocol and inches closer to me. He gently pulls my bangs back and tilts my chin up towards the light. "I still just see beautiful."

I half smile but still feel freaked out. I hadn't noticed the hazel earlier this morning when I was getting ready. This means my eye is getting more and more freakier by the second. "What's going on with me?" I ask him just above a faint whisper. I'm too terrified to ask anything else for fear he may know the answers.

"I don't know, but I'm sure you are fine. My eyes are changing too, so you aren't alone." He tries to comfort me.

I take a deep breath trying to chill out. I'm scared that tomorrow I will wake up and have another crazy color in my eye or perhaps it will just turn into a freaking rainbow! I know I'm totally setting myself up for a panic attack so I take breath several deep breaths trying to calm myself.

I look out around the cafeteria and my eyes stop

cold when I see Zack. He's standing about twenty feet away leaning up against a pillar. He gives me a wicked smile, then turns and walks away. I get goose bumps on my arms and an unsettled feeling as I turn back towards Alec.

"What's wrong?" He asks me, barely above a whisper.

"We need to talk." I reply simply.

"No." I hear someone yell in my head.

What in the world? That did not sound like Alec. Alec stares at me like I'm crazy. I look around the cafeteria and find Zack standing across the room near the exit of the cafeteria.

"Don't you dare tell him about me." He's staring at me boldly now.

I hear his thoughts loud and clear as if he's talking directly inside my head. How can I hear him? I couldn't hear him before!

"Are you okay Willow?" Alec asks. He puts his hand on my shoulder as if to steady me. He looks in the direction that I'm staring, but he's too late, Zack has already left.

I open my mouth but can't think of anything to say. "Um, I think I need to go to the restroom." I feel bad for lying but I'm thoroughly freaked out by now.

"Need me to go with you?" Claire asks.

"No, I'm fine." I say to her. "I'll be right back." I tell Alec. I give him a quick kiss on the top of his head and head out of the cafeteria.

"So does his dad know about the two of you? I mean, I would think that a little boss on employee action would be frowned upon." I spin around to see Zack leaning coolly against the doorframe of a nearby office. His blonde hair is spiked up with gel and his hazel eyes stare at me appraisingly.

"What does it matter to you?" I ask him snidely. I throw my hand on my hip to further show him my annoyance.

"Nothing, I just find it interesting. I wouldn't have pegged you as a 'go against the grain' type of girl." I don't like the way he stares me up and down as he says this. His voice holds a sly, snake-like quality that makes me on edge.

"Look, cut the small talk crap. What exactly is going on with you?" I try to open my mind up to hear his thoughts but once again they are non-existent.

"What's going on with me? I think a better question would be what's going on with you?" He raises his eyebrow and rubs his chin in a questioning gesture.

I don't like how he plays back the same question I asked him yesterday. I'm finding myself not liking a lot of things about Zack. "Uh-uh. I know something is going on here with you. You obviously don't want me to talk to Alec about what happened today. I'm not one for keeping secrets without a good reason. So spill it." I stand taller trying to look intimidating.

He laughs which makes my face flush with an angry heat. "You are kind of cute when you get all worked up, you know that sugar?"

I'm so flustered that if I were a two year old I'd throw myself on the floor in a full-blown tantrum, but I'm not going to do that. Not with Zack especially, because then he wins whatever pissing match this is. I count to ten in my head and then take a deep breath. "Look, I'm not your sugar and if you want me to keep my mouth shut then you'd better tell me exactly why you were able to do whatever you did in the hall yesterday. I've never seen anything like that, it's like you were compelling that man to believe whatever you said. And it worked!"

"Shhh." Zack looks around. Nobody is paying attention but he grabs me by the elbow and pulls me into an empty office. I look around and see menu boards, a computer and several stacks of paper. I'm guessing the office belongs to someone who manages the cafeteria. He closes the door. My heart starts racing as I remember the last time we were alone. I don't like whatever it is that he does to me. I feel unsafe around him, almost like I can't control myself.

"So?" I ask him. I put my hands on my hips and tap my foot. We are standing at least ten feet apart but it doesn't seem far enough for me. I step back for extra measure.

"So what?" He asks.

"Argh!" He's seriously a sicko and is driving me nuts. He's just toying with me and he knows it! He starts moving towards me and I scoot further back until I feel the desk meet up with my lower back. Backed into yet another corner by Zack; he moves to where he's only a foot from me. He stares in my eyes and I move to avert my gaze. I brace my hands back behind me and grip the desk tightly, trying to gain composure.

"Ouch!" I cry out as something sliced my finger under the desk. A shiver runs up me from the spike of pain and I pull my hand up to examine the damage. A half inch long slash runs along the pad of my middle finger.

"Are you okay?" He asks, seeing the bleeding.

"Yeah, something just cut me." I grab a tissue from a box on the desk and hold it against the wound.

Zack leans down to check the underside of the desk. "Oh, there's a nail sticking out here."

I lean down to see the sharp pointy nail sticking out. Realizing how close our faces are to each other I pop my head up and nearly hit his in the process. I dart a little too fast across the room.

Zack looks at me with an amused expression. "Hey, we should probably get that cleaned up. I bet there's a first aid kit in the hallway somewhere." He moves towards me and holds out his hand. "Let me see the damage." He says.

I shake my head and he walks swiftly to me and stares intensely into my eyes. I can't help but feel a bit hypnotized by the greens, browns and yellows that make up the hazel color of his eyes. An eerily similar hazel to the one that is now in my eye. I surprise myself when I hold my hand out to him willingly.

He grabs it gently and takes the tissue from me as well. He wipes away at the blood. "What?" He looks back at me incredulously. His hand grips my wrist tighter.

I look down to see that there is no longer a wound on my finger. I yank my hand back immediately and hide it behind my back. My heart starts pounding double time.

How did that heal so fast? That's Alec's thing, not mine!

"How is there no cut on your finger?" He asks again. He tries to pull my arm from behind my back to examine it and I yank away from him.

"Hey! Don't touch me." I snarl at him.

"Look, I know something is going on with you. I can help you if you let me." He says in a voice that is way to calm given the circumstances and my miraculous healing.

I look up at him in surprise. "You can help me?" I barely whisper. I doubt that a guy like Zack can really help me but maybe he knows something about what's going on. I mean, obviously he's got some freaky stuff happening with him too.

"Yes, I can." He stares deeply into my eyes. "But, I need to know what is going on with you."

Somehow I feel myself believing that he can help me and I show my cards way quicker than I normally would. "I don't know what's going on with me but things are changing." I say still staring into his eyes.

"Like what things?" He asks calmly.

"Like I can do stuff, like I could hear you earlier when you told me not to talk to Alec. I mean, I guess you already knew that, since that's how you told me to keep my mouth shut. But, I can hear everyone's thoughts." Why did I just tell him that?

"Interesting." He scratches his head as if contemplating the meaning of the universe. "And the healing, you can heal as well?" He asks me.

I look at him and then pull my hand out from

behind my back. I examine it and find that the cut is fully healed. "I guess so." I say shrugging my shoulders. Remembering what Alec told me about his gift and how his scars disappeared, I look down at my arm. Sure enough the scar from the surgery on my arm is completely gone. I withhold that information from Zack of course because I don't trust him as far as I can throw him.

He uses his finger to lift my chin so my eyes are staring at him again. "Your friends, have they been having these weird things happen to them as well?"

I open my mouth and am about to tell him about Alec but something tells me not to. I struggle hard because half of me wants to answer his question so badly and the other half is sounding the alarms, telling me to shut up. I jerk my head out of his hand and look away. I take a few breaths and then say, "No, it's just me."

He looks at me speculatively. "Really?"

I avoid locking eyes with him because something about his eyes hypnotizes me. "Really." I say trying to put on my best poker face. "So, what about you? What's up with you?"

He laughs, "What do you mean?"

"Seriously Zack? Don't be so coy. I know something is up with you. What is it? Can you hypnotize people or play mind games or what?" I look at him but keep darting my eyes away every few seconds.

"Hmm, I'm not really sure what is up with me. I just know that I can be very persuasive and people tend to do what I tell them to do." He smiles all cockily.

I make a fake gagging sound. He looks surprised at my audacity but then laughs.

"Hey, don't hate me cause I can make you want me." He jokes around.

"No, whatever it is that you do, it doesn't work on me." I say pointing my finger at him. I keep moving my eyes away from his occasionally because I know that it does in fact work on me, even if just a little.

He calls my bluff, "That's not what it seemed like earlier today in the hall. It seemed to me like you really wanted to kiss me."

Ugh, smug jerk. "No, I did not!" I say sounding like a toddler. I clench my hands in fists then say, "Look I need to go. My friends are going to wonder where I am." I turn away from him and head towards the door.

"Fine, but we aren't through yet. I told you that I would help and I will keep my word. That is, if you want to know what's going on with you."

I spin around and study him. I don't know if he has any information but I really would like to know what's happening to Alec and me. "How exactly do you propose you could help me?"

He smiles as if he already knows that he's got me in his trap. "I figure you haven't told Alec yet that your community service is cancelled. Is that correct?"

I honestly forgot to tell Alec, I wasn't trying to keep it from him. Never the less, I nod, not sure where he's going with this.

"Well, I think we need to start our own investigation.

There are some things happening in this shelter that worry me and I think that our new found powers are just the tip of the iceberg. Are you game to play a little Nancy Drew with me?" He raises his eyebrow in anticipation of my response.

I remember reading those extremely old Nancy Drew books when I was twelve. I loved the mysteries and found myself reading through the whole series in a year. "I guess." I say trying to be nonchalant. As long as he doesn't expect to play the part of Ned Nickerson.

"Sounds good. When's your next free day?" He asks.

I pull my tablet out of the pouch that I have it in on my hip. I slide the power on and pull up the calendar. "I don't ever know for sure but it should be Friday."

"Friday it is then. Meet me in the hall where you went for community service." He smiles big showing off his pearly white teeth. "You know, the hall where we almost made out."

I roll my eyes. "Whatever." I say, not giving in to his poke. I turn around to head out.

"Oh and Sugar, don't tell anyone about our little arrangement." Zack calls as I walk out the door.

I don't respond to him. I just head back towards the cafeteria.

"There you are," Alec says when I return to the table. "We were getting worried about you. Everything okay?"

I nod my head embarrassed by my dishonesty.

He wraps his arm around mine holding me close. All I can think about is how my life is seemingly spiraling out of control and how there's nothing I can do to stop it.

FIFTEEN

The next morning, as I'm getting ready for school, I notice my eye is looking increasingly more bizarre. The one eye is still a solid, plain old brown. The other eye is a kaleidoscope of brown interlaced with red, navy and two different shades of green. One of the shades looks remarkably like Zack's hazel eyes. Looking closer in the mirror there is a new color appearing next to the blue swirls. The color is so unique I can't put a name to it. What in the world? I run my hands over my eyes in frustration. It is becoming painstakingly obvious that my eye is a swirl of colors. I'm going to have to think of some other way of hiding this because my bangs are not covering it well enough. I grab my stuff and head out for the grueling two hours of school that lay ahead.

As I'm walking into the classroom I immediately spot Claire waving her hands at me trying to get my attention. "Willow, over here." She calls out as if she's really that far away.

I walk over to her and squat next to her desk. "Hey Claire, what's up?"

She looks at me and points to her left eye. Oh

no, I think to myself. I study her eyes and lo and behold there is a purple swirl lining her icy blue eye. It's not overly obvious...yet. I purse my lips not sure of what to say.

"What does it mean?" She asks me.

I shrug my shoulders having no idea what's going on.

"Places everyone, we need to start on time today. Lots to cover." "Oh, how my job sucks." I smile to myself, glad that Ms. Thomas is just as thrilled as we are to be here.

"We'll talk later," I say to Claire squeezing her shoulder.

I find myself getting so bored that I let my mental guard down hoping for some form of entertainment. I hone into the teacher first and listen. I become bored all too soon. All she's thinking about is pharmaceuticals and how they tie in to today's lesson. I look around the room at the other nameless faces. I sense love is in the air as I listen to their thoughts. I scold myself for invading their privacy.

My eyes land back on Claire who is punching something in her tablet, probably to Connor. Then I see it. My heart practically leaps out of my chest. How else can I describe this but to say Claire's arms have completely disappeared! I run my hands over my eyes and refocus on her again. No, I am seeing clearly! She looks like someone cut her arms off! It's like a bad magicians trick or like that game toddlers play when they run out of the room with their arms tucked in their shirts trying to scare their friends. Quickly, I grab the sweater I take with me on a daily basis since I get cold sometimes, and throw it at her.

Startled, she turns to me and mouths, "What the hell?" While putting what I'm guessing are her hands up in exasperation. I stare at the sweater and her pencil, which seem to be floating in mid air. All of the color drains out of her face as she realizes her arms are gone. Well, not really gone since she's still able to hold stuff, they are just invisible...or something!

I motion for her to put the sweater on. She just furrows her brows at me in shock. I keep motioning, hoping she will take the hint.

"Willow!" Ms. Thomas shouts my name. I whip my head around to find her coming towards me. She stares me straight in the eyes.

"Please turn around, please turn around..." I whisper over and over again under my breath so quietly, hoping that nobody notices.

She stops abruptly, looks utterly confused and turns back around. She goes back to the board and begins teaching again, right where she left off.

My mouth drops open in utter shock. I snap out of it when I hear Claire, "Psst."

I turn to look at her. Her face has turned an ashen shade of white. She put my sweater on and since it's longer than usual she's able to wrap the cuff over her 'would be hands'. I stare at her in awe. Her arms are still in fact there but we just couldn't see them. How is that even possible?

Part way through the class Claire starts twirling her fingers through her hair which I've noticed is her tell tale nervous sign. It would be fine but in this instance it looks like her hair is curling around in the air. It's so weird and strange to see her pale blonde locks wrap around what I guess is her invisible finger.

Connor must have noticed as well because he's just staring at her now, his jaw wide open.

She looks up at me and notices that I'm staring at her. Her eyes look wide and frightened.

"Stop twirling your hair." I whisper really low hoping nobody has noticed her yet. I'm not sure if she heard me or could read my lips so I start to send her a text when she abruptly stops.

I let my guard down to hear her thoughts. "I'm going to stop twirling my hair. I'm going to stop twirling my hair."

I immediately throw my guard back up. I put my head in my hands feeling an anxiety attack coming on. I haven't had one in such a long time, but I'll never forget the feeling. Taking deep breaths I try and focus on the here and now. Ignoring what just happened, I focus on breathing in and then out, in and then out.

I avoid looking at Claire's arms for the remainder of the class. It's really tripping me out. I have no idea what in the world is going on with us but I know that I need to find out soon. When the bell rings I hop up out of my seat and run to stand in front of Claire's desk blocking her from the view of other people.

I look down at her and am relieved to see her hands once again. "What was that?" I ask her barely above a whisper.

Poor Claire looks even more pale than usual. "I don't know." She says while examining her hands out in front of her. She looks unbelievably relieved to see them again. Who wouldn't?

"Let's go." Connor says. "We need to find Alec."

I nod my head and we all get up and head out. I text Alec and find out that he's working through his lunch break. We decide to stop in at the cafeteria and pick up some to-go lunches, then head in to work.

Alec meets us in the hall right outside of the office. I hand him a sack lunch.

"Thank you." He says, then leans in to kiss me on the cheek. While the kiss is sweet, I can't help but notice that he's looking kind of stressed out.

"Your welcome." I say.

Connor and Claire stand in the background quietly. I'm pretty sure they are at a loss for words.

Alec gestures for us to go into a nearby empty office. It's the same one that we were in when we first talked about our newfound gifts.

"So what's up?" Alec asks.

We all sit Indian style on the floor in a small circle with our lunches laid out before us. I look to Claire to see if she wants to talk but she just stares down at her fingers. Connor looks up at me and I can see the worry masking his expression. I notice something else. I lean in closer to examine his eyes a little better. His eyes have lightened up quite a bit. They used to be so dark that they looked almost black. Now they are mostly brown. Weird. He notices my stare so he darts his head down and starts opening his lunch.

"Um, are you all going to tell me what's going on?" Alec asks.

I allow a few seconds to see if Claire wants to speak up and when she remains quiet I blurt out, "Claire went a little invisible today."

Claire looks up at me, her face flushed.

I lean forward and pat her leg. "Hey, don't be embarrassed lady, you certainly aren't the only person around here who's been having some freaky stuff happen to them." I pull my bangs away from my left eye and point at it dramatically.

Her lip twitches up just a little but she remains quiet. She's reverting back to the Claire I first met. I wonder if it's one of her defense mechanisms. Almost like she tries to disappear when the focus is on her. How ironic that she could in fact possibly disappear now.

"That's really strange. Is this something you can turn on or off?" Alec asks Claire. I'm in awe at how calm he looks.

Claire looks up at him and finally talks. "I don't know."

"Why don't you try?" Alec encourages. I nod my head in approval. Connor just looks a little freaked out.

Claire holds her arm out in front of her. She stares at it for a bit, her eyebrows furrow in concentration. Instead of looking at her arm I stare at her eyes. The purple is starting to stand out more boldly. It's a beautiful color, one I've never seen in any eye before.

I hear Alec gasp and so I look back at her arm. It's gone again.

Claire's eyes water and she looks to Connor with a look of fear. "He's going to think I'm a total freak." I let my guard down to hear her say in her head. I hear so many other questions going through all of their minds so I close myself off again. It's amazing that I can easily do this now without even needing physical contact with Alec to do so.

Connor leans forward and wipes a tear away from Claire's eye then grabs her invisible arm with his hand and interlaces his fingers with her unseen ones. "It's okay Claire Bear. We will figure out what's happening to you. To all of you guys." He looks to Alec and I.

It takes a lot for me to not say 'awe' out loud. My heart is warmed by the affection that they share.

I lean forward and ask Claire, "May I?" My curiosity has gotten the best of me. When she nods her head I reach over and touch her imperceptible arm. "It feels just like normal." I say in surprise.

"Well yeah, I mean it's not like it just goes away. It's just you can't see it, that's all." She says really fast. I think that small qualification makes her feel like less of a freak.

"That's really cool. I wonder if you can do that with the rest of your body." Alec adds.

"Well, my arm is enough for now. I don't think I can handle much more for today." She gives her arm a concentrated stare and suddenly her arm slowly becomes visible once again.

"That's really cool babe." Connor says looking a

little disappointed.

"What's wrong honey?" Claire asks him.

"Nothing." He says then stuffs a bite of his sandwich in his mouth.

"Come on." Claire urges him.

He talks with his mouth half full. "It's just, you can turn invisible..." He finishes chewing then completes his thought. "Alec can heal really fast and Willow can hear people's thoughts." He frowns. "I can't do anything cool."

I laugh. "Correction, I can hear people's thoughts and heal really fast." Everyone looks at me strangely and I realize I never told anyone about my ability to heal. "Yeah, I don't know how but now I can heal myself like Alec does." I hold out my arm for them to see that the scar is completely gone from my surgery. The silence and odd looks they are all giving me makes me uncomfortable so I shift back to what Connor was talking about. "So, you want to be a freak like us?"

"Y'all aren't freaks. Y'all are like super heroes or something with newfound abilities." He counters.

"Yeah, maybe we need to find some more of those radio active spiders that have been biting us and hand them over to you." Alec jokes.

Connor seems a little frustrated, which I personally don't get. He stands up, brushes the crumbs off his scrubs and walks to the corner of the room. He lets out a huff as he takes a seat on an office chair.

Claire gets up to go try to comfort him but Alec puts his hand on her arm stopping her. "Hey, just let him chill for a second. He's a guy and sometimes when guys feel, well, inadequate they can sulk a bit. He'll get over it in a second."

"Ow!" Connor calls out. We all look over at him at the same time and a simultaneous gasp fills the room. I know my jaw must be on the floor but so is everyone else's. I'm staring at Connor who just happens to have landed on his butt with his legs out in front of him as if the chair was pulled out from beneath him. The key factor that makes this scene so jaw dropping worthy is that part of his body is still in the chair. His butt is on the floor but the upper part of his body from his shoulders up are sticking through the chair!

My brain has no idea how to contemplate this image that makes no sense at all. It's as if the chair is a hologram and he's sticking through it. If I hadn't seen so many freaky occurrences in the past few days I probably would have gone into complete shock.

Claire is the first to regain her composure and run to him. "Does it hurt?" I can hear the fear in her voice.

"No, but I need help up." He says.

Alec and I both head over to where he is. Up close it's even freakier because the chair still looks just as solid as before and so does Connor. He doesn't look invisible or anything. It just looks like part of his body passed straight through it.

Alec holds his hand out to Connor. He looks a little weirded out but he slowly lifts his arm up through the chair to accept his hand.

I stand there dumbfounded as I watch Alec help Connor to his feet. Connor's entire body passes through the chair until he's standing right in front of us.

"Oh my gosh Connor! Stop!" Claire cries out and runs to hold onto Connor around the waist. I look down to see that his feet are sinking into the floor.

"Crap! What's happening?" Connor yells his legs going further into the floor.

I worry about Connor falling straight through it so I grab his attention and stare straight into his eyes. "You need to stop right now. You need to become solid again or stop doing whatever it is you are doing that is allowing you to pass through stuff. Do you understand?" I ask calmly.

"I understand." Connor says stoically then steps up out of the floor and onto solid ground. Well, the ground has always been solid but I guess Connor made himself solid again...or something.

I'm surprised he listened to me that easily and so is everyone else because they give me a strange look. I shrug my shoulders to act like I don't know what's going on. Deep down I have an inkling this new ability has something to do with Zack.

"Well I guess you have some powers too babe." Claire says patting him on the back.

He shakes his head as if coming out of a daze and replies, "Yeah, I guess so." He runs his hands through his hair and then adds, "I don't think I like them very much."

We all laugh at that, which eases the tension in the room. A thought hits me and I blurt it out. "If Connor was able to pass through stuff, then why didn't your hands pass through him when you helped him up?"

We all contemplate it a little. Connor answers. "I don't know. Maybe I can control it like Claire can control the invisibility thing. I just focused on their touch."

"We should really work on this and try to see what all of it means." Claire says.

"Like practice using our powers?" Connor asks.

We all laugh again at him calling these oddities powers as if we are in a comic book.

"I think that's a good idea." Alec says. "I don't think we should tell anyone about this stuff though. At least not until we figure out what's happening."

Everyone agrees and my cheeks heat. I feel guilty knowing that I have talked to Zack already. I haven't told them about the others though, I tell myself, trying to make myself feel less blameworthy.

"Maybe we can go down to the cave on Friday. We all have the day off right?" Claire asks.

Alec looks at me, "Yeah, but Willow has community service." He looks like he still blames himself for my needing to do service.

Man, I feel needles of shame prick my heart. "Yeah, but you should all go and try this out. If I can get out early I'll join you." I lie. My bad conscience justifies it as doing my duty to figure out how all of this is happening.

"Okay, we better get to work." Alec says while typing something into his tablet. He leans in and gives me a kiss before he heads back to the office.

The rest of us follow in his footsteps a few minutes later. We still think it's best that the other workers don't know that Alec is fraternizing with his employees. The last thing we need is more attention shined on us.

SIXTEEN

I walk out of class on Friday to find Alec waiting for me.

He hasn't come to my class before so I'm pleasantly surprised to see him.

"Hey babe." He throws his hand over my shoulder.

"Hey!" I look up into his eyes, which look impeccably blue. The same color blue as my eyes now show.

Alec kisses me on my cheek then pushes my bangs out of my eye. "Beautiful." He says softly while staring at me intently.

I blush under the scrutiny of his gaze. I've been walking around half blind for the past several days ever since my eye has taken on even more freaky shades, including purple. Unlike the changes I've seen in my friend's eyes, mine is only occurring in that one eye. It looks almost like a marble and the colors have swirled together in a strange intricate design.

It didn't take me long to realize that the colors in my eyes correspond with the new colors of my friends eyes. What I haven't figured out though is why.

"I wish you could come with us." Claire calls from behind Alec. I gaze over at her and see that she's staring at my eye now too. I consider briefly allowing my shield to go down so I can hear what she really thinks about my eye color but I avoid invading her privacy.

"I wish I could too." I reply. My chest is tight with anxiety. I hate lying but I have to get to the bottom of this. My friends seem to only be exhibiting one newfound ability, but I'm somehow exhibiting multiple abilities.

I even realized that I have that gift of persuasion or compulsion or whatever the heck Zack calls it. I had asked the lunch lady for an extra dessert yesterday and she gave it to me for free. I know it sounds small and trite but that lunch lady has never given anyone an extra portion of food without charging for it.

"Do you want me to walk you to community service?" Alec asks.

My heart speeds up, that would not be a good idea. Man, I hate lying. "No, I'll be fine."

"Do you at least get to have lunch with us first?" He asks.

I think about it. I really would rather get this done with. I don't really feel hungry either; all of this lying has made me lose my appetite. "No, they will have sacked lunches there."

"Okay. I'll see you tonight at dinner then?" Alec looks hopeful.

"Yep! I want a play by play run down of all of the amazing comic book worthy stuff you guys do." I smile.

"Deal." Alec leans in and gives me a kiss before we part ways.

I find Zack leaning against the wall in the isolated hallway that leads to the assembly room. He turns to smile broadly at me when I start approaching. Zack is way too slick for his own good. His boyish good looks and big smile make him seem like a mix between a High School quarterback and a magazine model.

"Hey sugar." He drawls.

"I think you need to stop calling me that." I cross my arms over my chest feeling slightly annoyed.

"Why? Don't you like terms of endearment?" He raises his eyebrow at me.

"Look Zack. I'm not your 'sugar' so I prefer you don't use that term on me. We're not really friends or anything. This is a business arrangement and we are just working together this time to try and get some questions answered." I hope I've made myself really clear and have drawn that line in the sand for him.

"Hmm, okay." He moves closer to me then stares into my eyes. I swear that the colors, which make up his hazel eyes are moving around like clouds in a churning thunderstorm. He says slowly, "I can call you sugar."

I cock my head at him then say in a monotone robot like voice, "You-can-call-me-sugar."

He gives me a questioning look and I bust out laughing. I know it might seem sick but I get a bit of pleasure when I see his cheeks heat for once. He looks annoyed.

"Don't try that compulsion crap on me anymore. Are we clear?" I say. "Because it doesn't work." I flash my teeth and give him a prideful smile.

"We'll see." He says to which I just roll my eyes. No use trying to fight with him. After all, boys like Zack must always think they are right.

"Oh, by the way, I have a present for you sug... Willow." He pulls a small white box out of the front pocket of his scrubs shirt and hands it to me.

I accept it a little nervously looking down at it. "What is it?" I ask. Visions of strange jewelry and inappropriate gifts flood my mind.

"Open it and find out."

I open up the flip top of the box slowly and see several small colored contacts. "Ah! Genius!" I exclaim.

"I figured this would make it to where you could stop wearing your hair in front of your face. You do look a little ridiculous after all." He pokes.

I look back down at the contacts ignoring his off handed insult. "Um, I'm not sure I know how to use these. No one in my family wears them."

Zack takes the box from my hands. "Here," he says. "I'll show you." He walks over to one of the single person bathrooms along the wall and opens the door. He turns the light on and looks around making sure the coast is clear. He ushers me in, closes and locks the door. "Here, have a seat." He says, gesturing to the toilet.

"Eww, seriously?" I question.

His look gives nothing away. He puts the toilet seat down with his foot and takes ahold of my shoulders to sit me down. I squirm a little under his gaze. He hands me back the box of contacts and proceeds to wash his hands. "These contacts are special. You see, they don't need any contact solution like they used to. And, you can use them for up to thirty days at a time. Then you dispose of them and get a new pair." He dries his hands with paper towels and turns back towards me. He takes the box from my hands and reaches inside and grabs a pair of contacts. He holds them up to the light and looks back at me. "Yep, I picked just the right color."

My cheeks blush. It seems so intimate that he'd know my eye color that well.

He opens the package and balances a contact on the tip of his finger. "Lean your head back and hold still."

I do as I'm told. With one hand he holds my eye open so it's unable to blink; with the other hand he gently places the contact on my eye. The urge to blink is so strong but I fight it.

"Just give it about five to ten seconds for the glue to dry, then you can blink," he says. He lets go of my eye and my lashes blink rapidly. I furrow my brow. It feels like something is actually in my eye…like an eyelash or something. I go to rub it, but Zack stops my hand. "Whatever you do, don't rub it for at least an hour. You'll get used to it; don't worry."

I nod my head at him and stand up. I go to the mirror by the sink and move my bangs aside. My eye is a little blurry but already I can tell how much better it looks. "Wow, it looks…normal."

I see Zack's reflection in the mirror and he looks

mighty pleased with himself.

Suddenly the handle to the bathroom begins to jiggle followed by a loud banging on the door. I whip around and stare at Zack, wide eyed. He puts his finger to his lips and moves me by my shoulders to the corner by the sink. He walks back over to the door and opens it, releasing the lock.

"Hey man," some guy says. "I really need to go."

In that eerie voice Zack uses for compulsion he says to the man. "This bathroom's closed. The only one available is the one on the fourth floor, behind the cinema."

I gasp slightly and put my hand over my mouth. It'll take that poor guy at least fifteen minutes to get there. Ten if he runs. Zack slowly pulls the door closed and rearms the lock. I can't help it, I bust out laughing. Zack's eyes light up and I say, "I shouldn't be laughing you know. That wasn't very nice."

Zack tries to stifle a snicker. "What can I say?" He shrugs his shoulders. "Is it feeling any better?" He asks me, changing the subject.

I nod my head. "Yeah, it's just going to take some getting used to."

"Good," he says and then pauses. "I'm going to make sure the coast is clear, then you can follow me out, okay?"

"Okay," I respond. Do I really have a choice not to trust him?

Zack opens the door quietly and peers around it. After a few seconds he motions for me to come along beside him.

Once we're safely in the hall I say rather meekly, "Thanks for doing this for me." My guard around Zack is beginning to falter. He still seems sly and snake-like; but now, it's like there's another layer under him. Like maybe he really is nice and caring once you peel off that outer layer.

"Don't mention it," he says while looking both ways. He grabs my hand and hurries to the other side of the hallway. I don't even have a chance to protest before he lets go again. He takes his tablet out of his satchel, places it next to the wall and begins punching numbers in. It looks like he's scanning the wall…but why would he do that? I hear a click as something releases and I watch in amazement as the wall opens up revealing a hidden hallway. He grabs my hand and pulls me in with him and closes the …wall? I don't know if I should even call that a door.

"Um, Zack, what the hell was that?" I say trying not to yell.

He gives me a sly smile. "That," he says extenuating the word, "was something you," he pokes me with his index finger, "were not supposed to see."

I swallow hard and nod my head. I place my fingers up to my lips and pull them across imitating a zipper.

That must satisfy him because he turns and begins walking up the steep hallway. There is dim lighting coming from the ceiling. Some of the lights flicker like they haven't been on in a while. They emit a slight buzzing noise putting me on edge.

"Hey Zack, would you mind telling me where we're going?" I ask a little out of breath from the climb.

He doesn't answer me.

I don't like not knowing what's going on and I have a sinking feeling inside my stomach like something is out of place. Is it really safe for me to be in a secret hallway with this guy? I'm like putty in his hands here. I could scream but it's painfully obvious no one would hear. Having no choice but to follow the leader, I stay one step behind him and remain silent. We walk a little further up the twisting pathways until we come to a steel door with a small keypad adjacent to it.

Zack reaches his hand up to press in the code but stops abruptly, turning to me. "Do you mind?" He asks.

"Oh," I say. "Sorry, sure." I turn around and listen to seven numbers being typed in followed by a quiet beep after each. The door releases and I turn around. Zack is already halfway through the doorway so I follow behind him.

Inside is a large lab. It looks like something from a movie; with all the twisting tubes and smoke billowing out of glowing beakers. The room is illuminated in a dull blue light. As if on cue, Zack chimes in answering my unasked question. "This is my father's lab. You might know him."

"Oh?" I ask, suddenly curious. Why I would know his dad puzzles me.

"Dr. Hastings?" He asks it in more of a question than a statement.

Suddenly, I'm at a loss for words. His dad is Dr.

Hastings? "Dr. Hastings, as in the leader of this entire facility?"

He gives me a sinister look and turns away. "The very one." He says, not giving anything away in his voice. I guess that explains his living arrangements and the fact that he doesn't have to work.

Zack walks through the lab like he's been here a thousand times before. He starts checking on beakers, swirling different fluids around.

I begin to relax, just a little, and browse around. "So, what does your dad do in here?" I ask rather curiously.

Zack pauses and looks up at me. "You really want to know the answer to that?"

I think for a second. "Yeah, why not?"

Zack lets out a huff of air. He seems more amused than irritated. Zack drones on about his dad being in charge of the vaccinations that were given to each of us when we entered.

I lose interest when he starts talking about durable immunological responses. I run my hand along the shiny stainless steel countertop. Spotless. My eyes land on a file as I peruse around. I look down at its label: Immunizations. It's the same file I saw Dr. Hastings leave Alec's office with. I open it and find a large stack of paper, held together with a heavy duty staple. I scan over the papers, which consists of a very long list of names and other scientific mumbo jumbo. I scan it briefly and one name jumps out at me, my fathers! My eyes dart over to Zack who is still lost in his own world. I don't waste a second longer as I slip the stapled list inside my satchel, careful not to let Zack see or hear what I'm doing. I button it back up praying he didn't notice.

"...So, all in all, my dad and I tested different strands trying to see if we needed a monovalent or a multivalent Vaccine. We settled on a polyvalent hoping it could fight off more than one antigen."

He looks over at me and I nod my head feigning understanding. He lost me at Dr. Hastings.

Who would have guessed that Zack was so scientific? "Um, cool." I scratch my head and then add, "So, what does this place have to do with our new abilities?"

He looks thoughtful. "My dad hasn't always been very forthcoming about his studies so I figure it wouldn't hurt to do a little snooping. You never know what we could find."

"He's not forthcoming yet he allows you access to his 'secret' lair?" I ask quizzically.

"Yes, I help him here on occasion. I've had access to this lab since before this shelter opened its doors."

"But you think he might be hiding something here?" I ask.

"You never know. We needed a place to start." He heads over to one of the lab tables and grabs a needle and a few vials. "Plus, I want to take some blood samples." He brings the needle over to me and grabs my arm.

I yank it back from him. "I don't think so!" I stare back and forth at his eyes and then at the needle.

"What's your problem; scared of a little ol' needle?"

He prods.

I roll my eyes. "No but I don't really see the point in you taking my blood. After all, who exactly will be able to process the blood work? Don't tell me you know how to do that too."

"I actually do. I know someone who is better at it than I am though and I was going to ask for their help." He gently grabs my arm again. I look up into his eyes as he adds, "It will be fine. I will have them look at mine too and won't tell the person who the samples belong to."

I don't jerk my arm back this time for some strange reason so he takes that as a sign of my compliance. He swabs my arm with alcohol and applies a tunicate to my upper arm. Slowly, he sticks the needle in and I watch as my blood fills the vial. He takes three different tubes worth of blood then labels them with a letter A. He grabs a new needle and three new vials, then repeats the process on himself. He labels those with the letter B.

"So, who are you going to ask to help?"

"I think the less you know about that, the better." Zack disposes the needles and then carefully puts the vials in his satchel.

I have a strong suspicion that he's keeping something from me but I don't push it. I can tell that he's not going to give me a name and the way I see it, it doesn't really matter. We could use any information we can get our hands on and frankly I'm mighty curious to find out if anything unique shows up in our blood samples.

"Can you think of anything at all that could have

triggered the beginning of your abilities?" Zack asks.

I know that it all started when we were in the cave. I don't know if it was the water or possibly something in the cave that ignited it. I can't tell Zack about it though because then I'd have to disclose our secret place and tell him whom I was with. "I really can't think of anything out of the ordinary that would have brought it on. How about you? When did you start displaying the um, symptoms?"

He seems annoyed that I directed the question back at him. "It's been a little while now." He answers vaguely.

"And did you do anything unusual that could have sparked the change?" I ask.

He answers a little too quickly, "No, not that I know of."

I guess that's how it's going to be. We will both keep our secrets. This will make it harder to draw a connection to whatever ignites the abilities, but I don't yet feel like I can trust Zack with this information.

We hear a beeping sound on the other side of the keypad as numbers are being typed in.

"Crap, hide Willow." Zack runs to the door.

I look around frantically trying to find a hiding spot. Zack gets under a desk and looks at me with worried eyes as the door lock clicks. I'm still standing there out in the open. Zack seems to be looking right through me as the door opens and Dr. Hastings walks in.

I find myself frozen in place, like in one of those horrible dreams where you are paralyzed by fear and can't move. My heart starts pounding so loudly that I am sure

Dr. Hastings will hear it before his eyes lock onto me.

Dr. Hastings closes the door and stares right through me before heading to his computer.

What? He looked right past me as if I weren't here. I look down at myself and realize that I've gone invisible. I don't know how I did it, but even my clothing all the way down to my shoes has disappeared with me. I would assume that anyone who went invisible would be able to at least see their own bodies even if others can't. That's not the case though. I hold my arm out in front of my eyes, which work just fine despite the invisibility. I can feel my arms and even feel the muscles that I use to lift them but I can't physically see them. Cool!

I tiptoe over to check on Zack. He's pretty well hidden under the desk and he's running his hand through his blonde hair out of worry. I head over to check out what Dr. Hastings is up to. I walk by one of the lab tables and accidentally nock over a small test tube. I cringe as it rolls off of the table and crashes onto the floor.

I stand frozen in place as Dr. Hastings turns and looks directly at me. He starts walking towards me and I open my mouth to explain but I close it quickly when he reaches the table, bends down, picks up the test tube and sets it back in its place. He looks around a little then heads back to his computer.

I follow him, careful this time not to knock anything over. I steal a peak over his shoulder. The screen is full of a whole bunch of nonsense that looks like a mathematical equation. He types in some sort of formula before he logs off. He turns around so suddenly that I have to jump out of the way to keep from having him run smack dab into me. I hold my breath while he slowly makes his way out of the lab. I breathe a sigh of relief once we are in the clear.

Zack calls out, "Willow?"

There's a decision to be made here. I could show him yet another newfound power of mine or I could hide it. I decide on the latter. I crouch down behind the lab table and focus my mind on making myself visible again. I stare at my arm, which slowly comes into focus. Once I check that all my limbs are present and accounted for, I jump up from behind the lab table. "Wow, that was close!" I say wiping my forehead dramatically.

"Yeah, I think we should leave now." He says. If he suspects something, he gives nothing away.

I nod my head and follow him out of the lab.

"So," I say while leaning back on my heels. "I guess I better take off. My friends are probably wondering where I'm at."

I watch to gage Zack's reaction but he seems calm, a little too calm if you ask me. "Sounds good," he replies. "I guess I'll see you next week…same time, same place?"

I nod my head in response and turn to leave. I pull out my tablet and text Alec to find out where he is. I'm surprised when he immediately texts back and says he's in the library. I didn't expect him to have his tablet on him since he made plans to go to the cave today with Connor and Claire.

I prod him a bit by text as I walk towards the library

and find out that he felt too much like a third wheel and begged out on the practice day. Once again I feel that guilt make its way back up into my heart knowing that I very well could have joined them.

A few moments later, I find Alec sitting in the corner of the library on one of the couches reading a book. He has several stacks of reference material surrounding him. Curiosity gets the best of me as I saunter over. He doesn't see me approach so I place my hands over his eyes. "Guess who?" I ask playfully.

A smile creeps from his lips. Suddenly he grabs my arms and pulls me down in a cradled position in his lap. He envelops me in a way-to-passionate-kiss-for-public, but I don't care. His lips are warm and inviting and I melt into his arms. All too quickly he releases the embrace and sets me in the seat beside him. I blush as I see an audience of people staring at Alec and me. I turn my attention back to Alec and peak at the book he has propped open in his lap.

"Whoa, your eyes are back to normal." Alec stares at me amazed.

I am startled at first before I remember the contacts. "Oh, I found some contacts." I say.

"You found contacts?" He asks.

"Um, well, more so I stole contacts." I hate lying because when you tell one lie you end up having to tell a hundred lies. "I saw them in another girls satchel. She was at the community service. I took them."

"What? Did she notice?" He asks looking worried.

"No, I don't think so." I let my hair fall back in

front of my eyes feeling extremely uncomfortable. I switch subjects as fast as possible. "So, today I went invisible."

He gives me a stunned expression. "Like Claire invisible?"

I nod my head. "Yep, it's crazy right?"

"It's cool. I mean, I have absolutely no idea how you are picking up multiple gifts, but I think it's pretty awesome." He says sincerely.

"I'm not sure how awesome it really is. It's going to take a little getting used to. I'm turning into something straight out of an X-Men comic book and I have no idea how or why."

"Those X-Men girls are pretty hot so you would fit in quite nicely." He studies me from head to toe and whistles.

I can't help but blush. Averting the attention I ask quickly, "Whatcha reading?"

It looks like a bunch of tables and diagrams, definitely not a 'for pleasure' kind of read. He pinches the bridge of his nose. He must have been at this for a while. His eyes show strain with small bags forming beneath them.

I reach over and grab his hand in mine and give it a squeeze. He kisses the top of my head before talking. "I'm just trying to figure out what is causing all of us to exhibit these 'abilities' if that's what you call them. I've been in here most of the morning studying the vaccinations over the past few years. I'm going over the research but it's written so scientifically that I have to use a dictionary to even be able to read the manuscripts. It seems like I've been here forever and am getting nowhere, like I'm walking in circles."

I give his hand another squeeze. "I might have something that may help and it may not, I'm not sure. I found this while doing my community service today." I feel so guilty for lying to Alec, but I feel if I tell him the truth I may endanger him. Lord only knows what Zack is capable of doing. That single thought sets me on edge. I move to my satchel and pull out the stapled papers I swiped back at the lab and hand them to Alec.

Alec takes them from me and looks them over flipping the pages back and forth. "Do you know what this is?" Alec asks me. His tone is one of wonderment and awe.

I shake my head. "I didn't know what it was, but I picked it up because my dad's name was listed on the front page. I guess my curiosity got the best of me." I shrug my shoulders trying to make it seem like no big deal. Alec continues to flip the pages back and forth.

Finally, after several minutes of flipping, he turns to me. "These are the vaccinations records…I think," he whispers. "You found these?" He studies me.

I nod my head and he seems to believe me. What reason does he have to think I'm lying after all? Great, another knock out delivered to me by my good old friend: guilt.

I furrow my brow and change the subject. "Okay, so what is the significance?" I haven't been able to connect the pieces yet, but it looks as if Alec has already done just that.

He gives me a polite, excited smile. "If you flip

through these pages you can see that not everyone received the same vaccine. Do you have a pen?" He asks flippantly.

I dig into my satchel and find a pen. "Here," I say and hand it to him.

He removes the staples from the paper and begins scanning the list again. He circles his name, Connor, Claire and my name on the list. The numbers next to each of our names apparently indicates the type of vaccination we received upon arrival. We all have different numbers next to our names. He looks up at me. "I'm not sure if that makes sense. If the vaccinations are to blame for our abilities, then why do you have multiple abilities?"

I shrug my shoulders. "It's over my head. I can't seem to make the connection."

Alec runs his hands over his face thinking intently. "You only got the one vaccine right?"

I scan my mind looking for the answer. I only remember them giving me the one vaccine…and then my brain makes a connection I hadn't made before. My face goes pale as the blood drains from it.

Alec gives my shoulder a slight shake. "Willow, what's wrong?"

I take a few deep breaths preparing myself for the explanation to follow. "When I was first in the exam room, after I had got the vaccination I went into my brother's room. He was rejected," I say barely above a whisper. Alec pulls me into a hug and urges me to continue. "I couldn't bear the thought of them possibly giving the red shot to my baby brother so I took the red serum syringe and hid it in my hospital gown. The thought of that shot getting into the wrong hands....it just scared me." I take a deep breath and continue finding comfort in Alec's touch. "After we went to the dressing room I had to change into the new clothes; the lady startled me and I ended up poking myself with the needle. I wasn't sure if any of the serum got into me but it very well could have. Even just a trace amount." I breathe a sigh of relief. "It feels really good to be able to share that burden with someone else. I guess at the time it scared me so much I didn't want to tell anyone. I thought that if I didn't speak or think about it, it would just go away. Really though, I don't know if that has anything to do with it, but that's my best guess."

I watch Alec's face as he contemplates what I just said. His eyes crinkle as he tries to piece the situation together. "Well, for what it's worth, I'm glad the red serum didn't harm you like they said it would. The thought of not having you in my life is unbearable. You make this..." he looks to the air to find the words. "...this shelter that we live in, this situation we have been placed in, much more enjoyable. I find it exceptionally exciting when you're around. It's like you breathe life into me, allowing me to relax and let go. Let go of any worries or anxieties that I have and just...just be."

Having Alec share this with me makes my heart soar. I had no idea the effect I had on him was this strong. But, truth be told, I would have to say I feel the same way. Sure, I have Connor and Claire, but Alec is different. Alec is like my rock in this place. The foundation I need to keep my time here not only bearable, but meaningful and peaceful as well. I give his hand a squeeze. "I could never have summed up my feelings as well as you just did. You are an anchor for me here and I'm so grateful to have you in my life." I say with a shy smile.

Alec's eyes brighten with my sentiment. He kisses me gently on the lips.

"Okay enough of the mushy stuff; get back to work." I joke.

He goes back to looking at the papers scanning over them again. "I'll have to do a bit more research and see if I can find any other connections. But, thank you Willow, for telling me about that red serum. I know that must be hard to talk about."

I nod my head. I know that if I say anything more, painful memories of my brother will have to be relived in my mind, so I push the thoughts aside deciding to live in the here and now.

"Oh." I say when a question springs into my mind. "If everyone had vaccinations then how come we are the only one's showing symptoms?"

"I've been pondering that too. The only thing I can think of is the cave perhaps. I mean it wasn't until then that we started showing the changes. Maybe it was something in the water." Alec guesses.

I doubt Zack found the cave but I keep that information to myself for now. "Perhaps. By the way, how many different vaccines are on that list?" I ask scanning over the numbers next to the names.

Alec flips through the numerous pages. "I only see ten."

"Wow, I wonder if it really is the vaccines that have caused the powers or if it's something else. I find it hard to believe that everyone in here has a latent power now lurking in their systems waiting to be unleashed. It just doesn't make sense at all." I think out loud.

"I hear you. That would be total chaos at best. It's very possible that the vaccinations don't have anything to do with these changes, but it's the only semi-logical thing I can come up with. It's an easier pill to swallow than radio active spiders or magical stones." He massages his temples. "I think my brain is fried."

I move to sit back on his lap. "Awe, poor thing. We will have to fix that." I say with a big smile before I lean in and kiss his headache away. I follow it up with a light kiss on his forehead. "Better?" I ask.

"It might just need a little more mending." He says with a crooked grin. "What do you say you and I ditch this place and spend the last half of the day together."

"Sounds like a brilliant plan to me." I smile. We put away the books and I tuck the list back into my satchel and head out.

We decide to check out a movie and we end up watching some goofy vampire horror flick that makes us laugh. The special effects and acting were mediocre at best but it provided us plenty of cheesy lines to make fun of. After the movie we grab a bite to eat for dinner and then Alec walks me back to my room.

"Night." Alec says.

My back is pressed up against the door as he leans in to kiss me goodnight. "Eek." I screech as I fall backwards into my dad's arms. He opened the door so suddenly that neither Alec nor myself could keep me from falling backwards. My cheeks heat and I know my face must be hot pink or something close. Awkward!

My dad sets me back on my feet. "Hello Alec." He says a little icily. My dad likes Alec but I know that he certainly doesn't want to think of him kissing his little girl.

"Hello Mr. Mosby. Um, I was just escorting Willow home." He stammers.

"Mmhm. How often exactly do you escort my daughter home?" My dad interrogates.

"Dad, be easy on him. He was only doing the honorable thing." I say trying to save Alec.

"Oh, making out with my daughter in the hallway is the honorable thing?" He eyes the two of us.

"Dad!" My eyes widen in embarrassment.

"I'm sorry Mr. Mosby." Alec looks clueless on how to respond to my dad's prompt.

My dad breathes out a long breath then says, "You are respecting my daughter, right?"

"Yes sir, very much sir. I mean, I respect her very much sir. And you. I respect you too, sir." Alec stutters.

"Good. Well have a goodnight." He shoos Alec away.

Alec looks at me a little torn but I smile and say, "Goodnight." He gives me a sweet smile and then gladly retreats from this intensely awkward situation.

I turn to my dad. Any normal teenager would start a fight with their parent after being embarrassed in such a way. I open my mouth but close it quickly when I notice just how tired he looks. I rarely see him due to his intense schedule and I don't like what I'm seeing. He looks much older than he did when we first entered the shelter. His hair is more than fifty percent grey and his eyes look worn out and exhausted. His shoulders are slumped just enough to soften away all of my teenage angst. "I'm sorry dad." I say.

His look softens and he says, "Lets go inside honey." He looks down. My satchel must have crashed to the floor during my fall. My tablet and the paperwork I stole lies face up. My heart starts accelerating as he leans down and picks up my stuff. I try to take it back from him before he can look at it but I don't get the chance. He glances over some of the names and then quickly ushers me into the room and shuts the door. "What is this?" He waves the paper in the air and a look of deep concern lines his face. His eyes don't look tired anymore; they look wide and alert.

"Um, I found it?" I end up phrasing it like a question instead of an answer.

"Sit." He points towards the one chair that is in our room. I take a seat feeling like a child put in the corner. I watch as he flips through the papers. "Where did you get this?" He asks.

My brain thinks through what to say. Should I lie or tell the truth. Do I involve my dad in this mess or not? I want to protect him because he certainly doesn't need any extra stress. I open my mouth to make up a lie and am cut short.

"Truth Willow." He says cutting me off at the pass.

I look from side to side and then mutter, "Dr. Hastings lab."

His eyes nearly bulge out of their sockets. "Dr. Hastings lab? What in the world were you doing there?" He stares me down and adds, "I want the truth young lady and I want it now."

I accidentally let out a laugh. His eyes narrow at my outburst. "Sorry, it's just a long story dad."

"I have all night." He sits down on the edge of his bed to listen.

I sigh and realize that I have to tell my dad what's going on. I owe it to him. He is my family and his name is on that list. Plus, maybe he can help. I run through everything with him from the cave to the powers and then end with my under cover work that I've been doing with Zack. I even tell him about my eyes and the contacts. I wish I could show them but I don't know how to take the contacts out. When I'm done talking I feel relieved. I look up at my dad who has been silent the whole time. He has a strange pondering look on his face.

"Honey, you know that I always believe you right?" He asks.

"Yes." I say wondering where he's going with this.

"I believe you now but I have to say that I'm struggling a bit with the whole super power thing. It doesn't make sense Willow. Maybe you imagined it?" He says. "I wish her mom were here. I don't know what to do."

"She's not here dad and I need you to believe me." I say.

He looks at me incredulously. "You heard that?" "No, I must be going crazy. This isn't possible."

"It is possible dad and you aren't going crazy." I study him and decide he might need a little more convincing. I haven't tried out Connor's super power yet so I decide now is as good a time as any. If it's anything like the others it is all about concentration. I take my index finger and place it on the middle of the desk. I concentrate as best I can and slowly I watch my finger sink into the desk. Weird! It doesn't feel like I'm moving through anything. The desk just feels like air, or maybe it's my finger that feels like air. I plunge the rest of my hand through the desk. I giggle when I see it sticking out at the bottom. "Freaky." I say aloud.

"Oh my gosh." My dad says. I look up to see him hovering over me. He touches the desk and sees that it's not a magic trick or an illusion. "Okay." My dad says a little shaky. "I believe you. Can you please pull your hand back out. It's freaking me out a bit."

"Oh sure." I pull my hand out quickly and place both my hands in my lap.

My dad runs his fingers through his hair and pulls a little at it. "This is impossible. I don't know how..." He starts pacing the room. I watch patiently as he makes a few laps. He stops mid stride and turns towards me. "Okay Willow. Tell me what, um...abilities have you been noticing?"

Relieved that he isn't labeling me as a total nut job I answer. "So far I can read minds, heal myself, go invisible, pass through objects and I can convince people."

"Convince people?"

"I'm not sure what to call it. It's like I can tell someone to do something and if I concentrate just right they will listen. It's like I can hypnotize them or something but I don't use a watch or an object to put them under." I qualify.

"Compulsion. This is truly amazing Willow." A look of question pops on his face. "Wait, you haven't used this on me have you?"

I feel a little hurt but I understand his need to clarify. "No, I wouldn't do that dad. I try not to use any of this stuff. When I got each power it was hard for me to control it but after a day or so I can manage to turn it off and only use it if I have to."

"I'm sorry I asked. I love you and I know you wouldn't do that." He sits back down on the bed. "Why do you have this list?" He holds up the papers.

"I saw our names on it and I just grabbed it. I didn't know if it had anything to do with what's happening with me." I say.

My dad scans through it all. "These are the immunizations?"

"I believe so." I say.

"You think this has to do with your abilities?"

I nod my head.

"Well, I guess it's as good of a guess as any." He takes the list and hides it under his mattress. "Have you told anyone else about this?"

I shake my head. “Alec, Connor, Claire and Zack know.” I add, “I’m the only one who knows about Zack though. I haven’t told my friends about him and I haven’t told Zack about their powers either.”

“There are others?” He asks looking at me with a fixated stare. I nod my head. “That’s what we were doing tonight…trying to figure out why we’re exhibiting these symptoms when others aren’t.” He rubs the tip of his chin in thought.

“Smart girl. I don’t like you working with Zack at all though. I don’t trust his dad and I don’t think the acorn fell far from the tree in that family.” He says. “I will do some digging of my own for you. In the mean time, try to lie low.”

“Okay.” My heart feels relieved knowing that he believes me and is going to help. I catch on a moment later to what he just said. “You know who Zack is?”

He nods sadly. “Yes, I know Dr. Hastings son. That family is up to no good. There’s a lot of rumors going around about some past trouble they got into. I don’t like any of it and I don’t want you mixed up with that kind of people.”

“I understand.” I say not confirming or denying that I will spend any more of my time investigating with Zack. I already knew that Zack and his family seemed untrustworthy. Now, with my dad’s warning, I will be even more vigilant.

“I love you.” He comes over and places a kiss on the top of my head. “Everything is going to be okay.” It still astounds me how easy he is handling this. I would have expected more of a show; perhaps hysterics or fainting… something.

"Thanks dad." I say. I believe him. We can figure this out.

"Try to get some sleep honey." My dad says.

"What about you? Aren't you going to bed?" I ask.

"No, I think I need to look into a few things first." He helps me out of the chair, gives me a hug and then leaves the room.

My mind is so wound up that it takes me what seems like an hour to turn my mind off enough to fall asleep.

SEVENTEEN

I get a surprising message on my tablet when I wake up the next morning.

I've been given another free day. I rarely ever get two free days in a row. The sleuth of texts that follow up that notification let me know that my friends are off as well.

Since I didn't make plans to snoop around with Zack I tell my friends that I was given a day off from my community service. We text a little more and then agree to meet at breakfast to discuss our plans for the day. While my suspicions are rising as to why I keep getting free days I don't question it too much. I mean, to work or have a day off…is it really a question?

I quickly throw on a pair of purple scrubs and take a look in the mirror. Leaning in closer I check out my eyes. They are brown but not the same brown that I was born with; the contacts have altered them to look a little darker. I don't know if it's the contacts or what, but I look a lot older than sixteen. I know that inside I feel older too. I've been through a lot of things that a sixteen year old should not have to endure. I sigh and throw my wild curls into a loose bun, grab my satchel and head out, determined not to have a pity party.

Surprisingly Claire meets me outside of the cafeteria. She looks nervous and her purple eyes are darting back and forth through the crowd looking for someone. I realize that someone is me when she comes running up.

"Hey!" She looks tense.

"Morning." I say with a half-smile.

Claire is literally radiating anxiety. "Um, what's going on?"

I raise my eyebrow in question. "What do you mean?"

"Alec seems a bit perturbed this morning. I wasn't sure if y'all had a fight or something last night." She looks behind her checking to make sure nobody is listening.

"What makes you think we got in a fight? Maybe he's just having a rough morning." I'm surprised by her question.

"Yeah, that could be it." She bites on her lower lip. "But, I saw something this morning. I mean, something I probably shouldn't have seen."

I stare at her for a second expecting her to carry on but I guess she needs a little prodding. "Well, what did you see?"

She looks around to make sure nobodies within earshot then leans in close to whisper. "I was practicing my invisible skills this morning and ran into Alec and Zack in the hall."

I gasp. Crap-ola!

Claire looks at me suspiciously then continues.

"They were arguing pretty heatedly. I heard your name brought up. I couldn't hear everything they were saying because I had to turn visible again. I swear I thought that Alec was going to take a swing at Zack and I knew that I had to interrupt them. I ran to the next hall so I didn't just appear out of thin air in front of them and by the time I returned Alec was gone. Zack was standing in the hallway looking all smug with himself. He gave me a horrible stare that made me feel icky all over so I rushed by him as fast as possible."

She looks at me expecting me to say something. I just stand there staring at her with a blank look. My brain is running through the possible things they may have discussed. Does Zack know about Alec's abilities? Does Alec know about my snooping around with Zack?

"What did Alec say when you found him?" I finally ask.

"Nothing really. He's just been sitting at the table looking all agitated. I asked him what was up but he didn't seem to want to talk. I didn't tell him that I saw him and Zack. I just wanted to find you first." She looks worried.

"Well, I'm sure it's fine. Let's go in and see what's up." It's easier for me to say than to actually do. Everything in my being doesn't want to go into the possible thunder storm that all of my lying and sneaking around has potentially caused. I walk in behind Claire. Instead of going directly to the table I make my way to the cafeteria line. I grab a bowl of cereal, no milk and a glass of orange juice then head to the table.

Alec avoids eye contact with me until I sit down. He looks up at me and in that instant I wish he would have continued to dodge my gaze. His blue eyes are as dark as a midnight sky. They still take me back a bit seeing as how they were a bold emerald green when I first met him. I break eye contact first and feign interest in my food. My stomach doesn't feel hungry; in fact it feels a little sick. Probably sick with worry. I pick at the cereal with my fingers and eat anyhow.

Everyone remains uncomfortably silent while I finish my breakfast. The tension in the air is so thick you could cut it with a knife. I want to say something and start defending myself but I know I should wait for Alec to bring it up first.

"So, are you all ready to go?" Connor asks uncomfortably.

I look to Alec who is still appraising me with an intense, slightly angry stare. I dodge it quickly and say, "Sure." We leave the cafeteria silently. Once we are out in the hall Connor takes all of our tablets. I assume that means that we are headed to the cave.

The journey to our secret spot is agonizing due to the silence. I twiddle my thumbs and have to consistently try to tell myself to stop fidgeting. It makes me look guilty. Alec glances at me through his peripheral vision every once in a while. I tense up each time wondering when he's going to lay me out.

When we reach the drop off I consider asking Connor to help me down. I can't imagine jumping into

Alec's arms. I wonder if he could be mad enough to let me fall on 'accident.' I brush that thought off as absurdly ridiculous. Alec loves me and even if he hated me, he wouldn't be the kind of guy to let someone get hurt.

Connor and Claire make their way down the drop off first. Connor jumps down, not bothering with the ladder and Claire drops into his arms. He gives her a peck on the lips when he sets her down.

My heart starts racing as Alec jumps down. Connor and Claire have started heading down the next tunnel leaving Alec and me alone. He turns around and gestures his arms up to me. I can't see his facial expression because he's set his flashlight on the ground facing up towards me. I take a deep breath and allow myself to drop into his arm. He catches me. He hesitates for a second as he slowly sets me down. His hands remain planted on my hips as my feet touch the concrete. I look into his eyes and see a mix of emotions running wild. My heart is hammering fast and the butterflies that I always get around him are running rampant in my stomach. He leans forward only a fraction of an inch. I imagine he would have kissed me had it been any other circumstance. The fact that he slowly comes to some unknown realization and turns away from me hits my heart hard. It feels like a knife cutting right through it.

He grabs his flashlight and heads down the tunnel behind Connor and Claire.

I follow reluctantly, feeling horrible. Whatever went on between Zack and Alec must have been bad. By the look in Alec's eyes and the silent treatment he's giving me, I assume it was catastrophic.

A thought occurs to me. I work so hard to keep people's thoughts out of my mind that I haven't thought to listen in on what's going on in Alec's head. I feel a little torn about invading his privacy but I figure I can't do much worse than I've already done to him.

"I'm so mad at her. How could she do this?" Alec's inner voice says in a near holler. I cringe at the sound of it. I didn't know you could yell in your head.

Usually people's inner voices are rather calm but he seems really worked up. I listen hard to find out what he's mad about but he just keeps saying the same thing over and over. Sometimes he rephrases it in a different manner but never does he think about the reasons why he's actually mad.

At the next drop Alec stays behind me so that Connor has to help me down. That really tops the cake; he's mad enough that he doesn't want to touch me. I just wish I knew exactly what he's so mad about. Is it the sneaking around with Zack or lying to him? Or maybe a little of both? I mean either one of those things would be enough to make me mad but would it make me as angry as Alec seems to be? I don't know.

When we get into the cave Connor and Claire head directly to the later cave. Alec moves to follow them but I grab his arm and turn him towards me. He looks surprised at first but then his stare turns into an angry glare.

"What is wrong with you?" I throw my hands on my hips and stomp my foot. I can't believe I just stomped my foot!

Alec seems like he is going to ignore me but then he says, "Actually the question here should be what is up with you?"

I look at him appraisingly. "What do you mean?"

He laughs. "Oh, let me rephrase that for you Willow." I don't like the way he says my name. He continues. "What is up with you and Zack?"

Crappy-crappington! "What do you mean what is up with Zack and me?" I know it's a stupid mechanism to counter his question with another question but I want to know what he's heard. I open my mind but all I hear are the same phrases over and over again. He's mad at me and he can't believe I've done this. Done what?

"Don't play coy with me Willow. You know exactly what I'm referring to!" He puts both of his hands on his hips. I note that his hands are facing outwards. I remember learning in an elective psychology class that hands facing backwards on your hips represent someone taking a normal posture. Hands facing forward show aggression or anger, neither of which are a good thing.

I open my mouth to try and say something witty or to possibly counter with yet another question but I decide against it. I take a deep breath and tell myself that I need to be honest with him. I should have been honest with him from the very beginning. "I'm sorry Alec. He told me not to tell you. I know I shouldn't have listened to him but I thought that perhaps he would be able to help us."

A strange look flashes across Alec's eyes. He says,

"What do you mean? How could Zack help us?"

"I don't know how but he knew about me. I didn't tell him about all of you though. He said that he could help me investigate to try and figure out how we got these powers." I say quickly.

His eyebrow shoots up. "How we got these powers? You just said that you didn't tell him about us."

Oh touché! I consider it quickly and then realize that I don't owe anything to Zack by keeping his powers a secret. "Zack has a power too. He can compel people."

Alec seems to be processing the information when he asks, "Like make people do his bidding? Like those old vampire movies?"

I had never really thought about it that way but, "Yeah, I guess like that."

He scratches his head and I notice that his body language doesn't seem as rigid. "So did he help you?"

"Well, he got me these contacts." I point to my eyes and then cringe at Alec's expression. I forgot that I lied to him about that too. I take a long exasperated breath. This is the exact reason why lying is bad!

When Alec doesn't say anything I add, "We also broke into Dr. Hasting's office." Alec seems to look interested in that tad bit of knowledge. "Actually, Dr. Hasting's is Zack's dad." Alec seems surprised by that too. "We nearly got caught but I managed to grab that list before we left."

"Did you guys figure out what the immunizations have to do with this?" He asks.

"He doesn't know I took it so no, we didn't figure out anything. My best guess is that maybe it could have caused our powers."

"Then why hasn't everyone exhibited powers yet?" He ponders.

"I don't know that yet. I mean honestly, they could have squat to do with our powers but I figured it was a start."

"Okay, so I get that you and Zack were trying to do 'research,' but why did you lie to me?" Alec puts his hands back up on his hips.

"I don't know. Zack told me I couldn't tell you and I...." I feel frustrated tears come to my eyes as I realize how damaging my lies were to our relationship. I blink them away and look back at Alec. "There is no excuse for my lying to you. I shouldn't have done it. I'm so sorry Alec. If I had the power to go back in time I would tell him No!" I take a shaky breath and add sincerely, "I understand that you are mad, probably even livid at me. I understand as well that I've broken our trust. If you feel like we need to break up I would not hold it against you in any way." This time I can't blink my tears away. They start flowing over.

Alec seems to struggle against some sort of invisible barrier as he takes a single step towards me. He doesn't say anything but looks tortured. I open my mind to hear what he's thinking. "I'm so mad…aatt…hheerr." My eyes open wide at the way his thoughts sound. It's like each syllable is a struggle for him to think, or like he's thinking that thought but is also in a way trying to fight against it.

I blink a few times as I listen to his thoughts repeat the same struggling inner dialogue. Something clicks and I realize instantly what's going on here. "What did Zack tell you?" I ask boldly.

He seems to be surprised by my change in demeanor. "What do you mean?"

"What exactly did he say to you? Claire overheard you both fighting. I want to know what he said." I stand up tall and stare him down.

Alec looks puzzled and then thoughtful. He seems to be pondering it. I tune into his thought process. "What did Zack say? I can't remember. I know we talked. What was it? I'm so mad at her, how could she do this? What?" Alec rubs his temples.

I was right in my conclusion. I take a step towards Alec. I put both of my hands on his arms and then look deeply into his eyes. "He compelled you." I say simply.

"What? No." He says with very little conviction.

"Yes, he did. I've been listening to your thoughts and over and over again you've been saying that you are so mad at me and how could I do this? What exactly were you mad about?" I ask. "Did you know I had lied to you?"

He thinks about it and then takes a step back from me. "No, I don't think I knew. I mean, you just told me but..."

I step back towards him not letting him off the hook. I hold my hands to each side of his face and make him stare at me. "He compelled you Alec. He told you to be mad at me." I say it with force in hopes that he will listen to me.

"He had to have! I'm going to kill him. I'm…so… ma…no!" Alec cuts his own line of thinking off at the pass. He grimaces and jerks away from me again. "That bastard! I'm going to kill him!"

"Not if I get to him first! He had absolutely no right!" I'm feeling utterly furious. I don't know Zack's motive but it doesn't matter, I'm pissed!

Alec seems to calm down a bit. He looks remorseful. "I treated her so horribly."

"No!" I say. He looks confused at my having heard his thoughts. I continue. "You did not treat me horribly. Sure you were mad at me but Alec, I deserve this! I don't know why exactly Zack compelled you to be mad at me but you really honestly did have the right be mad at me. I lied to you and went behind your back. That is completely unacceptable! I'm so sorry!"

"Willow." He whispers.

A loud clapping erupts behind me followed by a sinister laugh that echoes against the cave walls. I turn to see Zack standing near the entrance to the second cave. He's clapping brashly. "Bravo! Bravo!" Alec takes me by the hips and moves me behind him. I stare over his shoulder grateful for the protection.

I glare at Zack. My insides feel like they are on fire and my heart starts hammering in my chest. How did he know we were here? Better yet, how did he find this place?

"That was such an impassioned plea Willow! I nearly yelled out that I forgive you for poor Alec." He sets his gaze on Alec. "She's a firecracker. I would think you might be a little too good for her. That whole gentleman thing you've got going on doesn't seem to mesh with her bad girl persona if you know what I mean buddy." He says laughing again. Zack seems far too comfortable in his own skin. Almost like he could take the world on his shoulders if he deemed fit.

I watch Alec's fists clench up and his muscles on his forearms tense. "I'm not your buddy and don't you dare talk about her that way." Alec starts walking forward but I pull his arm back.

"No Alec, leave him alone. He's dangerous." I whisper the last part hoping Zack didn't catch on. That was a very sensible thing for me to say especially when I really wanted to see Zack's face pummeled in. "What are you doing here anyhow Zack?" I ask vehemently.

"Well I heard this is where all the cool kids hang." Even though he is across the room I can still see that trademark sly smile of his. I want to slap it off his lips.

I start stomping his way but Alec keeps his arms taught, not allowing me through. "Willow, why don't you get out of here? I can deal with Zack."

"No way!" I say.

Alec spins around and tries to convince me with his eyes to leave, but I don't succumb. Knowing that I'm not going anywhere, he turns back and yells, "What do you want Zack?"

Zack holds his hands out, "Well I wanted to invite you to the party. Come on in." He gestures for us to join him. Neither of us move so Zack adds, "Hurry up now, your friends are waiting."

Connor and Claire! I forgot they were in there. A sick feeling knots in my stomach. Alec must have the same feeling because he turns and whispers in my ear, "Run Willow. Go get help." I look back up at him and slightly shake my head. I couldn't leave! Not now.

"Ah, ah, ah!" Zack yells catching on to what Alec is trying to get me to do. We turn to see him shaking his finger at us. "You're both invited to this party. He looks behind my back and I turn to see a large, bouncer worthy man blocking the tunnel that leads to our freedom. "Come on!" He yells more impatiently this time.

Alec grabs my hand and we slowly make our way towards Zack.

"Ah, lovebirds. It's sickening, really." He turns and leads us down the narrow tunnel, leading us to the other cave.

I crawl through it. I have to take several breaths as my chest starts constricting. The walls seem to be closing in on me and my heart skips a beat. I feel the dizziness wash over me as a panic attack starts. Alec squeezes my hand ever so slightly and a warm feeling succumbs me. The panic subsides. I wonder for a second if it was just my knowing that I'm not alone or if it is Alec's healing ability that made it go away.

I don't have time to ponder it much when we step out into the cave. The sun is shining brightly on the pool of water. This cave feels more warm and humid than the inner cave does. I wonder how much hotter it must be outside if the small amount of sunlight in this cave can heat it even though it's still several hundred feet below ground.

"Ah, our guests have arrived." I look up to see Dr. Hastings staring at us. Next to him on the floor are Connor and Claire. Another man stands next to them. He's holding a gun to Claire's head.

"What's going on?" I direct my question towards Zack who has come to stand next to me. My heartbeat picks up seeing that cold steel barrel pointed at my best friends head.

He looks at me with an amused expression. "We are just cleaning up some loose ends here."

"Over here." The man with the gun waives at Alec. "You sit."

I look to Alec. We silently agree that now is not the time to fight.

We start moving forward but Zack puts his hand on my shoulder stopping me. "Not you sugar." My blood boils! It must have set Alec off as well because he lunges at him. I get knocked over by them and I watch the fight from my place on the ground.

Alec pulls his hand back and takes a swing for Zack's face. I inwardly cheer as it makes contact with his jaw. Zack recovers quickly and punches Alec in the eye. Alec tackles Zack and they both go plummeting into the water. I hadn't realized how close they were to the edge.

Dr. Hastings walks over to the man with the gun and takes it from him so that the man can go and retrieve his son. Or Alec, whichever one came first. The man splashes into the water and pulls Alec out by the back of his shirt. Alec is still swinging but the man outweighs him by nearly double. He pulls him out of the water with minimal struggle and pushes Alec to the ground next to Connor.

Zack rubs his jaw as he climbs out of the water. He's soaking wet and his shoes make a squeaking sound as he walks. I expect him to go after Alec again but he does something even more dangerous. He walks to my side and throws his arm around my shoulder. The cold water dripping off of him seeps into my clothes and I shiver. Alec tries to jump up but the sound of the safety being removed from the gun makes him rethink his next move. The man must have grabbed it back from Dr. Hastings because he now points it directly at Alec's temple.

I stand frozen underneath Zack's arm. Worry for Alec and my friends paralyzes me. I must look scared because Alec ignores the gun pointing at him and tries to stand up again. A gunshot rings out. It echoes dangerously through the cave as Alec falls to the ground.

"No!" I yell out. I unfreeze in that second. I stomp with all my might onto Zack's left foot and elbow him as hard as I can in his stomach. I take satisfaction in hearing the air whoosh out of Zack's lungs.

I don't take time to savor the slight victory though. I run to Alec and slide down in front of him. His head is slumped forward and I worry at first that he may be unconscious or worse yet, dead. I look around trying to find where he was hit. The blood is seeping out of his right shoulder. His eyes look glassy and disoriented. My heart is beating so frantically that I can feel it in my throat. I have to blink away the tears that are blurring my vision. He can't die!

The man aims his gun towards Connor and Claire when they try to come help me. "Move away." The man orders to me.

I ignore him and start ripping at Alec's shirt. The bleeding has soaked through.

"Let her be." Dr. Hastings chimes.

I find the bullet hole. I'm guessing the bullet exited his body by the size of the wound. In movies and on television that always seems to be a good sign. Alec grunts in pain so I try to lay him back on the ground. I imagine that Alec's healing abilities would probably heal this size of a wound in a few minutes. I can't stand the pained expression on his face though so I decide not to wait on his inner healing abilities.

I've never tried to heal anyone before so I don't know if I can, but I figured it wouldn't hurt to try. I pull him up into my arms and then I press both of my hands on each side of his shoulder over the entry and exit wounds. I focus with all that I can on healing him. I feel a type of energy going out of my hands. A slight tingling sensation reaches all the way up my arm. I don't know if what I'm doing is helping until Alec takes a deep breath. I pull my hands back and examine the wound. It's closed up completely. I let out my own sigh of relief and my heart starts steadying out.

Alec sits up next to me slowly. He still seems sore, which makes sense; what, with having just been shot and all. He leans his forehead against mine and says, "Thank you," in a breathy whisper.

A few tears escape my eyes as I realize he's going to be okay. I'd never been so scared in my life than when I heard that gunshot ring out.

"Remarkable." Dr. Hastings breaks the silence. "Is there anything you can't do Willow?"

I glare up at Dr. Hastings who seems to be eyeing me like he would a multi-million dollar experiment. "Apparently not. You should let us go now before I bring down the wrath of my powers on you." I stand up and try to look menacing hoping that my cheesy fake out line will work.

He eyes me appraisingly and then smiles. "I don't believe you have that type of power yet my dear."

Urgh! What is it with these Hastings men and their use of not-so-endearing terms?

"Anyhow. I'm not done with you yet." He looks down at his tablet. "Oh, we better get going. We have a lot to do."

"Yep, time to go sugar." Zack says with venom in his voice. I don't move and a second later he grabs a handful of my curly hair and pulls me by it. I yelp as I feel my hair pulling at my scalp. Tears spring to my eyes and I hastily jump up.

Alec tries to help me but the man puts the gun against his temple. He says in a low terrifying voice, "This time I'm going in for the kill. I recommend you don't move."

Alec looks so torn so I say, "I'm okay."

Zack throws his arm around my shoulder again but squeezes me uncomfortably tight against him. He's making sure there is no room for an elbowing of any sort. I wouldn't have done it anyhow. I don't want to do anything that would make Alec tempt the man with the gun again.

"Let's get on with it." Dr. Hastings says rather bored. He waves his hand over his shoulder as if shooing us off and then exits the cave.

"Yep, I've grown bored with this party. I recommend you stay as far from the exit as you can." He says to my friends. He turns and looks at me, "Shall we?" He doesn't wait for a response. He grabs my arm tightly and starts pulling me towards the exit.

I plant my feet into the ground and try to hold my place but he just drags me a long. "Let me go!" I scream looking back at my friends.

The man with the gun is backing up but continues to have his gun trained on them. When he reaches us he turns it on me. "Move and she's dead." The man calls to Alec who has already gotten to his feet. "Sit!" The man demands pressing the gun into my temple. I can feel the cold steel and it sends prickling goose bumps cascading down my arms.

"Willow." Alec calls.

"Alec!" I yell as Zack pulls me into the tunnel. I fight him but it's no use. I hadn't realized how strong Zack was. He drags me through the tunnel. I feel the cold earth slicing at my body but I refuse to make this easy on him. I kick and scream. The man with the gun crawls through the tunnel backwards, ready to shoot anyone who tries to follow.

When we are all out on the other side, Zack calls into the tunnel again. "I really recommend that if you are near this tunnel that you get as far away from it as possible!"

The bouncer looking guy who blocked our exit to the first cave is standing near us now. In his hand is a stick of dynamite. He lights the long cord and realization strikes me cold. They are going to trap my friends! "Get back!" I yell into the tunnel. "They have explosives!"

Zack pulls me away from the tunnel towards the main cave's exit. The man throws the dynamite into the tunnel and we all hastily retreat. A minute passes before a deafening explosion rings out and the ground shakes. I nearly lose my balance but Zack rights me back up and continues dragging me out of the cave. My entire body goes numb and my heart drops! My friends were in there! I have no way of knowing if they are dead or alive. They have no escape, that's if they're even alive.

Think, think, think! I have to make my brain work if I have any hope of surviving this. As of now it's three against one and those odds are surely not in my favor. I think about all the abilities I have exhibited over the past few weeks. My only guess is I must have all the powers of my friends combined. I try and make a list in my head.

- Hearing inner thoughts (my original power)
- Healing (Alec)
- Compulsion (Zack…shiver)
- Invisibility (Claire)
- Changing molecular structure…if that's what you call it (Connor)

If my theory is correct and I do in fact have all these powers, I may just make it out unscathed. As to my friends…I just don't know. One thought that crosses my mind is about Connor. If he is able to change his molecular structure maybe he will be able to walk through the wreckage caused by the explosion and get help. A spark of hope ignites within me…a very tiny spark, but nonetheless a spark.

I'm brought back to the present as Zack pulls my arm again jerking me around yet another corner. I should have been paying attention to where we were going because now I have no idea how we got where we are. The tunnel has become smaller and Dr. Hastings and the other man have turned into a narrow walkway that's offset to the side. It's so small one might not see it if they didn't know what they were looking for.

Zack shoves me in first and follows right behind me, never letting go of my arm. I'm sure that I could try and use Connor's ability right now to move straight through Zack's grip but I should probably save it for a time when I wouldn't get immediately caught. Plus, then they would know more than they already do about me. At this point that is probably the only power Zack doesn't know about and knowledge of that is definitely on my side.

We round a few small turns and come to a door. There is a single bulb light flickering haphazardly above us. Dr. Hastings walks up to the door and punches in a code. It's nine digits in length…too long for most to memorize…and it's an odd number. I hate odd numbers. My photographic memory steps in as the numbers become ingrained in my brain: 4-2-6-8-4-9-0-1-2. Who knows, that may come in handy later.

A small beep sounds and the door releases. Zack pushes me into the room after the other two had gone before me. A light turns on illuminating Dr. Hasting's lab. I can tell this is where Zack had taken me in the past because the layout is identical. The only difference is the bed that is fixed in one of the corners…that wasn't there before. A small feeling of panic escapes my lips as I see the restraints they are probably going to be using. Large leather belts with multiple belt holes reinforced by large silver rings. They look impenetrable…well at least for normal people. An IV pole stands to the side of the bed with a clear solution hanging from a bag. On the other side is a heart monitor and some other machine I have yet to identify. It all looks so wrong, it scares me to death. I begin shaking and my feet won't move. I feel myself slowly sinking to the ground, shaking and sweating.

"Oh no you don't," Zack says forcefully. "You can do that over there if you want."

I shake my head and feel a scream of panic rising from my lungs. I dig my heels in the ground realizing that if they get me where they want me, I might never leave here alive. I begin scratching frantically and pulling at anything I can from the counters throwing it on the ground. I scream and flail my arms trying desperately to get Zack to let me go.

"Stop Willow…relax a little would you!" I feel a sting in my neck and my eyes open wide in surprise. Then the world around me grows dim as I slip slowly away into nothingness.

EIGHTEEN

I wake to the sound of beeping machines.

It takes me a second to remember where I am and all the memories come flooding back. I keep my eyes shut to try and assess the situation. I hear at least two people in the room. One is scribbling on a pad of paper in the corner while the other is typing something on some sort of device…I can't tell. I listen for a few minutes concentrating on keeping my heart rate down. I know that if I panic, my heart rate will go up, and it could go from bad to worse really fast.

Someone taps a pencil against a piece of paper. "When is she going to wake up? She's been out for over three hours." I can tell that the voice belongs to Zack.

"The serum is different and is contingent upon the person. It could take another hour or so, or it could take a few more minutes. Try and exhibit some patience, would you?" I recognize that voice as that of Dr. Hastings.

A chair scrapes against the floor and I listen as feet begin pacing the room. "I'm going to try the smelling salts again." Zack's voice reverberates off the walls of the room.

"You must get your impatience from your mother's

side." Dr. Hastings remarks.

Zack's footsteps stop suddenly. I wonder to myself if that's a sore subject…Zack's mother. I hear him coming around to the side of my bed. I try not to breathe or move. I know what smelling salts can do, and I know for a fact it will give away the fact that I'm awake.

I feel something tickle under my nose. I try and hold my breath, but one of the machines starts beeping. My oxygen levels must be dropping. I can feel the machine clipped to my index finger. When I can hold my breath no longer I breathe in the smelling salts and immediately cough and sneeze at the same time. Realizing it's over, I open my eyes.

"Well, well, look who's up," Zack says with that sinisterness back in his voice. The hairs on my arms stand on end as he leans over the bed assessing me. I open my mouth and he cuts me off. "If you scream, I'll gag you," Zack says simply.

I hear Dr. Hastings chair scoot back and see him come into my peripheral vision. I try and move my body but I'm held down by the straps. I even have one around my head and my middle making it impossible to move even an inch. A single tear slips down my face. "What do you want with me?"

"We want to know why you are possessing more than one power." Dr. Hastings says rather matter of factly. "Your blood work was inconclusive."

"Why are you doing this?" I ask.

"Well to find out how to duplicate it of course.

We are going to do several tests and some require you to be awake. Don't worry, they won't last too long but they may hurt. I will put you out as soon as we are done." Dr. Hastings says.

Put me out? Like a dog or like a light? My heart races and I hear the monitor tattle tell on me by beeping ferociously.

"Well sugar, you could always tell us how you came to possess these additional powers...That is if you know." Zack chimes in, smiling creepily down at me.

I try to shake my head, but it's no use. I don't know how and even if I knew some special secret I wouldn't share it with these guys. The type of power I've come across could be extremely dangerous in the hands of the wrong person. In my peripheral vision I see Dr. Hastings pick up some sort of scary looking metal instrument. My heart starts raging war again and the monitors go wild.

Zack seems pleased when he sees this. "What's the matter sugar? Are you scared?" He makes a pouty face at me and then laughs. "This will only hurt a bit." This last statement must seem even funnier to him because he laughs harder.

I close my eyes trying to regain my composure. I can't seem weak in front of Zack. It's like adding fuel to the fire. He likes it, and it makes my stomach recoil in disgust. I force my heart to move into a steady rhythm.

"Hold still," Zack demands. "I need to remove your contacts. We need to run a few…tests." He says the last word with more venom than I'd like to admit.

Zack pries my eyes open with his fingers and puts a few drops of liquid in my eyes. It burns like crazy for a few moments, and then the sensation subsides. He does the same action to my other eye, then removes the contacts with the tips of his fingers. I watch as the world comes back into focus. Zack's eyes are wide with shock. "Dad, you might want to take a look at this…"

I listen as Dr. Hastings footsteps approach. His footsteps stop abruptly and my eyes meet his. We stare at each other for what seems like forever. I watch him appraise me; he approaches with what seems like caution. "Brilliant," Dr. Hastings whispers. "Just…spectacular!" He seems at a loss for words.

I glance back over at Zack and he has the same wonderment in his eyes. Far too soon the both of them snap out of their appraising trance and look at each other. "You ready to start?" Zack asks his dad.

He nods and I hear them beginning to clank metal instruments around in a drawer. I clench my fists knowing I'm about to become a lab rat. There is no remorse in their beady stares. I know they will show no mercy or pull out any stops for me. I am just an object to them…an object on which to study. Well, at least I'll go with my pride, I think to myself. I'm not going to cry, no matter how bad the torture. I. Will. Not. Cry.

I begin to hear the sharpening of metal objects to my right and I stare straight up at the ceiling. Even if I was able to get myself out of these straps I wouldn't be able to get out of the room…or would I. A plan begins to form in my brain. And before I have a chance to think it through I begin to put it into action. It's now or never in my mind. These two will show me no mercy and I have to act now… or I will surely die. I concentrate hard opening my mind up to channel Connor's gift. Silently and swiftly I lift my arms up from the straps and set them back down on top of them. I do the same with my feet. I take a deep breath and allow the head restraint to fall below my head and the waist restraint to do the same. I listen intently and hear Dr. Hastings and Zack still perusing through the various drawers and cabinets. I take this time to go completely invisible. I wait a few seconds and then look down at my arm. I lift it but see nothing. I glance over at Zack and Dr. Hastings. I realize I only have seconds before they realize what I've done. I quickly and silently get up from the table. My head is still woozy and I try and make sure that I don't fall. I'm not very graceful but I manage to get back on my own two feet. I inch away from the two of them when I hear the sound of numerous metal objects clatter to the ground.

"Zack," Dr. Hastings says in a panic.

Zack looks over and seems surprised for a second to find me 'not there.' "Dad, I told you she can turn invisible. She's still there." He goes back to what he's doing, but it doesn't look like Dr. Hastings is buying it. I inch my way quietly through the room getting as far away from the two of them as possible.

"If she's only invisible, then why are the restraints not holding their shape?" Leave it to Dr. Hastings to realize this.

Zack stops what he's doing and lunges for the bed. He grabs for the strap and feels around it. In a furry of anger he slams the empty strap back down on the bed. His face turns red and he turns facing right at me. I have to keep whispering in my head that he can't see me. "Where are you," he yells. "I know you're in here. There's no where you can go."

I inch closer to the door as he begins searching the room. He flails his arms out making sure he covers every inch of the room. Dr. Hastings joins him in the search. My heart pounds in my chest as more than one time I catch Zack's eyes with mine. I'm sure he doesn't know it, but it still puts me more on edge. I find the doorway. Dr. Hastings is only a few feet from me at this point. I'm scared to death because if this doesn't work then I know I am done for.

I take a deep, silent breath and concentrate on becoming nothing. Concentrate on not only being invisible but also allowing my body the ability to pass through the door. I've never tried to use multiple abilities simultaneously before. It's a feeling like no other when I finally manage to slip past the solid oak. I watch the wood splintering past my eyes as my body melts through the door, first one leg, then the other. My body is almost through it when Dr. Hasting's hand hits the remainder of my arm. He grabs on and holds it like a death grip. "Got her," he says.

I don't panic at all. I know that won't help me here. I just allow my body to calm and focus. I know I can get away from his grip; I'm doing the same thing with the door. Slowly, ever so slowly I inch my arm from his grasp and through the door. "What the…" Is the last thing I hear as I slip into the hallway.

I take off in a sprint and make my way down the long, winding tunnels. I have no idea where I'm headed but I continue to run away from the sound of footsteps and shouting. By the sound of it I can assume that I'm not only being followed by the Hastings men but by at least two other people. I approach a fork in the tunnels and make a gut choice to take the path to my left. I pray that it's the right one as I hurry through it.

My heart starts pounding as I reach a dead end. What the heck? Why would any tunnel have a dead end, I mean why even build that portion of the tunnel?

"Ah, Sugar. I can see you again." Zack says from behind me.

I look down at my body. The panic must have been what made me lose my concentration. I slowly turn around. Zack is standing only a few feet away looking smugger than ever. "Why are you doing this to me?" I hate it when the victim says that in movies but I couldn't think of anything better to say. Plus, I need to stall until I can calm myself down enough to possibly move through this tunnel wall. My heart is beating way too fast to control any of my powers.

"It's nothing personal Sugar. You see, you have a few things I want." He looks me up and down.

I do my best not to show any emotion. Instead I

just raise my eyebrow and ask, "Like what?" I take a few non-exaggerated breaths willing my heart to calm.

"When I found out about my dad's little experiment he had to do a lot to keep me quiet. The most important demand I made in order to promise my silence was that he give me the strongest power of them all. He obviously hasn't kept up his end of the bargain."

I try pushing my hand through the wall at my back but it doesn't go through. Crap, I have to keep him talking. "Why would your dad have to bribe you to keep you quiet? You're his son. Are you saying you would have thrown him under the bus?"

His hazel eyes turn dark and I worry that I just made him even angrier. "Let's just say that some of his experiments didn't turn out so well."

"Zack! Did you find anything?" Dr. Hastings voice echoes through the tunnels.

Zack walks a short distance to the mouth of the tunnel and yells, "Yep! I've got her!"

This is my only opportunity. I take a deep breath and focus my mind on being fluid. I push my hand into the tunnel wall and it passes through. Yes! I take a few more deep breaths and push my full arm and leg in.

"No!" Zack yells. "Stop!"

Yeah right, like I would really stop. Instead I focus on pushing the rest of my body into the cold rock. I close my eyes and literally walk through several layers of dark sediment until I see light behind my eyelids. I open them again and find myself standing in a hallway somewhere in the shelter. Feeling a bit disoriented, I lean up against the wall and take a moment to get my bearings straight. I have never passed through anything that thick and it really wore me down.

I focus my healing powers internally and soon I feel back to normal. I look around and notice that I'm in the school wing of the shelter. Thankfully nobody was around to see me materialize from the solid wall.

I run past a few classrooms and into the stairwell. I reach my room a few minutes later. I know it's not the safest place to be but I don't know where else to go. I shut the door behind me and lock it.

"Warning! We have a high risk red alert. Please proceed to lock down mode. I repeat high risk red alert." A female announces through the intercom system.

A second later a new voice takes over, this one I recognize. "Please proceed to follow lock down instructions. We are currently looking for a suspect, Willow Mosby. She is a five foot seven Caucasian teen with light brown curly hair. She was last seen wearing purple scrubs. This suspect should be considered dangerous. If you believe you have seen Willow Mosby please report her through the emergency app on your tablet. Please do not approach her as she may be dangerous." Dr. Hastings announces.

What? My heartbeat starts running frantically again. They are going to hunt me down! I feel the panic attack coming on strong so I sit down and place my head in between my knees while taking deep breaths.

The female voice comes onto the intercom again.

"High risk red alert. Please proceed to follow lock down instructions. I repeat, High risk red alert."

What the heck are lock down instructions? I must have missed that part of orientation!

The lock on the door jiggles. No! I don't have time to react so I throw myself under the bed. As if that weren't an obvious place to look. I watch as a single set of shoes enter the room. The door closes behind them and I hear the lock click back into place. I will my heart to calm down so I can go invisible but it's beating way too frantically.

"Willow?" My dad whispers.

My breath whooshes out of me in a loud sigh of relief. My dad must have heard it because he kneels down beside me.

"Willow! Are you okay? What are they talking about?" My dad asks as he helps me out from under the bed and to my feet.

"Dad, it's Dr. Hastings and his son! They knocked me out and were trying to do tests on me to find out why I have these powers. They hurt my friends. We were in a cave and they blew up the entrance leaving my friends there. They are trying to find me! They are going to kill me!" I mumble so quickly that I don't have time to keep the tears from falling down.

"I knew that he was up to no good!" My dad says. He starts pacing the room. His face is red with anger and he keeps clenching his fists. He stops in front of me. "I won't let them hurt you. Do you understand?" My dad says as reassuringly as he can. He stares closely at my eyes and seems awed by them. I forgot he's only seen me with the contacts on.

"Dad, I love you but you are only one man. They have the entire shelter after us. They will hurt you. They threatened my friends with a gun. They shot Alec!" Suddenly worry for my dad consumes me. I can't let him get caught up in this!

"They shot him?" He seems amazed that this was even possible. We rarely hear about shootings now a days. Officials still carry weapons but rarely is it ever necessary to use them.

"Yes, but I healed him. Well he helped too with his own healing powers." I run my hands through my hair. My body is alert with nervous energy.

My dad looks awed again at my powers. "Honey, you are so strong, you know that right?"

I start to shake my head but my dad's gaze tells me that he believes in me so I nod.

"This is so hard for me to say, but you need to go. You need to leave this shelter. If anyone can make it out there you can. You can use your powers. I will try to get out as soon as I can but you need to get out of here now." He looks torn at sending his daughter out into the elements. "You can make it through the walls cant you? Isn't that one of your gifts?"

I stifle a sob and nod. I can't imagine leaving here, leaving my dad. Leaving my friends trapped. Alec.

"Then you need to do it." My dad pulls me into his arms.

A series of thunderous knocks pound against the door.

My dad whispers in my ear, "I love you. Go now."

I look around frantically. I have to calm my heart rate first so I climb under the bed. My dad must realize that I need a moment because he pushes his blanket so it covers the area under the bed where I'm hiding.

The knocking persists. "Mosby family, open this door immediately or we will open it by force.

I hear the toilet flush and then my dad calls out as he opens the door, "Sorry, I was in the restroom."

I hear several footsteps enter the small room. "We are looking for your daughter Mr. Mosby. She is a dangerous suspect and we must see her immediately. If you are harboring her here you will be implicated as a party in her crimes as well." A man I don't recognize calls out.

"My daughter is not dangerous. What exactly is it that you think she did?" My dad asks.

The man clears his throat. "Murder."

"Murder?!" My dad yells. "Impossible. Who do you think she murdered."

"Three of her friends."

I nearly gasp out loud but catch myself. They are saying that I murdered my friends? What a convenient out to explain why they are missing! Rage fills me.

"She would never!" My dad demands. I can hear the outrage in his voice.

"I will not discuss anymore information with you sir. Do you wish to give up your daughter willingly or will we have to search the room?" This voice I recognize as the evil Dr. Hastings.

"She's not here." My father says confidently.

I look down at myself. I'm obviously still here. I work hard to focus on melting through the floor. My heart is still beating too fast.

"Well then, you don't mind if we search the room?" Dr. Hastings says.

"Be my guest." My dad says.

With that I change my tactics and focus on trying to turn invisible. I don't want my dad to suffer for this, so they can't catch me. I look down and feel my heart calming as my arms disappear before me.

"Thank you Mr. Mosby." Another man says.

"Candy, please proceed." Dr. Hastings orders.

Candy? Why is Candy here?

"Why do you need her to search? This room isn't that big. You can obviously see that she's not here." My dad says.

Dr. Hastings must hesitate a second but then deems it okay to spill the beans. "We know about your daughters abilities Mr. Mosby." He chuckles and says, "Don't pretend with me and act like you don't know." I guess my dad gives up his false look of question because Dr. Hastings says. "My daughter has an ability too. She can see through any type of facade that these abilities can create. That means she can see the invisible and a lot more than that."

Oh no! My heart starts racing now. Chill out Willow, chill out. I focus everything I have on moving through this floor. I feel myself slowly sinking. That's when the blanket pops up. I look down at my arms and see that I'm invisible. Then I look to the side at Candy's big blue eyes staring at me. My heart races again and just like that the floor becomes hard again beneath my body. No! Now not only am I in this mess but my dad is too!

Candy opens her mouth and I expect her to call out that I'm here but instead she mouths the word 'Go,' to me.

My mouth opens and I find myself in pure shock. She drops the blanket back over the bed and tells her dad. "I don't think she's here father."

"Are you sure?" Dr. Hastings asks.

"Yes father, of course I'm sure. I would have seen her if she were here and she's not." Candy plays the act of annoyed teenager well.

I can't take time to consider exactly why Candy is letting me go. I calm my heart and then find myself melting through the floor again. This time I focus on my feet going first. I can feel my feet dangling from the ceiling in whatever room is below me. I allow myself to slowly drop through. I nearly lose my focus when Dr. Hastings flips back the blanket again and looks right at me! His eyes dart back and forth because, to my relief, I'm still invisible.

"I told you father!" Candy wines.

Dr. Hastings reaches his arm under the bed and swipes it around. I push the rest of myself through to the room below just before his hand catches me.

I hit the ground feet first but fall to my knees from

the drop. I knock a metal tray off of a table at the same time and I cringe as it clashes to the floor with me. Looking around I realize I'm in one of the patient rooms of the nurses station.

"What was that?" A nurse runs into the room and looks around. I'm still conveniently invisible.

Another nurse comes in. "Is everything okay?" She asks.

"Yeah, this just fell? That's strange. Do you think someone was in here?"

"No Silvia. Look around, where would they hide. You need to stop being so jumpy." The older nurse chides.

"Sorry, it's scary though. I don't know what that girl did but I don't want to run into her." The nurse leans down and starts picking up the items that fell to the ground.

I take that as my cue to exit. I walk as quietly as I can out of the nurse's station.

The most obvious question I have to ask myself is how the heck do I plan on getting out of here? I don't know the answer yet but one thing is for certain. I have to go back to save my friends.

I stealthily make my way through the halls trying my best to remain undetected. Luckily the halls seem pretty much deserted. The same female voice comes on the loud speaker every five minutes reminding people that there is a high risk red alert. She also continues to remind everyone that I'm a dangerous fugitive. Hearing my name repeated over and over again doesn't help my nerves. I keep going though. I figure if I can make my way to the area above the cave, I could drop through a couple of floors and be there in no time. I can't chance taking our usual route through the tunnels since they are likely to be heavily guarded. The only problem is that if I'm right, the cave is two floors below the commons area. I just hope that the place that is usually bustling with people is as deserted as these hallways.

I look down and realize my hand is coming back into focus. I stop mid step and regain my composure. My hand becomes invisible again. I breathe a sigh of relief. I'm not sure how much longer I can keep this up. My body is trembling from using my powers this long. I find the will power to keep going. My friends need me.

A moment later I find myself turning the corner of a hallway that spills out into the commons area. I stop suddenly seeing all the people struggling to make their way into the auditorium. Seas of people take small steps towards the far entrance on the opposite end of the room. People are packed in tighter than a sardine can. Is this the protocol for a high risk, red alert? There is no way I can weave through all these people and still remain undetected.

Think, Willow think... I have to find somewhere to hide before I materialize out of thin air in front of all of these people. I suddenly remember the very first time my father and I made our way into the mountain. There was a hallway that has since been closed off. I move along the wall as stealthily as possible making sure I don't bump into anyone. My hand accidently hits a lady's bottom. She turns around and slaps the man behind her. I hold my breath as I watch the two of them yell back and forth at each other. A small hole opens up in front of me as people meander over to where the argument is taking place.

Soon I come to a spot in the wall that looks to have been recently sealed. There is a light grey substance, almost like grout, surrounding the outline of a door in the mountain wall. I look down making sure I am still invisible. I pray that I have enough strength to make it out alive. My knees are threatening to buckle from weakness of using my gift of invisibility. I place my hand up to the middle of the newly made wall. I slide it through and am pleased to find it is only as thick as the stone itself. I concentrate on pushing myself the rest of the way through. I feel someone ram into me from behind and I am thrown to the ground on the other side. The wind is knocked out of me and I just lay there for a few moments, in the dark corridor, catching my breath. I let my powers go allowing myself to get a break from using them.

I hone in on my healing gift for a few moments and feel the shakiness reside. I don't think I'll ever get used to the idea that I can regenerate myself. Soon I feel back to normal. I focus on going invisible first. It's too dark in this corridor to know if it worked so I'm just going to have to hope for the best.

I start allowing my body to melt through the floor. I move much faster than usual this time. I fall down into a small patch of leafy green stuff. Looking around I realize I landed in a row of spinach in the garden level of the shelter. Usually I hate spinach but I feel a little more affection for it now that it cushioned my landing. The sprinklers come on and they start soaking my scrubs.

I move as fast as I can through the floor and only fall a few feet before I land with a thud on top of one of the storage containers. I throw my hands over my mouth worried that someone might have heard the fall.

I wait a few minutes and when nobody comes running my way, I jump down. One more floor to go! I focus again and this time I try to move much slower through the floor. My biggest fear is I'll land in the cave and go falling four stories to the ground.

As I continue to move through the dense mountain matter, I get a panicked feeling inside. I try to focus on staying calm and eventually I feel my feet touch the ground. I have to drop to my knees because when I come out of the wall all together I'm in the small tunnel that we had to crawl to in order to get to the main cave.

I can't believe I did it! I crawl in the direction of the outer cave quietly. When I reach the entrance I peer around and find that the cave seems to be empty. It's extremely dark inside so it's hard to tell for sure. I remain invisible just in case and stealthily move towards the entrance to the second cave.

The rock debris left over from the explosion cover the mouth of the tunnel. My heartbeat starts picking up as I think of my friends on the other side. I have no idea how damaging the dynamite was. I don't know if they even survived and that thought sickens me. I clear my head and try not to focus on the worst possible outcome. Instead I imagine the most gorgeous pair of navy blue eyes waiting for me. I push my hand through the rock. I think of Alec the whole time I move through to the second cave. Our cave.

I let go of the invisibility and when I step out on the other side my heart soars. The cave isn't completely collapsed in. I look back at the tunnel and see that only a few rocks lie there. The explosion must not have gone as deep as they thought it would.

"Alec!" I call out excited to see him. The sun is still shining through the opening in the ceiling. Nobody answers me. I look around for my friends but I don't see them.

"Claire? Connor?" I call out unsure. My brain starts going through all of the possible scenarios. This cave is a good size but there isn't an area that they could hide in. I would be able to see them. Why aren't they here? I look back at the rubble. There's no way that all three of them were in the tunnel when it exploded. Right?

I walk around looking for any sign of them. I must look around for at least an hour because the sun shifts in the sky. I walk back and forth along the water's edge trying to think of what to do next. Maybe Connor found a way to get them out using his gift. If I could use my gift on Alec what would keep Connor from using his gift on other people.

Something catches my eye. In the corner near the Western cave wall is a grouping of rocks. Why hadn't I noticed it before? I run over to them expecting to see some sort of message written out that tells me what happened to my friends. Instead I find a single arrow made out of small rocks. It points towards the wall. Why would it....They went outside! The epiphany strikes me and my heart soars. They are trying to let me know that they went outside! Excitement overwhelms me as I think of my friends making it out of here alive. I'm going to find them after all!

I have no idea what lies on the other side of this mountain, if it's scalding hot temperatures or unlivable conditions. Not knowing makes me leery but it's not enough to keep me from reaching my friends.

I put my hand up to the wall and slowly start moving through it. The wall feels warm as I make my way through the rock and sediment. Sweat begins to accumulate on my brow. I'm not sure if the temperature is increasing, or if it's my anxiety that causes this stifling condition. Eventually I feel the heat prickling at my fingertips and I let the rest of my body follow.

NINETEEN

On the outside, the sun beats down relentlessly and I close my eyes against its blinding light.

I haven't seen the light of day in...how long has it been? Weeks, months, years? The first thing I truly notice is the lack of heat. It's hot, don't get me wrong but it is definitely not unbearable. This isn't one hundred and seventy degrees like they predicted with the shields down. It feels more like ninety degrees.

I cup my hands over my eyes and slowly allow them to adjust to the daylight by staring downwards. The bone-dry ground is cracked beneath my feet. The sight of it makes me suddenly thirsty. Soon, I'm able to make out some different bushes and wildflowers scattered about on the surface.

My eyes adjust enough that I am able to finally look up and see at eye level...every hair stands at attention down my arms and legs. My scalp grows cold regardless of the pressing heat. About fifty yards in front of me lay a group of people, at least seventy to a hundred in number. They all wield different weapons: spears, knifes, swords... guns. I swallow hard noticing my throat has tightened up considerably. Their eyes press into mine. The light reflects off these strangers revealing their beady red irises. They stare at me and I at them. No one moves...no one breathes.

In the matter of a split second a war cry calls out. All eyes turn toward the East, including mine as a second group of people descends upon the first. They drop down from the mountain scape above me. Each person holds a different weapon similar to the other group. Someone lands directly in front of me. I catch a glimpse of his eyes before he turns away. They startle me almost as much as the crimson eyes that were looking at me just moments before. Their color is the most vivid yellow I have ever seen. It has a look that is almost radioactive.

A gunshot rings out and I fall to the ground, curling up into a ball. I try and filter out the sounds of the war around me, but the task is impossible. Clanking of metal on metal, gunshots and screams echo off the mountainsides. There's growling and gnashing of teeth as one man falls after another.

Frightened doesn't even begin to describe how I'm feeling. I am utterly helpless as I remain curled up in my ball, with the sun beating down on my back. I feel as if I entered an alternate reality, a different world. I wish to escape but can't bring myself to move.

A body falls to the ground next to me. I feel the persons blood soak into my shirt and I look up in that moment to see yellow, pain filled eyes staring at me. They aren't just any eyes though. Gasping for breath I call her name before she passes out, "Mom!

To Be Continued...

Rebecca and Courtney are downhome country girls powered by chocolate and other random late night cravings. Coined in southern twang they bring new meaning to the word y'all. BFI's since the 6th grade, with a knack for getting into sticky situations, has resulted in countless ideas to write about for years to come.

ACKNOWLEDGEMENTS

First thanks goes to our awesome God and His Son for all of his amazing blessings. A million hugs and kisses to our wonderful supportive family and friends whose love and encouragement make us who we are. A special thank you to all of our fans and book blog sites that have supported our books. You encourage us more than you could ever know. You are why we write! A big thanks to the most amazing book cover designing genius: Marya Heiman from Strong Image Editing. You rock our socks! A million thanks to Mandy Buchanan from LEO editing for making our book sparkle brighter than a vampire in the sun! A huge shout out to all of our fellow Indie authors! There is so much teamwork and support that goes on between fellow authors in the indie community and we are so grateful for it.

PERSONAL ACKNOWLEDGEMENTS

"Thank you to my amazing husband Adam, who listened to endless ranting about our new apocalyptic series and who gave me ingeniously creative ideas to implement in the series. A dozen thanks to my kiddos Trinity and Aiden, who put up with my 'cave' time and my endless hogging of the computer. I love y'all more than a trillion dark chocolate Godiva truffles! A paw shake goes out to my not so little puppy Neo for laying by my side on my late night writing sessions. Ps: Thank you Red Bull for my writing wings."

~Rebecca

"Thank you to my hubby Kevin who has supported my work even when I work through the night. Thank you to my kids: Cameron, Chloe and Kaleb, who are the inspiration for many of the silly scenes in the book. Thank you for your understanding when I have to write causing us to do our homeschool at night. You three are the best! Thank you to my two doggies who keep my feet warm while I write. Wintertime just wouldn't be the same without you. And a final thank you to my extended family...my mother and grandparents specifically. You supported me from day one on this crazy adventure of mine. You are ALWAYS there when I need you and for that I am truely greatful. So, it's this book that I dedicate to you. Thank you for bringing me all the happiness and joy in the world. I love you both to pieces.

~Courtney

We would love to hear from you! Please come visit us:

Facebook:
http://www.facebook.com/eleseries

Twitter:
Courtney: http://www.twitter.com/nuckelsc
Rebecca: http://www.twitter.com/midnitebeckie

Webpage:

http://www.eleseries.com

CPSIA information can be obtained
at www.ICGtesting.com
Printed in the USA
LVHW02s0501120518
576944LV00001B/6/P

9 781940 534787

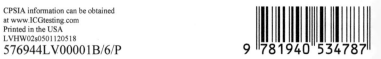